SECESSION

A Republic Reborn

Philip M. Fishman
And Don King

Foreword by Chris Martineau

This work is dedicated to two youngsters—Griffin Wilson, our grandson; and to Kaylee King, daughter of my deceased co-author, Don King, and his wife, Kathleen. They are a bit young right now, but I hope that when they are of age they will read, enjoy, and possibly gain some inspiration from it.

—*Phil Fishman*

Foreword

When I first received this manuscript, I prepared myself for a delightful evening of scholarly research on conservative theory, and a well-reasoned argument for a Convention of the States. I expected a treatise on how secession of southern states from the Union might one day become a reality.

History, people, and philosophies of nations tend to move in cycles, and Phil Fishman is a gifted enough historian and researcher to follow and chronicle both. Elections have consequences, and laws and policies passed with even the most noble and well-meaning intentions can have a profound ripple effect on history. And as Winston Churchill once famously noted, "The further back you look, the farther forward you can see."

So, coffee in hand, I delved with relish into what I anticipated to be a work of scholarly nonfiction.

I quickly found myself involved in an engrossing chronicle of what I hesitate to call fiction. After a succinct historical analysis of the causes, consequences, and implications of nations and peoples seceding from their governments, the work transported me seamlessly to the year 2042. There I found myself sitting in the same room with men and women just as real, relatable, and inspiring as anyone you would meet on the street or know and love from your childhood. The events which form and shape these characters occur in a story that eerily and disturbingly mirror the events we are seeing in our country today. In fact, the story that unfolds in the author's narrative could just as easily take place in 2017 as they do in 2042.

Lon Whitt, and Jonas O'Leary, our protagonists, find themselves caught in the cost and consequences of a global and geo-political drama. The events leading up to the main story line find their origins in the successful war on coal by the secular left wing of the United States government.

The worldwide consequences that ensue involve the results of skyrocketing energy costs, and the ripple effect on industry, unemployment, currency devaluation, and the impacts. Ordinary people find themselves enmeshed in extraordinary and seemingly overwhelming, untenable geo-political forces.

Events of a sheering and overwhelming nature develop quickly. What ensues is a thoroughly enjoyable story that not only engrosses the reader, but provides a decidedly disturbing and unsettling glimpse into the unintended consequences of potential events that find themselves rooted in today's headlines.

Hence my hesitation to call it fiction.

Philip M. Fishman and Don King

From a reader's perspective, what Phil Fishman and his co-author, Don King, have accomplished here is remarkable. The fact that they have done their homework reveals itself very early in the story. They demonstrate a keen intuitive knowledge, and deep familiarity of all opposing theories of climatology, micro and macroeconomics, US Constitutional Law, and even the intimate details of US juridical proceedings and law enforcement.

This work clearly represents the culmination of a life time of expert research, scholarly knowledge, and deep thought. The authors' ability to tie together in a logical, plausible sequence, both the predictable and unintended consequences of current events is as enrapturing as it is chilling. Every writer who puts pen to paper hopes to one day create a "magnum opus" which not only chronicles and comments on their times in an engaging and entertaining way – but also helps to impact and shape their readers and those times for the good. Secession—A Republic Reborn is just such a work. The authors set out to tell a story which will have their readers talking about not only the events in the novel; but will spark a dialog among all those who read it long after they have set this book down.

They have absolutely succeeded. For anyone who is invested in the wellbeing of the first and greatest Constitutional Republic ever conceived in human history (and intrigued with learning more about the forces which oppose that Republic's founding principles and continued success) Secession—A Republic Reborn is well worth your time, and deserves a prominent place in your library.

—Chris Martineau

Prologue

Nothing ever happens without at least one underlying cause, and often, several causes. The precipitating event that led to the start of World War I was the assassination of Crown Prince Franz Ferdinand of Austro-Hungary by a Serbian radical. But the kindling was there with the growing nationalism, militarism and alliances, only awaiting a spark, which turned out to be the assassination.

Similarly, the catalyst for the start of World War II, was Hitler's invasion of Poland, but the stage was set at the end of WW I by the extremely harsh treatment of Germany exacted by the Versailles Treaty.

And so it is with the current state of affairs in the fall of 2042. It is impossible to know when it all began. Spontaneous combustion by definition starts when fire breaks out, but in actuality, spontaneous combustion is a misnomer. *Spontaneous* suggests that something occurs without cause. The fire occurs only when there is a build-up of heat in a combustible material in an atmosphere that supports combustion. In other words, there are three components that need to be present for spontaneous combustion to occur.

Secession had been a favorite topic of discussion many times throughout the history of our country starting with its founding, but rarely since the mid-eighteen hundreds had the discussion been any more than academic and rhetorical. After all, the issue was supposedly settled once and for all by the Civil War. But did the Civil War really prove that the right of secession did not exist, or did it prove that the right of secession exists only when the party attempting to secede has the power to make it happen?

The thirteen colonies managed to secede from Great Britain by winning the Revolutionary War, and then were able to seal the bargain by winning the War of 1812.

If the Confederacy had won the Civil War, secession would have been fact, and questions on the right of secession would be moot. Numerous books and scholarly papers have been written on the right of secession, but the most powerful argument resides in our Constitution. There is nothing in the Constitution stating that secession is illegal, and the Tenth Amendment clearly states that *"The powers not delegated to the United States by the Constitution, nor prohibited by it to the States, are reserved to the States, respectively, or to the people."*

As stated, it is all but impossible to ascertain the starting point. There are those that point to the New Deal of Franklin Roosevelt and the beginning of the ever expanding welfare state. Others refer to Lyndon Johnson's Great Society. Each of these administrations increased the numbers of welfare recipients exponentially, but neither resulted in anything close to the racial and class divisiveness of the Barack Obama administration from 2008 to 2016. After Obama, a succession of Democrat Presidents continued the direction of the country into a more powerful central government and European style socialistic state through executive order, and similarly minded judicial appointments.

The system of checks and balances that the founding fathers had wisely put in place to counter the tendency of power to concentrate and beget more power was being whittled away by the leftist executive branch , happily enabled by a legislative branch of like mind. Two remaining bastions against the concentration of power, the Supreme Court and the Senate's filibuster rule, had been in place for several years, albeit precarious, and even more so at this time, since the oldest conservative justice had passed away in early September, resulting in a situation eerily similar to that of late 2016 except that in 2042, the older justices were conservative and it was a mid-term election. Now, heading into the election of November 2042, the Supreme Court consists of four aging conservatives and four younger liberals, while the Senate is near a liberal super majority, which could close down filibusters and allow the Democratic President an unimpeded choice of a replacement justice, who most assuredly would be liberal.

Beginning perhaps in the late 20th century there had been a mounting frustration and resentment among a relatively small but politically active portion of the population toward the steadily increasing power of the Federal Government and concurrent erosion of personal liberties. A political movement, protesting the growing socialist state and calling itself *The Tea Party,* hearkening back to *The Boston Tea Party* of 1773, began in December 2007. Its aims were honorable, but the party actually ended up hurting more than helping its members' cause. The Tea Party's *Achilles Heel* was its refusal to compromise, with the effect of electing the liberal parties' candidates. Often, when its favored candidate failed to win the Republican Party's nomination, the Tea Party would run its candidate as an Independent, thereby splitting the conservative vote. Other times as in the Nevada and Delaware Senatorial elections of 2012, the Tea Party was successful in winning the Republican nomination only to be defeated in the general election.

After that the word *secession* began to be heard, not infrequently, among certain conservative groups; but despite the frustration, conservatives remained too splintered to have any kind of lasting positive effect. The kindling was there. What was needed was a catalyst to ignite it.

Chapter 1: The Project

The two were huddled together in a far back corner table of the almost deserted diner at the late hour. The employees had already been sent home, and aside from the proprietor, who was busy cleaning up, the only others in the place were an older bearded gentleman, apparently finishing his meal, and a young couple, oblivious to anything happening around them. In the recent past the two men had met at either of their apartments, but now it was becoming ever more dangerous for a link to be established between certain individuals.

Lon Whitt, who had initiated the meeting, was an imposing figure, six feet four inches tall and lean with a well- toned muscular physique. He had been a civilian for many years, but his military background was obvious from his appearance. His ramrod straight posture, clean shaven face, extra short haircut, and neat appearance left no question. Except for the deep scar across his left cheek, beginning at his ear and ending just below his left eye, he would be considered by most females to be movie star handsome. In fact, even with the scar, his deep blue eyes were so focused and penetrating that when he looked at someone, they tended to forget that he had any disfigurement.

He had received the scar during the Second Syrian Campaign of the Middle Eastern War, when as a recently promoted captain, he was commanding an infantry company that was chasing a group of insurgents through a valley. Almost like General Custer's experience at The Little Big Horn, except that this enemy had advanced weaponry and vastly superior firepower, Whitt's men found themselves surrounded.

The situation would have been similarly hopeless but for the resourcefulness and courage of the commander. The logical reaction would have been to retrace their path, which probably would have meant the total annihilation of his command due to the overwhelming numbers of insurgents at their rear. If he had instead advanced, he would have faced a similar number of the enemy, in addition to being unfamiliar with the terrain. He would have called for air or artillery support except that his radio man had been killed and his radio rendered useless in the first contact.

His executive officer, First Lieutenant Robert J. Stephens IV, said, "Lon, I don't think we're going to make it, but we...I see you're shaking your head; just let me finish."

"Go ahead, but keep firing, Bob."

"Thanks.. But we're going to give them a fight they will never forget." Stephens and Whitt were good friends, dating back to their days as fraternity brothers at Pitt, and classmates in ROTC. Their academic pursuits were 180 degrees apart with Whitt majoring in chemical engineering and Stephens in philosophy, but otherwise they had remarkably similar interests.

Whitt replied, "You're half right. This will be a fight they won't forget, but I think that most of us will be around to tell our grandkids about the battle. All we need to do is take the high ground away from them."

Whitt had noted that the grass and brush on the steep hills on either side of the narrow valley were extremely dry due to several weeks without rain and that there was a strong updraft. He ordered his men to ignite the tinder with phosphorus grenades and his two flame throwers. As the flames ran up the hills and engulfed the entrenched enemy on the hills his men were able to follow just high enough so that they now had the high ground. Now it was the enemy at a disadvantage.

The fighting was intense, and at times the fight boiled down to brutal hand-to-hand combat, which was the source of Whitt's tell-tale scar. It came from the tip of a combat knife wielded by a Mujahedeen who had come at Whitt from behind. His enemy might have drawn first blood in their short lived encounter, but Whitt drew last blood, taking the knife away from his adversary and skewering him with it. The battle continued for several hours until the rest of the battalion, seeing the smoke and hearing the din, arrived to reinforce the beleaguered company. At that point air and artillery support was called in and the battle was over shortly thereafter. The final count was 16 dead and 87 wounded of Whitt's 100 man company. Whitt came through with only his scar, while Stephens suffered a severe shrapnel wound that resulted in the amputation of his left leg just below his knee. Enemy losses were 210 dead and 438 captured, including a number who were wounded. For this action, Whitt received his first decoration, a bronze star. His unit was also cited for bravery.

Whitt had been waiting in the diner only a few minutes when his companion joined him at the appointed time. He was confident neither had been followed since the other occupants were present before he had arrived. Nevertheless, he spoke in hushed tones and avoided certain words and phrases. His counterpart, who presented a stark contrast in appearance, followed suit. After the greetings and pleasantries, Whitt spoke first. "Jonas, please join us. With your academic background and gift of communication, you would be of immense value to the 'project'."

Jonas O'Leary, at age 46, had recently resigned from his position as chairman of the law department and Constitutional law professor at Georgetown University. He had been chairman for only a little more than a year after an exemplary teaching career of twenty years at Georgetown, and of course had earned tenure many years earlier. A number of his friends had wondered if he might have succumbed to a virus or perhaps had a brain tumor, which could account for someone in that position to give up such a prestigious position and comfortable retirement. He assured them, however, that he was of sound mind, and had thought through his situation and options. He would have preferred to teach, but since being promoted to department chair, he had little time for the classroom he loved. He was an acclaimed author so would have little difficulty in lining up lectures where he could once again interact with students.

He was dressed neatly as well, but that was about the only similarity in the pair. O'Leary looked the part, wearing a dark brown bow tie with matching vest over a pale blue shirt and khaki trousers. His sandy hair with specks of gray was neatly cut, but a little on the long side with long side burns. He had thick glasses, probably as a result of a lot of reading, and his physique displayed the result of years of good eating with too little exercise. He was probably thirty or forty pounds overweight for his height of about six feet.

"Lon, we have been over this too many times. You know my thoughts on the matter."

"I do, but the situation has radically changed."

"In what way?"

"Every day it seems, more and more of our freedoms are disappearing. Riots are increasing and the government is using that as an excuse to clamp down further. Inflation is getting worse and taxes are unbearable. And the scariest thing of all is that welfare rolls are expanding so fast that it won't be long before more than fifty percent of the people that are of voting age are on government assistance."

"I hear you, Lon, and I agree that things are not looking good, but there has to be another way."

"Dammit, Jonas. Tell me another way."

"I'm afraid I don't have an answer to that."

"OK, Jonas. I know that you fear a conflict if the project is implemented. I don't really want a repeat of history, so let me make this proposal: Help me to come up with a series of incremental steps that will move me towards my goal and at the same time slow down the movement to what I feel is inevitable."

"Come on, Lon. That sounds like 'Heads I win, tails you lose.'"

"Not really. Small incremental moves are not likely to stimulate a drastic response. You know well the analogy of boiling a live frog."

"Let me think about it and get back to you."

"Fair enough, Jonas. I'll be waiting."

Chapter 2: Boyhood Friends

They had been life-long friends, dating back to childhood, but as so often happens, they had found other interests and grown apart. Now, perhaps, fate was intervening and drawing them back together. Whitt and O'Leary had grown up together in an Irish Catholic lower class, but proud Charleston, West Virginia neighborhood. They both came from large families and their fathers worked in the nearby coal mines. Although Lon's name wasn't Irish, for which he took a lot of ribbing from his friends, he was probably more Irish than most of them. His father's paternal grandmother had married an Englishman named Whitt, but that was the only defect in an otherwise perfect four generation genealogy. When they were youngsters they played lots of cowboys and Indians, and war with the marines against the *terists*. The only problem with that game was that no one wanted to be a *terist*.

The two boys were inseparable when they were young and actually looked and acted so much alike that a lot of people thought they were brothers. They both had sandy hair and infectious smiles, with big dimples and lots of teeth showing. Both also were very extrovertive and smart although neither spent much time studying. As they entered their teens, a tragedy occurred, however, that resulted in their growing apart, not only in interests, but in appearance. When the boys were twelve, Jonas' father was killed in a mining accident that nearly killed Lon's as well, but miraculously his Dad survived.

After the accident, Jonas' big smile began to recede, as there was a lot less time for playing in the O'Leary household. Jonas' mother first started taking in laundry for wash and ironing, but when that wasn't enough she began taking housekeeping jobs in some of the wealthy neighborhoods miles away from their neighborhood. Jonas's older two sisters took on the mother's duties, and Jonas being the only male in the seven person household, began mowing lawns in the summer and shoveling snow in the winter, anything to bring in a buck or two to help the family survive.

About two years later Mrs. O'Leary remarried a Quaker history teacher, and the divergence in the boys' interests really set in. Brantley was a recent widower whose only child had been killed several years earlier in an automobile accident. He obviously had a lot of love bottled up and transferred all that love to his new wife as well as to his step children. He was an excellent father, but he insisted on the children doing their homework and studying hard. Then after homework was done, two or three nights a week, he would gather the family together for a history game. One of the children had to pick either a date or incident in history and tell the rest about it. After the child was finished, Brantley would fill in the blanks and embellish the story a bit. It was a lot of fun and what the kids thought was just a game became an excellent learning exercise. Jonas and his siblings would spend a lot of time trying to come up with something that their father would not know much about, but they never succeeded. They learned about the fall of the Roman Empire, the Magna Carta, the Renaissance, the Revolutionary War, The Civil War, the history of the Quakers and more.

One night after having studied the topic for a week, Jonas thought he had a subject about which he would know more than his father. The subject was global warming. Jonas told the group that the earth was heating up, which was obvious from the disappearance of the Arctic ice cap, melting of glaciers around the world and the record high temperatures in recent years.

He explained that the atmosphere acted like an insulating blanket, keeping the area of the earth warm at night where there is no direct sunlight, and that scientists had calculated that the average global temperature is 59^0F warmer than it would be without an atmosphere. Jonas continued, "The insulating effect is commonly called the greenhouse effect, named for its resemblance to a giant greenhouse surrounding the earth. And the gases that trap the heat are known as greenhouse gases. The most important greenhouse gas is carbon dioxide (CO_2), which is the main by-product of the combustion of fossil fuels, like coal, gasoline, and natural gas. Since 1850 when the industrial revolution began, and large quantities of coal began to be used, followed by the invention of the automobile in the early 1900's and the use of gasoline, atmospheric CO_2 levels had almost doubled. Global temperatures had followed the same path during that time after remaining fairly constant for one thousand years. Scientists are predicting that if the CO_2 level goes much higher, we will hit a 'tipping point' at which time there will be no turning back and we will have runaway global warming with sea level rising so much that low lying coastal areas such as Florida, New York City, and many islands in the Pacific will be completely under water."

At that point, Jonas finished his presentation and it was time for Mr. Brantley's critique. "Jonas, my son, you have studied well. Your presentation was very well done and convincing, but let's talk about the greenhouse effect. Who can tell me what a greenhouse is?"

Most of the children raised their hands. "OK, Kathleen."

She was the youngest of the five sisters at eleven years old. "A greenhouse is a glass house used for growing plants in cold climates. Sunlight is able to enter through the glass and then the heat is trapped so the plants remain warm at night."

Brantley replied, "Very good, Kathleen. So the heat is stored up during the night, waiting for the sunlight of the next day?"

Kathleen and several of the others nodded their heads.

"So can someone tell me why the heat doesn't build up from day to day until nothing can survive?"

There were a lot of puzzled looks around the room, but no words of response.

Brantley was on a roll now and was thoroughly enjoying it. "Could it be that some of the heat escapes somehow?"

More puzzled looks, but some nodded heads, and one, "I guess so."

"Well, you are right. There happens to be a tiny window at the top of greenhouses that can be opened and closed. Hot air rises because it is lighter than cooler air, so it moves through the open window and in so doing controls the temperature. This is called convection and it operates in the atmosphere as well to keep global temperatures from getting too hot."

Jonas chimed in, "So there is no such thing as the greenhouse effect?"

Mr. Brantley replied, "No, Jonas. You were right the first time. There is a greenhouse effect, but convection weakens it. You might call convection 'Nature's thermostat'. Do you and your sisters remember our trip to visit your cousins in Los Angeles last year when we had to travel through the desert?"

The children nodded attentively.

Brantley continued, "Who can tell me what it was like when we went through the desert?"

Another show of hands with several shouting, "Cold." And one or two, "Dark and cold!"

Brantley was smiling broadly now. "Well, I thought deserts were very hot places."

He didn't have to even ask a question before Jonas chimed in, "That's only in the daytime."

"But I thought the greenhouse effect kept temperatures from falling too much at night. Is there maybe something about the desert that keeps the greenhouse effect from working?"

Jonas knew he had the answer and blurted out, "No CO_2 in the atmosphere because there are no smokestacks in the desert!"

Brantley's smile had grown even wider. He was visibly pleased. "You are thinking, my son. But unfortunately, that is not the answer. CO_2 like the other gases in the atmosphere are spread evenly due to the winds. The difference in the desert is very low humidity. Water vapor is actually a far stronger greenhouse gas than CO_2, but because it condenses to form rain it is not spread evenly." And so ended the session on global warming.

At first, Jonas thought his step dad was just making things up as he went along, but when he checked some facts in the library, he found they were right on. From that time forward he never doubted his Dad, and he decided that he would study hard and become a history teacher. Jonas went on to surpass his dream, receiving a full paid scholarship to Yale where he achieved Summa Cum Laude for his bachelor's degree with a double major in history and economics, and then earning a PhD in Constitutional Law. Unfortunately, Brantley did not live long enough to see his son graduate, but Jonas knew he was there in spirit with that big smile.

Chapter 3 Sharon Eleazar

After high school, Lon Whitt and Jonas O'Leary went their separate ways. Lon didn't make it to Yale, but he did just fine at University of Pittsburgh, where he majored in Chemical Engineering. He took ROTC and was commissioned a Second Lieutenant in The U.S. Army Infantry.

Israel had been under continued attack from Hezbollah in the north and Hamas in the west for years. But only after Syria attempted to regain the Golan Heights in late 2016, did the incursions escalate into a full scale war. Whitt had been stationed in Israel for two years as part of a U.S. regiment in support of Israeli IDF forces when the battle in the valley occurred. He was at a party at the Tel Aviv officers' club celebrating his bronze star when he first saw the beautiful dark eyed 21 year old Israeli graduate student. Whitt managed a quick introduction through her father, Simon Eleazar, who was a major in the IDF and who knew Whitt from the joint American- Israeli operations.

Sharon Eleazar was not only a beauty, but had the brains to match. She had double majored in psychology and linguistics, and was fluent in Arabic and English in addition to her native Hebrew. Not surprisingly, she had several eager suitors, and Whitt instantly joined the crowd. He had had an active social life in college and dated a few times since he had been in the Middle East, but he had never met anyone like her. She had it all- beauty, intellect, charm, and a great sense of humor. Their first date was a week later and after that, he didn't give anyone else a chance. They became engaged in three months and married twelve months to the day they had met.

She was Jewish and he was Catholic, but neither took religion too seriously and for that reason felt that their religious differences would not be problematic. She, like a lot of Israeli Jews, came from a secular Jewish family. They had attended services on Rosh Hashanah and Yom Kippur, but that was about it. Similarly, he generally made it to church on Easter, but the last time he had attended mass other than for a holiday or funeral, he could not remember.

Early in their courtship, when they were discussing religion, Sharon asked Lon if he knew how Jesus would be able to differentiate between Jews and Christians. Lon was thrown a little bit off guard since the conversation to that point had been serious.

He asked, "Are you speaking only of males?"

She smiled, shaking her head, no.

"OK, Sharon. He would just know, but I don't think it would matter."

Sharon said, "No, Lon. He would know by how they responded to the question, 'Are you a first timer or a second timer?' "Sharon laughed and Lon, after hesitating, followed.

"Lon, from your facial expression, I surmise that you may not have gotten it."

"O.K, smarty psych major, explain it to me."

"Well, Christians believed Jesus was the Messiah, but Jews didn't accept him. Jews are still waiting, so when the Messiah comes, it will be the second time for Christians…"

Lon interrupted, "so Jews would be first timers."

"You got it, Lon, but I think you had it half right; it shouldn't matter."

Lon then told her that he was a CEO Christian and asked her to guess what that meant. When he told her it stood for Christmas, Easter, only, she laughed and responded, "I guess that makes me a 'Hiho', that's a High Holiday Jew."

He agreed to be married by a rabbi in a Jewish wedding for the sake of Sharon's parents, but they would raise their children to know both faiths and let them choose when they were old enough to understand.

When she completed her Master's degree a few days after they became engaged, Sharon joined the IDF and entered into the rigorous officers' training program. Six months later after successfully completing the course she received her commission, but then was quickly transferred to the Mossad, which had been actively recruiting her for over a year based on her educational background and intelligence.

About that time Whitt was assigned as attaché to General Max Hershon of the IDF, who also was a hero of several campaigns. Hershon had been impressed with the young captain's courage and resourcefulness and had asked Whitt's regimental commander, Colonel Larry Donahue, who was a good friend, for his services. He also requested that Lon be promoted to major, which would be more befitting a General's attaché.

Shortly after the newly promoted Major Whitt joined the General's staff, he proposed a radical and controversial approach in the battle against the Islamic extremists, since the strategy to date had been unsuccessful. He had broached the subject before, but his U.S. superiors had brushed it off as some wild and unworkable scheme. The plan was to begin a massive psychological warfare program to empower women and turn them against the men who viewed them as nothing more than chattel for their own pleasures. The program was contentious to say the least, since most of the Moslem countries were Western allies, supposedly, and one of the tenets of Islam held that women should be subservient to men. The messages would be delivered by radio, leaflet, internet and VID Discs. Small WiDi or Wireless Display players would be air dropped along with the leaflets for those who had no access to VID players.

The new program was eagerly accepted by the Mossad as it was ideally suited to its mode of operation. Lieutenant Sharon Eleazar Whitt was put in charge of its implementation. The information was conveyed in Arabic with considerable quotations from the Quran mandating kind treatment of women and heavenly rewards for men who obeyed those commandments. Moderate Muslim women from Israel and other countries, so long as they were fluent in Arabic, were recruited to appear in the VIDs. There were also a few participants who had been raised as Muslim, but had converted due to the harsh treatment they had been subjected to.

Before long, rumors began to surface about beatings and worse, of

Muslim wives who apparently had gotten the message. At first it was just a trickle, but shortly thereafter it became a stream, and within a year it was no longer rumor, but confirmed fact, and the stream had become a flood. Muslim women were standing up to their husbands and taking the drastic step of appearing in public without their Berkas.

This revolt was occurring not only in the Middle East, but around the world. Islamic Mullahs everywhere were protesting what they called a war on Islam. King Suliman bin Abdullah of Saudi Arabia protested vehemently as did other royal heads of state and ambassadors to Israel and western European countries that had jumped on the bandwagon with their own version of Major Whitt's approach. The U.S. had tried to stay out of the fray, but it was drawn in due to the administration's reluctance to condemn the program.

To be sure, there were still suicide bombings and other attacks, but the number and severity were decreasing steadily. Ever since the program began, there had been death threats against Lon and Sharon as well as leaders of countries that were participating. Because of that, the IDF had provided the Whitts with round the clock security personnel. There had been at least three foiled attacks, but nothing for at least three years.

Perhaps that explained the lapse in security on a beautiful Tuesday afternoon in May, five years to the day they were married.

Whitt had been in the military just short of eight years and had just been promoted to Lt. Col, a meteoric rise for a young man not yet thirty years old. And if not for the incident that occurred when on a four day leave, it would have been reasonable to predict his eventual rise to the rank of three or four star general.

The incident occurred in Jerusalem when Lon and Sharon were on a shopping trip, planning their fifth wedding anniversary party scheduled for that evening. He had left her in the car for a couple of minutes while he ran into the grocery store to pick up some champagne for the party. As he was returning, there was a terrific explosion that blew him off his feet. He could see the remnants of his car, which was ablaze, but miraculously, Sharon had not been killed in the explosion. He could see her struggling to get out before the gas tank erupted for what would have been a sure death. Although injured, Lon leapt to his feet and was able to pull the passenger door open and extricate her just before the second and final explosion destroyed the car and all its contents. She was rushed to the hospital and survived but had numerous fractures, internal injuries and second and third degree burns over 80% of her body. After months in the hospital, numerous skin grafts, and extensive physical and occupational therapy, she was finally released, a paraplegic who would live for only another fifteen months.

Whitt had resigned his commission to care for her rather than commit her to a nursing home, which all of his friends and family had recommended. Until she died, Whitt had forced himself to keep his mind off the terrorist act that had claimed his wife in order to focus on her care. But now that she was gone, he could not put the incident out of his mind. Until the incident, to him as a military professional, the enemy had been just the enemy. Undoubtedly, he would kill them without hesitation, but now it was personal.

Understandably, his impulse was vengeance, but Sharon had made him promise that he would make sure that the program continued after her death. She was convinced that it would result in the eventual eradication of Muslim extremism, and it was already having a significant effect at the time of her death.

By the time she died, Whitt had exhausted all his financial resources and was heavily in debt. He considered going back into the Army, but because he had resigned his commission and there had been major cutbacks in the military, he would have had to take a reduction in rank back to Captain.

His father-in-law, Simon Eleazar, now a full colonel, and General Hershon both tried to get him to join the Israeli army, offering him the rank of major with a high probability of promotion to his former rank of lieutenant colonel in a matter of months. He strongly considered accepting the offer, but came to the realization that if he stayed in the Middle East, vengeance would sooner or later overtake him causing him to break his promise to Sharon.

He felt that he had to get back to the U.S. to start networking with his extensive list of friends. He fully intended to honor Sharon's wishes, but short of continuing to live in Israel, which he had already ruled out, he felt it would probably have to be on a part-time volunteer basis since he believed it unlikely that he could find any similarly minded organization that would pay him enough to live on and extract him from the deep financial hole he found himself in

Fortunately, one of those friends was his subordinate from those early Army days, Robert Stephens, now recovered, who was able to pass along a very interesting lead. Stephens' father was the CEO of Atlas Energy, the second largest energy company in the U.S. That the company was headquartered in Pittsburgh, where he went to college and only a three hour drive from Charleston, his home town, certainly were not negative factors, but the key attraction was coal, Atlas' main business.

Stephens senior was as impressed with his potential new employee as Whitt was with Stephens and the company. The situation could not have been more perfect. Whitt had grown up in the coal industry and his college major fit well with the situation that the industry found itself in as well as Stephens' plans for dealing with the situation. The interview lasted for over an hour, but in truth it was over in the first ten minutes since Stephens knew Whitt was the man he had been looking for, and Whitt had a mutual feeling about the company and his future boss.

Chapter 4: The Enemy

Lon had been working at Atlas Energy for five weeks, visiting the scattered Company operations and getting acquainted with company personnel and protocol. He was now back in Stephens' office reviewing his observations and recommendations. When Lon was finished with his presentation, Stephens spoke, "Lon, I felt when I hired you that you were the right man for the job. I am now more certain of it. Did you ever wonder why I hired you?"

"Sir, I suppose because of my engineering background and maybe my family connection."

"They were part of it, but your military background was the clincher."

Lon laughed, "To fight the competition?"

"No Lon, we are at war, but our competition is not the enemy…"

"Who then is the enemy?"

"It's not the usual type of enemy that can be easily defined. In this case, it's the EPA…, you know- the Environmental Protection Agency. And in a broader sense, even our government and the U.N. You undoubtedly have heard of global warming and climate change?"

"Of course."

"What do you know about it?"

"Not much. I hear it mentioned all the time, but really have not thought that much about it. I recall having it explained to me by my best friend when we were kids, but I didn't pay that much attention. Somehow, I must be missing something. How does climate change or global warming relate to what we're talking about.?"

"Lon, don't feel lonely. I don't pretend to know that much about it, but there is the confounding notion that coal is the source of all of the weather problems, whether it be hurricanes, tornadoes, drought…heat waves, you name it."

"Sounds like a bunch of bull. What do scientists say?"

"According to the media, an overwhelming number of scientists agree. I frankly don't know if I believe it or not. I am not as concerned about my personal or family situation. We will still be able to live comfortably if Atlas Energy goes under, but what I do know is if the coal industry disappears, there are going to be an awful lot of people without jobs and a lot more people suffering from the cold in the winter."

"Sir, I can see that the situation is serious, but I am not quite clear on what you would like me to do. In a war the mission is to defeat the enemy. With the enemy being EPA, our government, and the U.N., what would you have me do?"

"I want you, very simply, to save our industry. I will leave it to you to figure out how. You have demonstrated resourcefulness in your military career. I have confidence that you will come up the answer. As you may have heard, I am currently the chairman of the North American Coal Industry Trade Organization. I've discussed you and your background with my colleagues and we are all in agreement. With your permission and acceptance, I am relinquishing my position in that organization and turning it over to you. It is an unpaid position, but you will continue to be an employee of Atlas Energy and receive your paycheck from Atlas. I may ask for your input from time to time on company operations, but I want your main focus on the organization and mission. Just keep me informed."

"I am honored and of course I accept, but I can't help wondering if I am the right man for the job."

"I have no doubt. "Stephens handed Lon the contact information for the trade organization and the meeting was concluded.

Lon left the meeting with a very strange feeling. He had never before felt so unsure of himself. He was in a war, but it wasn't even clear who his enemy was. Stephens had said it was the EPA, our government, and the U.N. But it sounded more like it was a war with science, and he knew that was a war he couldn't win.

Chapter 5: The Enemy (part two)

Lon knew he had to be brought up to speed on global warming and climate change, and who better to talk to than his old childhood friend, Jonas O'Leary? It had been years since they had spoken, but Lon hoped that he could track him down, either through family members or mutual friends back in Charleston.

Since he wasn't able to find any O'Leary's in Charleston, he concluded that all of Jonas' sisters had probably married. But then Lon remembered the step-father's name. Fortunately, Mrs. Brantley had not moved or remarried, and after learning that her son was a professor at Georgetown University, he left a message for Jonas to call him at his earliest convenience. That evening Lon received the call. After an hour of catching up on a lot of years, Lon broke in, "Jonas, it's been great, but I know you probably have other things that you need to attend to."

"I do have some preparation for classes tomorrow, but I too have enjoyed it immensely. Perhaps, we could get together sometime when you have business in the area."

"I'll take you upon that, but before we hang up, let me tell you the reason for my call. I recall when we were kids, you telling me about global warming. It went right by me then, but now I find that I need to know what that's all about."

"Lon, I would love to help you, but I am not a scientist. I certainly have been interested in the subject for a long time and have followed developments, but I think you would be far better off speaking to an expert in the field."

"Jonas, I understand, but if you have an evening free in the next week or so, how about dinner on me at a restaurant of your choice?"

"That would be hard to refuse, given my meager income and getting to see my old friend in the bargain, but let's go Dutch."

"I'm on expense account, Jonas, so pick a nice restaurant. Just tell me when and where."

"Okay. The Epicurean in Georgetown this Saturday at 7 PM, if that works for you."

"That sounds terrific. Looking forward to seeing you in a couple of days."

Jonas was already seated when Lon arrived a few minutes early and leapt up to greet his old friend. They hugged, sat down, and reviewed the menu. Jonas passed on an appetizer and ordered the least expensive item on the menu. Lon reminded him that the tab was covered and urged his friend to reconsider. As they ate and drank, they rehashed a little of what they had covered on the phone, but then Lon moved the conversation over to global warming. Jonas then gave him an introduction to the subject, which was similar to the presentation he had given during one of those family history games back in 2007.

Jonas continued, "…back then it was already an important political issue, but over the years it has become far more important. The EPA declared carbon dioxide (CO_2) a pollutant in 2009, and with that action the war on fossil fuels had begun."

"Hold on a minute. Robert Stephens, my boss, had referred to it as a war on coal. Which is it?"

"Lon, you are an engineer, so you have had a lot more science than I, but the war is really on CO_2. Coal is only the first target because it is perceived by the general population as being dirty and unhealthy."

"Makes sense, so go on."

Jonas continued, "After the EPA proclamation, a succession of anti-coal measures came into being, some by EPA and others by law. At first, the measures were relatively mild in an effort to have industry move away from coal voluntarily, since political interests favoring coal were so strong. But when the first steps resulted in only driving up prices for all energy sources and leaving coal relatively unaffected, it was decided that stronger measures would have to be put in place. The most recent was the enactment of a tax on CO_2 itself, called the Federal Carbon Offset Surcharge, passed in early 2023."

Lon interrupted, "So just two years ago and if I may ask, how much is the tax or surcharge?"

"$50 per ton of CO_2."

"$50 per ton?!"Lon's raised voice brought stares from some of the people at adjacent tables. "What an ingenious ploy?"

"I'm not sure that I understand. How do you mean, ingenious?"

"Jonas, that is just the point. Even you as a well- educated man, probably do not understand the financial implications."

"Lon, I still don't understand what you are driving at."

"Simply this, Jonas. CO_2 is a gas and is awfully light, true?"

"Yes."

"If it is awfully light, it should take an awful lot of it to add up to a ton, right?"

"Correct."

"So how much CO_2 would you think is given off by burning one ton of high grade coal?"

"I would have no earthly idea."

"Take a guess in pounds."

"I would have guessed maybe a pound or two, but since you put it that way, twenty pounds?"

'Nope, not even close, but don't feel bad. I suspect most laymen might have ventured a few ounces. In actuality, the answer is over three tons."

"Incredible!"

"Yes, but it's a fact. This leads to another question. How is it that the government intends to assess the tax?"

"I'm not clear on that. I do understand that each coal user is required to submit paperwork periodically, I assume to report how much coal they consumed. And then there are periodic inspections to make sure everything is in order."

"This gets more and more interesting, Jonas."

"How so?"

"Simply because the quantity of coal does not directly correlate to the quantity of CO_2."

"Lon, you have totally lost me. I knew you would be better off talking to a scientist."

"Not at all, Jonas. The reason that there is no direct correlation is that different grades of coal yield different quantities of CO_2. The purer the coal, the greater the percentage of carbon, therefore, the greater amount of CO_2. This complication leads to another plus from the standpoint of big government adherents. Since coal has varying carbon contents, the only way to fairly assess the surcharge is to analyze the coal being used. I suspect that the periodic inspections you referred to involve sampling and analysis any time a source is changed. Lots more bureaucracy and lots more headaches for the coal user."

"I understand, but I still feel you could learn a lot more by speaking to maybe someone from EPA."

"I highly doubt that, Jonas. You have filled me in pretty well. One last question and then we can order dessert. Stephens indicated that scientists are in agreement on global warming. Is that a fact?"

"Hardly, Lon. While it is true that a great number of scientists agree, it appears that there are a sizable number who disagree. One who I know personally is Dr. Kent Stratton, Virginia State Climatologist. I don't have his number, but you should be able to reach him by calling the Climatology office in Richmond."

"Thanks, Jonas. I'll give him a call." At that point, the discussion on global warming ended, and the two friends finished their meal and departed.

Monday morning, Lon was able to reach Dr. Stratton by phone and have a lengthy discussion on the subject of global warming. Stratton was able to fill in some blanks that Jonas had been unable to supply. After hanging up, Lon felt relieved in knowing that his mission would not involve fighting science.

Chapter 6: Economic Reverberations

Global cooling had been going on for three consecutive years when the Federal carbon offset surcharge went into effect, and one might have rightly asked what Congress and the President were thinking. By any logic, the theory of anthropogenic global warming belonged in the waste can of history. Atmospheric carbon dioxide levels had continued to go up while average global temperatures had remained unchanged for over twenty years before beginning their three year decline, and yet, those scientists who had been promoting the theory held on like gamblers certain that their current run of bad luck was about to change.

The many scientists who had spoken out against the theory over the years and had been branded crackpots and hired hands had been vindicated. But too many in government were beholden to environmental and alternative energy lobbyists so the war against fossil fuels continued.

Natural gas for now was not being targeted in the U.S., but only time would tell how long that would last.

The energy sector is too large a part of the economy for there not to be major repercussions from any disruption of supply. The CO_2 surcharge was only one of many costs added to the consumption and production of coal, but it was the final straw. The stock market, anticipating the demise of the coal industry, had been in a steady decline since the Dow Jones Average had hit 22,000 back in 2020. On the opening bell of June 23, 2023, the date the surcharge went into effect, the Dow was at 18,334. At the close, it stood at 16,459, the biggest one day drop in history. The good news was that the percentage decline of 10.23% was less than half the largest drop back in 1987.Over the next few weeks and months, however, further declines erased any happiness concerning the comparison.

But the stock market was only anticipating the effects to come. Electricity rates from those utilities still using coal went up almost immediately, as state boards allowed them. Nonetheless,, as the summer of 2023 was a mild one and power demand was low, consumers hardly noticed the slight increase in their bills. When cold weather arrived in early autumn and record cold temperatures ensued, the rate increases became apparent and there was shock.

Within two years of the CO_2 surcharge, the two largest coal companies, Atlas Energy and Olympic Coal were the only remaining U.S. coal companies, and no one expected them to be in business much longer. As demand dried up, coal prices fell, but ironically they could fall only so far until they hit the artificial floor established by the taxes. So, although there were few U.S. companies still using coal, its price was considerably higher than a short time before

There still remained twenty or thirty foreign coal companies around the world, but their total production amounted to less than twenty percent of the previous year's numbers, and with worldwide pressure mounting, it was only a matter of time before they fell and coal became an obsolete commodity. Nevertheless, the foreign producers saw an opportunity to exploit the price disparity. Since they weren't burdened by the CO_2 surcharge, they could absorb the ocean freight and still make a handsome profit. Generally, Congress is slow to act, but when it saw its revenues threatened by foreign interests, the action was swift, with a Presidential signature on the same day he received the bill. The law then assessed the same surcharge to imported coal and that problem was solved.

Meanwhile, as Stephens had predicted in his conversation with Lon Whitt, thousands of coal miners found themselves in the ranks of the unemployed and facing higher utility bills Workers, who had never before had to rely on government assistance were being forced to register for food stamps and government checks. Aside from the disastrous financial effect on families, morale plummeted and suicides sky rocketed. The suicides were almost always the male head of household, causing family cohesiveness to disappear. Juvenile delinquency rose sharply and riots broke out everywhere. Law and order had become an empty sounding phrase. Small towns whose entire industry was coal were instantly devastated.

Retail stores, relying on coal miners' paychecks, closed. Then like dominos, wholesalers saw their sales going down, with the weaker ones going under, and in turn, distributors and then manufacturers. In the beginning, the financial ruin was pretty much confined to coal mining areas, but what started as a regional effect in time became a national problem.

By the start of 2026, national unemployment had hit 20% with the country in a severe recession and headed for worse; the cold weather only adding to the misery of being unemployed, Twenty-six states had been declared disaster areas by their governors, triggering state assistance funds as well as requests to Washington to declare a national emergency and martial law. Riots in the big cities were a daily occurrence so much so that they did not even warrant first page news. Looting and arson were rampant and many stores had to close because of damages and stolen merchandise.

By May of 2026, direct losses due to the rioting were estimated at over four billion dollars and this did not even take into account the damage to the country's economy. Unemployment was most likely over 30%, but with layoffs occurring daily and many staying home from work afraid to venture into areas where rioting was worst, it was impossible to have a reliable determination.

Finally, on May 15, President Markham declared martial law, nationalizing the National Guard and directing them to the areas hit worst. Curfews were put in place and many civil liberties were suspended. The ACLU and other left wing groups naturally complained, but as ringleaders were arrested or shot, civil unrest dwindled. A few governors and mayors, however, did not wait for the President. Among them was the young mayor of Phoenix, Florence Zimmerman.

Back on January 26, shortly after riots had begun in downtown Phoenix, Zimmerman called a special session of City Council and asked them to implement a 10:00 PM curfew. Any individuals other than police out after that hour were subject to be arrested and searched. If it was their first curfew violation, they did not resist and had no weapons or drugs, they would spend the night in jail on a misdemeanor charge. The second curfew violation would warrant two nights in jail. If the individual resisted arrest, had weapons, which included knives, or possessed drugs, he or she would be tried with the minimum sentence six months. There were the usual outcries but most of the population supported the tough curfew law.

Phoenix was one of the few large cities spared of the wide spread damage. Midterm Election Day of 2026 had probably the lowest percentage voter turn- out in history at 32% of the electorate. The low turn-out could not be attributed to apathy; there was widespread discontent. It was more a malaise of pessimism that had pervaded the country, and most people could not see that either party had any answers.

Most of the general population had also lost faith in science after hearing for years about global warming and then climate change. They were witnessing climate change alright, but somehow the connection to global warming escaped them. Still, the Theorists were standing behind their theory, stating that the theory was still valid; the cold temperatures were only a short term aberration due to unusual natural influences and that if not for CO_2's contribution to the greenhouse effect, the cold would even be more extreme. (At least finally, they were acknowledging that CO_2 was not all bad after all.)The scientists who had not bought into the theory pointed out that the "unusual natural influences" mentioned above were a result of natural solar cycles that they had been talking about for years to an essentially deaf audience. Their prediction: thirty years of more cooling due to a quieter sun; after that returning to more normal temperatures. Their recommendation: reverse the predatory taxes and regulations that had strangled the coal industry since coal would be needed to deal with the harsh winters to come. But no one was listening.

Chapter 7: Depression

By the end of June 2026, lawlessness had subsided and martial law was lifted. But there was still the problem of the deteriorating economy. As the economy worsened with more and more people out of work coupled with increased outlays for unemployment, the Federal deficit rose correspondingly and politicians proved they were no better at economics than they were at science. Somehow, it escaped their thinking that government cannot create wealth. Sure government can create jobs, government jobs, that is. But where does the money come from to pay their salaries? Nevertheless, the summer of 2026 saw more government programs put in place than the nation had experienced during the first year of the Great Depression of the 1930's. The main emphasis was in getting people back to work, so an updated version of Franklin Roosevelt's WPA, referred to as the employment assistance program

(EAP) was enacted on July 15. Where the WPA had employed about 2 million a year, the EAP made it look puny in comparison. Over 2 million were put to work in the first three months and by the end of the year 14 million were at work repairing roads and bridges, but that was in addition to the vast bureaucracy needed to administer the agency. Each state would apply to the EAP for funding and then put its jobs out for bid to private contractors, who would then hire workers to complete the job.

Theoretically, the low bid would get the job with the government benefitting from the lowest price. However, as so often happens, there were unforeseen events that led to cost overruns and shoddy work that required re-work, all of which cost more money. But with the government footing the bill and having seemingly endless money, who was worrying about another million here and another million there?

One of the brilliant job creation concepts was greening Death Valley with desalinated ocean water. This brain child was conceived by Lester Parsons, CEO of Consolidated Energy, an international industrialist considered by many to be one of the richest and most powerful individuals in the world.

Consolidated was a conglomerate, owning electric utilities in thirty states, vast natural gas reserves with pipelines over most of the country, a steel pipe plant to serve his needs and a reclaimed steel plant to supply the steel pipe plant. In addition he had significant holdings and options in solar power.

Parsons had the well- deserved reputation of an unscrupulous manipulator, having no less than five fulltime lobbyists doing his bidding in Washington. Among their projects was promoting natural gas as the low carbon alternative to coal, and subsidies for the solar panel industry.

His idea was to lay pipe for the 352 miles from the Pacific Ocean at San Diego across the Sierra Nevada Mountains to Death Valley. Since Death Valley is almost 300 feet below sea level the only pumping required would be to fill the line. After that, siphoning would take over. The ocean water would empty into a gigantic sealed concrete pool at the low point of the valley and then be distilled for freshwater irrigation. Periodically, the siphon would be closed to allow bulldozers in to remove the salt.

Cost of construction of the project for material and labor was estimated at $5 billion, to be funded privately by a consortium of investors headed by Parsons with a federally guaranteed loan. After completion, maintenance and operating costs, primarily labor, were estimated at only $5 million per year. Projected income from the reclaimed desert was $250 million per year, so ignoring interest cost the project would pay for itself in slightly over twenty years. Not a very good deal for private enterprise, but not bad from a government perspective, particularly if inflation were taken into consideration.

It was the kind of sweetheart deal that Parsons was expert at and that had contributed to his immense wealth. There was no way he could lose on the deal. If it failed for inexplicable reasons, taxpayers would foot the bill, but Parsons would make out just fine, being assured a 5% net profit on the pipe. On the other hand, if successful, the consortium would also be paid a continuing royalty of 5% for their participation in this community- minded endeavor.

The project was doomed from the start because of the extreme corrosiveness of salt water, but no one thought it necessary to have any scientists or engineers do a feasibility study. The one bright spot was that the project resulted in the employment of 10,000 steel workers at Parsons' steel pipe plant for the twelve months it took to produce the 400 miles of twenty inch pipe as well as the thousands of workers required to lay and weld the pipe.. As the pipe was produced it was delivered to the sites for government employed workers to lay the pipe and weld the sections together.

When the water started flowing, there was great rejoicing, but it was short lived when the flow quickly dwindled down to a trickle and then stopped due to the many leaks along the way resulting from corrosion. At first, the remedy was to patch the leaks with rubberized cement, but it became obvious very quickly that patching the leaks was not going to work since the leaks were occurring faster than they could be patched. Various alternatives were suggested, including replacing the carbon steel with stainless steel, but when the cost of stainless steel in place of carbon steel was figured in, the time to break even would take in excess of one hundred years, even if the project was successful. In retrospect, aluminum probably would have been a better choice and PVC maybe best of all, but Parsons didn't have any positions in either aluminum or PVC.

It was boondoggles like this that got a great many more people working, but at the same time increased deficits exponentially since a lot of money was being spent with no corresponding increase in production.

During the early years of the 21st century the inflation rate had actually subsided due to recession, but it didn't take long for that to reverse as the politicians used their standard cure for recessions by deficit spending. The annual deficit had climbed from $1.26 trillion in the year 2010 to $5 trillion by 2024, an increase of almost 300% in fourteen years. Inflation at that point was slightly over 10%.The recession had brought that back down to 5%, but by 2029, the annual deficit had exploded to over $30 trillion, the inflation rate had crossed 20%, and interest on the Federal debt accounted for more than a third of the budget. Sales were climbing even faster as individuals and corporations were spending at an accelerating rate to try to keep ahead of the shrinking dollar.

Government's standard response to escalating prices has been price controls, and this was the case once again. That they have never worked has not kept the politicians from repeatedly implementing them. Some may actually have believed that they would work "this time"; probably the rest knowing the truth, but price controls were the easier pill to swallow for a gullible public. The rational approach of drastically reducing expenditures would be too painful and likely lead to a depression. The politicians had ignored the fact that price controls lead to scarcity and ultimately to even more severe depressions when they are removed and the resultant bubbles inevitably break.

Chapter 8: Independence Day

It was a beautiful clear Independence Day in most of Hawaii. Maui had a few clouds, and a brief afternoon thunderstorm crossed the northern tip of Big Island, but that did not dampen the enthusiasm and spirit for most Hawaiians. Fireworks were going off at such a pace that one could hardly hear the many high school bands.

It could not have been more different for the rest of the United States, which was frigid except for the southernmost cities. Miami and Houston were the warmest cities in the country with very pleasant daytime highs at 74^0 F, but the lows were just slightly above freezing. As would be expected, Death Valley beat those highs, coming in with a very livable (despite the place's name) 81^0F, but by sundown, the temperature had already plunged below freezing, and by 3:00 AM, had matched the all-time low of 15^0, originally set in 1922, for the third straight year. The new all-time low was 12^0 when it stopped falling shortly before sunrise. Much of the rest of the country considered themselves fortunate if the mercury even went up into double digits. Nighttime sub-zero temperatures were prevalent across the northern tier of states and emergency rooms were full of people suffering from hypothermia. Although smallpox had been declared eradicated years earlier, it somehow had survived and was rearing its ugly head again so that hospitals were having to deal with it as well. Hospitals were being forced more and more to fall back on emergency generators because of power rationing by the utilities.

The cold temperatures outside were bad enough, but ever since the EPA had declared carbon dioxide to be a pollutant, fossil fuel companies had been under relentless attack. The coal industry was the first victim of the surcharges, coupled with the fines from violations of draconian rules for mining put in place by their buddies at MSHA (Mining Safety and Health Administration). The two largest coal mining companies in the US, Atlas Energy and Olympic Coal, had managed to continue to operate by buying up their smaller competition and slashing overhead, including personnel, which in some cases ironically exacerbated the safety problems and added to the fines. Finally, Olympic Coal succumbed to the pressure and was forced into bankruptcy, leaving a severely crippled Atlas Energy as the sole survivor of the once mammoth industry. Atlas had a monopoly of sorts, but the irony was that every ton of coal the company sold put the company deeper in debt.

As soon as stockpiles were used up, coal burning utilities either had to convert to natural gas or oil, or stay with the much higher priced coal. It was a painful choice either way. On the one hand, there was a significant capital outlay with no assurance natural gas and oil would not be EPA's next targets, on the other, higher fuel cost and the almost certainty that the attacks on coal would not subside. In each case, the effect would be higher utility rates. The few domestic steel companies left that had not already been driven out of business by foreign imports found one of the basic materials used in the making of steel prohibitively priced. Railroads which had depended on low cost coal to drive their locomotives also were forced to convert. In addition to the added cost of fuel, there were capital costs as well.

So the mood across the land was far from celebratory on this February 14, 2029, which was the 136th anniversary of Hawaii's forced annexation by the U.S. and which now had been declared Independence Day for Hawaii. That this date had been chosen was certainly ironic since the annexation had been affected by force, and normally anniversary celebrations commemorated happy events. In this case, the celebration was for the undoing of a sad event. Most of the population outside Hawaii could not have cared less since they had far more pressing problems to think about, among them putting food on the table, staying warm, and avoiding death from the cold or disease.

The cold temperatures were not confined to the U.S. or North America. Europe and Asia were in a deep freeze as well. The tropics were enjoying mild weather, albeit cooler than normal. Equatorial and near equator Southern hemisphere areas were close to normal , but the rest of the Southern hemisphere was experiencing cooler temperatures than normal for their summer. Record cold temperatures had been outnumbering record warms by ratios as high as 20 to 1. Snowfall records were being shattered as well. So, what to make of it all? The IPCC (International Panel on Climate Change) had just met in Copenhagen and congratulated themselves on being vindicated in their belief that the increase in atmospheric CO2 levels was responsible for the climate change that was so apparent around the world.

According to the IPCC, the worldwide effort to reduce CO2 emissions was obviously working. One had only to look at the cold. Although atmospheric levels had continued to rise, the rate of increase had decreased significantly. The recent cold weather, however, was considered to be an anomaly, and it was the general consensus that global temperatures would cease falling and continue their rise, perhaps as early as this summer.

All was not gloom and doom, however. There had been an unlikely coalition that had come together in support of Hawaiian independence.

Many members of The Tea Party had become so fed up with what they perceived as a dysfunctional country that they were ready to separate from the U.S. to form a new country dedicated to the ideals of the Founding Fathers.

Several American Indian tribes had rallied to the cause thinking that they might gain some recourse for the way they had been mistreated and relegated to reservations. The ACLU and other left leaning human rights organizations had supported the cause and lastly, the UN, which had been anathema to conservatives almost since its beginning was probably the most instrumental force in Hawaii gaining its independence.

A large Tea Party Patriot chapter in Georgetown of about 200 was having a grand time celebrating with champagne. Lon Whitt, National Chairman, had been working with the diverse groups to get this done. Although he agreed that Hawaiians had been done wrong by the annexation and had the right to regain their independence, the group was not without a secondary and more important motive, that being secession and the formation of a new country based on the Founding Fathers' concepts.

However, until there was a single instance of a successful secession, the idea was merely hypothetical. Now it was fact that secession was possible.

Chapter 9: An Unholy Alliance

People were working again due to all the government programs, which gave the impression of a robust economy, but it was all an illusion based on fiat money with no backing. History shows that whenever government resorts to fiat money, there are two consequences. Initially rabid inflation, followed inevitably by severe depression so that the supposed cure leads to an even worse condition.

As inflation raged and individual's savings was being wiped out, there were those who profited mightily from the dollar's devaluation. Among those were Lester Parsons and his Washington cabal, who had invested in gold, which was soaring as a result of the inflation they had created. Price caps had been placed on a huge number of items, including natural gas, but the cap on gas had not been implemented before its price had doubled

Parsons was in a meeting with Bradley Sims, his counterpart at Solinco, a subsidiary of Parsons' Consolidated Energy rejoicing over the news today of Olympic Coal's bankruptcy six years after the implementation of the CO_2 surcharge on coal.

Not only was one of their largest competitors gone, but Parsons and Sims had raked in enormous profits from their short sales of the company's stock. Now they were poised to repeat the same thing with Atlas Energy, the company of Parson's long-time nemesis, Robert J. Stephens, III.

Their rivalry dated back to their college days at Yale where they were fraternity brothers. Both men were fiercely competitive, but it seemed that there was no situation where both were involved that Stephens did not come out on top. Whether it was academics, athletics, or love life, Parsons was always second best. The only area where Parsons had a lead was in their family finances, but Parsons knew he couldn't take credit for that since he came from a family that was wealthy as far back as the Revolutionary War. That none of his family are mentioned in the history of that time, makes one wonder, however, about the source of the wealth. Nonetheless none of Parsons' family going way back had to concern themselves with dirtying their hands for a living.

Stephens' grandfather, on the other hand, was a coal mine worker at the time of the Great Depression. When the company was on the verge of bankruptcy, Stephens got several of his friends to pool their meager savings to buy the company and thereby save their jobs. Stephens like his co-worker friends had a very limited formal education, having had to drop out of school in the seventh grade to support the family after his father had a stroke, but he had been a voracious reader even before the stroke, and somehow found the time to continue to read. He was the one man among his co-workers who could intelligently discuss current events as well as how history had impacted today's news. It was therefore no accident that his co-workers sensed that he was the man for the job and elected him president of the company. But this president didn't take a salary. Instead he worked alongside of his employees and in time by scrimping with his own finances was able to purchase the stock of those co-workers.

Stephens foresaw the skyrocketing demand for energy that the war would bring and was able to buy up a number of struggling coal companies for pennies on the dollar. By the late 1950's, Atlas Energy was already the most profitable domestic coal company and well on its way to becoming the largest in the world. Most of its active mines were in the U.S., but Atlas did hold extensive mineral rights in China as well as producing facilities in Australia.

Now with the relentless attack of the government agencies, it appeared that the creation of the first Stephens' sacrifices and hard work was about to die.

"So what's up, Les? We should be celebrating today. Gold is near record levels at $7600 and climbing again. I'm up two million on gold and raked in at least five million on Olympic today and I am sure you did far better. Every dollar that Atlas stock goes down is another $75,000 in my kitty, and I know you're short at least two or three times my position. Yet you look awfully serious."

" Yeah, I did OK, but I've got concerns."

"Like what, Les."

"Brad, you need to pay attention to what's going on. All of a sudden, since Hawaii's secession, there are people talking seriously about future additional secessions, and then there is this foolishness about a call for a Constitutional Convention. And finally, never take Stephens for granted."

"Les, it's only a matter of time before Atlas bites the dust, and Stephens along with his company."

"True, but the question is when? By all rights, Atlas should be gone as well, but Stephens keeps going. I'm beginning to wonder if it's just to spite me."

"And your comments about secession and a Constitutional Convention? So what? How could either of those affect us?"

"Brad, I don't know and that's what concerns me."

"Les, you're beginning to sound paranoid."

"Bradley, I'm not afraid of Stephens, or future events, but I didn't get where I am today, by ignoring even the most trivial of threats."

"So what could they do, Les? Those coal companies are dead; they are not coming back."

"True enough, but that coal is still in the ground, and it is said that America is the Saudi Arabia of coal. Supposedly, there is enough coal in this country to supply all the power companies' needs for the next thousand years."

"You don't think they would try to reopen mines?"

"I don't know what I think. All I know is that they are making too much noise. "

Parsons and Sims had been the primary benefactors of the demise of the U.S. coal companies, and they had been the ones instrumental in the manipulation of their stocks, but they had not been the ones that actually drove the companies out of business. Competition had not done it;

utilities other than Consolidated loved coal. It was by far the most economical fuel available.

It was the combination of regulations, taxes, and fees that had killed the industry. Politicians, domestic and international, had been the executors, but behind it all was the global warming scare, concocted by the environmentalists and implemented by the IPCC, which was a creation of the UN in the early 1990's. The academic world seeing the opportunity, came on board and it quickly became a gravy train for university scientists in climatology and related fields. The media, sensing a sensational new story, jumped in with both feet and the movement became an unstoppable train.

Parsons was right to have a foreboding of the future, but the one element that Parsons had not thought of was climate and how climate change might impact politics as well as the energy industry.

Chapter 10: The Trial

"Jonas, I wouldn't advise it. You are a Constitutional law professor and you know full well that you will be giving up your Fifth Amendment rights if you take the stand. The prosecution will twist and distort your words and quote excerpts of your writings out of context."

"Ron, I appreciate your concern, but I want to testify."

In pre-trial plea hearings with O'Leary's attorney, the prosecutor had offered to reduce the charge of sedition to the misdemeanor of disturbing the peace, carrying a maximum fine of $200 and no jail time. It was obvious to Haynes that the Government by making such an offer had a very weak case, and did not want to suffer the embarrassment of either an acquittal, or even the unlikely result of a conviction on such flimsy evidence. Nevertheless, Haynes had tried unsuccessfully to get O'Leary to accept the plea and avoid the risk.

After the prosecution had finished its case over a multitude of objections, most of which had been overruled, it was time for the defense.

The judge nodded to Ronald Haynes and said, "Defense counsel, you may now present your case."

"Thank you, Your Honor. Defense calls its one and only witness, Professor Jonas O'Leary."

Several jurors looked at each other questioningly;

"Did I hear you correctly, Mr. Haynes? The accused is your only witness?"

"Yes, Your Honor. The professor is our only witness."

It had been more than eleven years since Hawaii had become independent and almost two years since that meeting at the restaurant with Lon Whitt, but events began moving rapidly after that. There was more talk of the dreaded word, secession, and the government was getting ever more paranoid.

O'Leary had scores of friends who had wanted to testify, including Lon Whitt, but he had told them all to desist. Some had begged and pleaded, but O'Leary refused. He knew that anyone who came to his defense could be placing themselves in jeopardy, either harassment by the IRS or other Federal agencies, or worse (being pursued by the new dreaded Homeland Security Police).

After the professor was sworn in, Haynes began his questioning. "Professor O'Leary, you have pleaded not guilty to the charges. Would you in your own words explain to the court why you feel you are not guilty?"

"Gladly. I have been accused of sedition. The legal definition of sedition is incitement…"

Gary Andrews, the lead prosecutor, arose quickly. "I object, Your Honor. We do not need a lecture from the accused on his interpretation of the law."

"Objection sustained. The definition of the charge is the purview of the Court. At the conclusion of the case, the definition will be part of my instructions to the jury. Jury is to disregard Defense Counsel's question and Defendant's response, and both are to be stricken from the record. Next question, Counselor."

"Professor, do you love your country?"

Andrews again sprung up. "Objection, Your Honor! It's immaterial whether or not the accused loves his country. A man may murder the woman he loves, but he is still a murderer. The issue is whether or not he is guilty of the crime."

"Objection sustained. Next question."

"But, Your Honor. The question goes right to the issue of whether or not he is willfully hurting his country."

"Mr. Haynes, you heard my ruling. Jury will disregard Defense Counsel's question and response to my ruling. Also the remarks will be stricken from the record. Counsel, ask your next question."

After several more attempts to continue his questioning, each time cut off by a sustained objection, Haynes asked for a sidebar. Request was granted and both attorneys approached the bench.

Out of hearing by the jury, Haynes addressed the judge, "Your Honor, with all due respect, I am concerned that my ability to defend the accused is being impeded by your continued sustaining of the prosecution's objections and overruling of mine.

"Mr. Haynes, I do not appreciate your veiled attempt at impugning my integrity. I want you to know that I pride myself on being fair. Ask a pertinent question and I will sustain it; otherwise, I will overrule. Now, may we get on with the case?"

When they were back at their places, the judge asked if Haynes had any more questions. He was frustrated and angry, but swallowed his pride. "I have no more questions at this time, Your Honor."

Andrews began his cross examination. "Professor O'Leary, I hold exhibit one in my hand. Do you recognize it?"

"Of course. That is a copy of my latest novel, titled, The Second Confederacy."

"Thank you, Professor. You saved me asking my next question."

"No problem, glad to oblige."

"Your Honor, would you request the defendant to only answer my questions?"

"Professor, please refrain from speaking until the prosecutor asks you a question, and then all he wants is a direct answer to the question. Is that clear?"

"Perfectly, Your Honor."

"Good. You may proceed, Mr. Prosecutor."

"Thank you. Now with the Court's permission, I would like to read from Exhibit 1."

The judge told the prosecutor to proceed.

"On page 2, second paragraph, of the preface, I quote, 'As to the right of secession, there is nothing in the Constitution that forbids it. Furthermore, if the words and concept of the Declaration of Independence were valid in 1776, what has changed to render them invalid today?' Professor O'Leary, these are your words, are they not?"

"They are."

"Did I misquote anything or take anything out of context?"

"No."

"If you had the opportunity to rewrite your novel, would you change anything?"

"That's a very interesting question, Mr. Prosecutor. I am sure it is not perfect and could be improved. Is there nothing in your life that you would change if you could do it over?"

"Professor, I am not the one on trial here. Besides, you know what I am referring to. Some say your novel is subversive. Would you change the thrust if you were to rewrite it?"

"With all due respect, Mr. Prosecutor, you are confusing the book with the plot. The plot is a story of subversion; the novel itself is not subversive. The author of a murder mystery is not an accomplice to a murder just because he wrote about a murder. No, I would not change the thrust as you put it. To do so would be to trash my novel, which I happen to feel is a pretty good work."

"Professor, there is a term referred to as the 'project' in conjunction with what we are talking about. Are you familiar with that term?"

"Am I familiar with the term, 'project'?"

"Yes, in conjunction with what we were talking about."

"In conjunction with my novel?"

"No Sir. In conjunction with subversion."

"So in conjunction to the plot of my novel?"

The prosecutor was working hard to keep his facial expression from divulging his exasperation with O'Leary's responses as well as preventing his uttering of words that would be certain to draw a rebuke from the judge as well as turn some of the jury members against him.

"No, Professor. This is a serious matter. We are not here to play word games."

The judge interjected at this point. "Mr. Prosecutor, may we move on?"

"Fine, Your Honor. Professor O'Leary, I assume you have heard of a secret organization, calling itself, "The Second Confederacy?"

"I have."

"Are you aware that it has been characterized as a subversive organization?"

"I have heard some people refer to it as such."

"Do you believe that it is subversive?"

"I do not know enough about the organization to be able to make a judgment."

"Well, are you aware that there are those who believe it is?"

"They have a right to their opinion."

"Professor, you have been advised by the judge stated that you understand not to speak unless you are asked a direct question and then only to reply in answer to the question. Would you say it is only coincidental that the name of the organization is the same as the title of your book?"

Haynes rose to object, but was overruled.

O'Leary answered, "That would be difficult to say."

"If not coincidental, what would explain it then?"

"Perhaps they liked the book."

"Come on Professor. There are lots of books from which they could have borrowed the title. Isn't the real reason that the mission of the organization parallels the plot of your novel?"

"I suggest you ask one of the members."

"Do you know any members, Professor?"

This time Hanes sprang up and shouted so loudly that it startled several of the jurors. "I strongly object, Your Honor! That question is absolutely irrelevant."

Andrews spoke, "Your Honor, the accused invited the question by his response."

"Objection overruled. Defendant is to answer the question."

Haynes, red-faced now, arose and spoke. "Your Honor, may we approach the bench?"

The judge granted the request and both attorneys came to the bench where they could speak off the record and out of hearing by the jury. Since Haynes had been the one making the request, he was the first to speak. "Judge, the question suggests that my client is a member of a conspiracy, but he is not being tried for conspiracy. If you allow that question to stand, I will be forced to move for a mistrial."

The prosecutor disagreed, saying that O'Leary's association with an organization known to be subversive coupled with his novel, which encourages insurrection, should be admissible. Before Haynes could respond, the judge replied, "Mr. Andrews, that strikes me as a very weak connection. I will sustain Mr. Haynes' objection."

When the attorneys went back to their places, the judge announced that he was sustaining Defense Counsel's objection and asked if the prosecutor had any more questions.

"None at this time, Your Honor."

The judge asked Haynes if he had any additional questions of his client. About to respond that he did not, he caught a signal from Jonas on the witness stand indicating that he wanted to speak. Haynes would have preferred to rest at that point, but he had to defer to his client. "Yes, Your Honor. "He approached the witness chair. "Professor, is there anything that you would like to add?"

"Yes, Counselor. You and I both know that the Government's case against me was frivolous."

Haynes' face reddened again, but this time from embarrassment, not anger.

While Jonas spoke, the Judge was pounding his gavel. "Counselor, if your client continues along this line I will hold both of you in contempt."

Haynes attempted to restrain Jonas, but he kept talking. "The whole idea of this trial was intimidation of free speech…"

There were gasps and muffled laughter throughout the court room. The judge, while pounding his gavel and demanding order, interrupted, "That does it! Bailiff, remove the accused from the courtroom. And Mr. Haynes, I am holding both you and your client in contempt.

As the bailiff escorted him out of the courtroom, Jonas continued to speak. "The Government knew that it had no case or in plea negotiations I would not have been offered the reduced charge of disturbing the peace."

The trial drew to a close a short time later and Jonas was found not guilty of the sedition charge. For the contempt charge, he and Haynes were fined $500 each, which Jonas promptly reimbursed to his attorney.

A few days later, Jonas was relaxing in his apartment while reading the Sunday edition of the New York Times. He broke into a smile and thought about sending a thank you note to the lead prosecutor. The

Second Confederacy had just made the best seller list, and he calculated that the royalty from his book sales for the week was about twice the combined fines. He wondered too if at some point in the future, certain events in his book might actually come to pass.

The ringing of the telephone broke into his reverie and he answered.

"Jonas, it's Ron Haynes."

"Yes, Ron?"

"I just got off the phone with a buddy from the Justice Department."

"Don't the two of you have anything better to do on a Sunday afternoon?"

"Jonas, this is serious. I didn't call him."

"So what's up? You know that they can't try me again."

"Yes and no, Jonas. Gary Andrews, the lead prosecutor in your case has requested a warrant for your arrest to investigate the charge of misprision ."

"WHAT?"

"the deliberate concealment.."

"Ron, I'm well aware of the meaning of 'misprision'—the deliberate concealment of one's knowledge of a treasonable act or a felony. That guy is crazy. He couldn't get me on the sedition charge, so..."

"Jonas, the Justice Department considers 'The Second Confederacy' organization to be involved in insurrection. If you know any of the members he might have a case."

'I'll just refuse to testify under the protection of the Fifth Amendment. No jury will convict me with my prior acquittal of sedition."

"But you will be forced to testify if you are granted immunity."

"Okay, Ron. But a grand jury would be a big waste of time."

"What do you mean- 'would'?"

"I think I can cut this short and save us all a lot of time. Do you think you can arrange a meeting with the FBI?"

"And tell them what?"

"I will be happy to testify if granted immunity."

"All right, but I'm sure you know this is highly unusual."

"Ron, unusual times call for unusual actions."

"Fine, but you still have not told me if you know any members."

"Ron, there are may be some things you need to remain ignorant of."

"All right Jonas. Have it your way. I will get to work on the requested meeting first thing tomorrow."

Chapter 11: FBI interrogation

After Jonas hung up from his call from Ron Haynes, he dialed Lon Whitt. Fortunately, he caught Lon in his apartment. "Hi Lon. Sorry to bother you on a Sunday afternoon…"

"You know better than that.. Always good to hear from you and by the way, congratulations on the trial".

"That's what I called about. Now they are charging me with misprision of insurrection."

"What in the hell is misprision?"

When Jonas explained, Lon responded. "I knew they were not thrilled with the idea of secession, but I didn't know that campaigning for it was a crime."

"Constitutionally, it is not. But, unfortunately, the Constitution and our rights are being subverted."

Lon responded. "BINGO! And that is what we're all about. He then asked if Jonas couldn't just invoke the Fifth Amendment. Jonas pointed out that the Feds could offer immunity, forcing him to testify.

Lon replied, "I see. I guess I need to drop out of sight for a while."

"That might be best. And Lon, I'm sorry."

"Don't sweat it. I'll be fine and thanks."

Lon in turn called his boss and filled him in on the situation. Lon offered to resign, but Stephens wouldn't hear of it. Lon would be given a leave of absence but continue to draw his salary, which would be wired to a Swiss account in his name.

After the phone call, Jonas tried to relax again with the Sunday paper, but was interrupted again, this time by a knock at the door. He answered.

"Yes, who's there?"

"FBI."

As Jonas opened the door to the two agents showing their badges, he pretended to be ignorant of what he had learned just a few minutes before, "May I ask what is going on here?"

The senior agent, Stanley Rhodes, spoke, "You are Professor Jonas O'Leary?"

"Yes."

"Professor, you are under arrest for misprision of insurrection against the Government of the United States. You have the right to remain silent and anything you say may be used against you."

"I assume that I still have the right to a lawyer?"

"Of course."

"May I have him come over here?"

"Yes."

Jonas picked up the phone and dialed Ron Haynes. "Ron, if you aren't busy right now, I would like you to come over to my place. There are a couple of FBI agents here that have informed me that I have been charged with misprision of insurrection."

Ron told Jonas that he would be right over and Jonas relayed that to the agents.

When Haynes arrived, he huddled a few minutes with Jonas and then spoke, "Gentlemen, we have reason to believe that Professor O'Leary is not the primary target of this investigation, and that if he were to cooperate in the investigation, he would be granted immunity."

Rhodes replied, "We would be willing to drop the charge if the professor agrees to cooperate."

Jonas spoke, "I will be happy to cooperate if I am also granted immunity from the charge of accessory after the fact, and of course, in writing."

"Professor, you surely know that only a federal judge can offer immunity from a federal crime."

"I am aware of that."

"Okay, Gentlemen. I will contact a judge to get the immunity document and be back in touch. In the meantime, Professor, you will remain under house arrest."

Late the next morning, Jonas received a call from Haynes, advising him that a meeting had been arranged at the Georgetown FBI field office for 2:00 that afternoon. The requested documents had been prepared and a federal judge would be present to offer immunity.

Jonas and his lawyer arrived shortly before the appointed time and were greeted by Rhodes, "Gentlemen, I appreciate your cooperation in this investigation." Rhodes then introduced the two to Judge Earl

Grayson.

Haynes responded, "Mr. Rhodes and Your Honor, my client and I are happy to cooperate. We just hope that we can make this short and sweet as both of us have far more important things to attend to."

Rhodes replied, "Mr. Haynes, I assure you we will not be wasting time for either of you. His Honor likewise has an important agenda. We will make this as swift and painless as we can." Rhodes led them into a small windowless room, whereupon the judge handed Haynes the signed immunity document. Haynes looked it over and handed it to Jonas. Rhodes began, "Professor O'Leary, do you know any members of the organization calling itself 'The Second Confederacy'?"

Jonas whispered to Haynes a request to speak in private and Haynes forwarded the request to Rhodes. Rhodes was a bit perturbed at the request, but he and the judge excused themselves. Jonas spoke, "Ron, this document only grants me immunity from the charge of misprision, but as I had indicated, I also want immunity from the charge of accessory after the fact."

Haynes then signaled for the two to re-enter the room. Haynes spoke, "My client desires to also have immunity from a charge of accessory after the fact."

"Mr. Haynes, your client has not been charged with accessory after the fact."

"We are aware of that, but would like to take precautions against that arising in the future".

Judge Grayson angrily responded. "Mr. Haynes, you and your client surely know, that I cannot and will not offer immunity from the charge of a crime that may be committed in the future."

"Your Honor, with all due respect, my client is not requesting immunity from the charge of a future crime."

"Okay, so long as that is understood. Mr. Rhodes, would you ask your secretary to come in so that I can dictate the additional document?"

After that was done and the secretary brought the new document back to the judge, he signed it and handed it to Haynes, who in turn handed it over to Jonas. The document read in part, 'Professor Jonas O'Leary is also granted immunity from a charge of accomplice after the fact for any action or actions that may have occurred in the past.'

Haynes thanked the judge and asked Rhodes to proceed with the questioning.

"Professor O'Leary, do you know any members of 'The Second Confederacy'?"

"Yes."

"May I have a name or names?"

"Lon Whitt."

"Do you know any other members?"

"No."

"Do you know his whereabouts?"

"No."

"How do we get in touch with him?"

"I have no idea."

"You don't know where he lives?"

"Not now."

"So he just recently moved?"

"I believe so."

"When did you last speak to him?"

"Yesterday."

"What's his phone number?"

"I can give you his phone number from yesterday, but I suspect it has been changed."

"Did you tell him that you were to be questioned by the FBI?"

"Yes."

Rhodes sternly responded, "Professor O'Leary, you must know..." Rhodes abruptly stopped mid-sentence. What he was about to say before he realized the professor had outwitted him, was that O'Leary could be charged with accessory after the fact. Frustrated and red-faced, Rhodes concluded the interview.

Chapter 12: The die is cast

It probably would be a stretch to say that O'Leary's book was somehow responsible. But, how can we be certain? It may well have planted a seed, but why an event occurs is of importance only from an historical perspective to, hopefully, prevent the repetition of mistakes.

Almost nine years since Hawaiian Independence Day had passed, but the day had finally come. To be sure there were many in the movement that had wanted it to come a lot sooner, but saner voices prevailed. Election Day of 2042 was the determining event that had hastened the timetable.

Going into the election, Democrats controlled both houses of Congress as well as the Presidency, but the Party was three votes short of the 59 votes required for a super majority in the Senate. The House was safely in Democratic hands with close to a 2/3 majority and only ten or twelve Democratically held seats in real contention.

The Democratic Congress had been trying to pass a bill that would grant immediate citizenship to undocumented (illegal) immigrants, primarily from Mexico after they had been in the U.S. five years, provided they had no criminal record. (Coming into the U.S. illegally obviously didn't count as criminal activity.) It was estimated that this would apply to 30 million individuals, 20 million of whom were of voting age. The Republicans had been able to block this legislation with filibuster, but if the Democrats achieved a super majority in the Senate, the Republicans would be powerless to prevent the bill from becoming law. It would then mean the Republicans would be relegated to permanent minority status, with an unrestrained Federal Government.

By 1:30 AM Central Standard Time on November 5th, enough races had been called to make it a done deal. At that point, the Democrats had their 59 Senate seats with six races yet to be decided, and as expected, the Democrats handily retained control of the House. But from that moment on, at least for Texas, all the rest was irrelevant.

Governor Richard Houston and his chief of staff, Jerry Collins had had dinner together that evening and were tuned into national news from the time that the first polls closed in the east. The pre-election polls and Las Vegas odds makers had both predicted that supermajority control of the Senate was a toss-up. Five states were in contention, two held by Democrats and three by Republicans. If the Republicans could capture only one of the Democratic seats, they could lose all three of their contested seats and still have the 41 required to prevent cloture by the Democrats. In the end it came down to Nevada. The Republicans had lost their contested seats in Virginia and Missouri, and the Democrats had held their seats in Arkansas and Minnesota.

When Nevada was called for the Democrats, the Texas governor spoke, "Well, Jerry, the die is cast."

Collins responded, "Yep, Rich. I will have to say, though, I'm not surprised. It almost seems that fate is in control."

"I hear you, Jerry, but enough philosophizing tonight, let's get a good night's sleep so we will be sharp in the morning. We've got some thinking to do."

"For sure, boss. What time tomorrow?"

"Let's make it 10 AM in my office."

"I'll be there."

Two months earlier on Labor Day, in anticipation of the election result, the Texas legislature had met in an undisclosed session and had decided that if it appeared imminent that the "Fair Immigration Act" was to become law, Texas would secede. The vote was taken by secret ballot to prevent anyone from knowing how any other member had voted unless, of course, it was unanimous, which was highly unlikely. The vote was overwhelmingly in favor with only thirteen dissentions and three abstentions from the one hundred fifty member House, and four dissentions from the thirty-one member Senate There was one more ballot that day that had the same number of affirmative votes, stating that the results of the ballots would remain confidential until secession was officially declared and any violation of the confidentiality to be punishable by a sentence of no less than five years in a Texas penitentiary. The bills were sent by courier to the Governor's mansion and signed into law that evening.

But Texas was not alone in its concern with the immigration bill and its political ramifications. The Republican dominated states of Arizona,

Mississippi, Alabama, Tennessee, South Carolina, Kentucky and Indiana all had large enough undocumented immigrant populations to potentially tip the political balance. When Texas made its announcement, word spread rapidly, and secession was the main topic of discussion among the various legislatures.

Moreover, the immigration bill was not the only issue of significant interest, nor were the above states the only ones considering their options. There was a rumor that the EPA would soon be coming after the gasoline industry as it had done earlier to the coal industry. It did not matter that most scientists by then had conceded that anthropogenic global warming was faux science, and that attempting to control CO_2 emissions was a gigantic waste of money and an economy killer, but also a futile exercise in any event, since the largest fossil fuel users, China, Brazil, India, and Russia had no intention of cutting back. The narrative, therefore had to change, but that presented little difficulty as the Green movement showed once again how nimble they were in justifying the attack on gasoline by changing their focus to carbon monoxide, the poisonous product of combustion, as well as trace amounts of noxious nitrogen oxides.

The long term goal was to eliminate gasoline powered automobiles completely but the pressure would have to ramp up slowly since there were so few all electric cars and the number of battery charging stations were few and far between. As the price of gasoline was forced up, totally electric vehicles would become more and more attractive until gasoline, like coal, would become an obsolete commodity.

Chapter 13: Texas

Collins greeted Houston on the way into the Governor's mansion, "Good morning, Rich, hope you had a good sleep after that late nighter."

"I did and hope you did as well."

"I did and as a matter of fact was up early enough to get the latest election results, not that anything mattered after the Nevada call."

"You're right, but I am curious. What are the final numbers on the Senate?"

"It held at 59 to 39, Rich. Like I said, almost fate."

Texas Governor Richard Anderson Houston was proud of his lineage and all that it stood for. Born in 2002 and having been told all his life about the indomitable Sam Houston, a man eight generations back in his bloodline, Richard Houston took his allegiance to the great state of Texas very seriously.

That was one reason why he had taken the lead on crafting the secession legislation that his state had recently passed. It wasn't an undertaking that he took lightly. As a matter of fact, he looked upon it as his calling. After all, why would fate place him in the Governor's mansion at this time in history if not to lead his beloved state to break away from the bloated, near socialist, nanny state that the United States had become?

But he also knew that his responsibilities didn't end there. He had to take special measures to ensure the safety of his state - wait, make that his country - and all the citizens in it.

By 2042 the population of Texas was just over 61 million people, with nearly a third of that population being in the 18 - 35 year old demographic. That meant that for Gov. Houston to increase the size of the Texas National Guard from its current 38,000 personnel to his projected goal of 150,000 members he had a good sized pool to draw from. His only question was did he institute a draft or try and expand his military that much with a strictly volunteer force?

Houston for sure didn't want to go to war with the U.S., but he also had to be prepared. Aside from having the largest active National Guard, several other factors were in Texas' favor. Its strong and diverse economy, its access to the sea, and its favorable climate bode well for an independent Texas. Last, but not least, energy independence was crucial. And, in that regard, Texas was in excellent shape, given its massive petroleum and natural gas reserves, and the fact that Texas' power grid was entirely self-sufficient. It was, of course, attached to the national power grid, but it was not dependent on it.

The Governor's Chief of Staff was a longtime friend from college and confidant, and a man he considered a brother to him. But he wasn't a "yes" man, bowing to the Governor's every whim. No, Jerry Collins was a man who would look you straight in the eye and tell you that your latest idea was either crap or the best thing since sliced bread - and he'd mean every word of it.

Despite growing up in a lower middle class single parent household, he had good genes, at least from his mother's side. She had made a major mistake in marrying the truck driver who was to become Jerry's father, but she was determined to make the best of a rotten situation and ensure that her son would not grow up to be the low life that her husband was. By working two jobs, she was able to afford a small two bedroom basement apartment in affluent Scottsdale so that her son could have a quality education.

She lived long enough to see her dream come through when Jerry graduated from The University of Texas with a major in economics. Unfortunately, she died before he earned his master's degree in political science from Georgetown University. He was therefore a natural pick for Chief of Staff when Houston won the office in his landslide victory. Many times since then, Jerry and the Governor butted heads on the best course of action in whatever situation had arisen. But those tough sessions brought out the best in both men and, given the offices they held, produced the best results for Texas.

"I just don't know about this, Rich," Collins said, "I mean, are you trying to provoke a war with the US?"

"Of course not, Jerry. I just don't want to get caught with my pants down if Campbell decides to flex his muscles. We've already thumbed our nose at them by claiming the state guard for ourselves."

"Campbell is a dim-bulb and he isn't going to make any rash decisions. He's more worried about his "legacy" than anything else,"

Collins offered.

"I know. He's been that way forever, it seems. I remember at college when he was paying nerdy freshmen girls to do his homework for him so he could be the big man on campus. But what has me worried is if he feels like he's backed into a corner on this and has to do something, probably a blockade. We've got to be ready to counter that."

"Okay, now I see where you're coming from. We need to expand our military capabilities, but I don't like the idea of a draft, at least, right now. I'd suggest we ramp up our recruiting effort and tap into some of that Texas pride to get our numbers up," said Collins.

"Alright, see to it. As I recall, you have a lady friend who is a wheel at Josephine Strickland and Associates, a very reputable public relations firm."

"You're right, Rich. Kristen Walker, who I have known since college, is a partner in the firm. She majored in Public Relations and minored in Economics. Sharp as a tack and a Texan through and through."

"Perfect, Jerry. Give her a holler and let's see what she can do for her Lone Star Sta…, I mean Nation."

They both laughed.

"I will check with her, Rich, but I have little doubt that she would want to be on board."

"O.K. Just let me know. In the meantime, of only slightly lower priority, we need to be thinking about currency and probably a host of other things that haven't come to mind."

"Will do." Collins turned and left the Governor's office.

Chapter 14 Secession

"We, the citizens of the great state of Texas, and up until now, citizens of the United States of America, have determined as our forefathers did in 1776, that we can no longer tolerate the abuses of power and infringement on our rights, and therefore have concluded that it is our right, nay, not only our right but our duty to put an end to the abuses of power and intrusions into our liberty,…"

The congressional winter recess for election years had been expanded to the Friday before the week of Thanksgiving until the day after New Years' Day a few years earlier since very little significant legislation was ever accomplished during lame duck congresses. Hawaii with the mild winter weather, typically had been the preferred vacation venue, but ever since Hawaii had become independent, it was considered bad form to spend their vacations there. The beaches of Florida and the Gulf Coast states were way too crowded causing the favored destination to move to Puerto Rico, but now it also was becoming too crowded as people from areas that previously had experienced generally mild winters were being forced to seek refuge from the cold weather due to the increasingly frigid winters and electricity "black-outs". So now, the Washington politicians were looking for out of the way places even if they were foreign venues.

The recess was chosen as the ideal time for the declaration of secession, since it would be all but impossible to recall enough of Congress for a quorum, delaying any possible reaction to the situation till early January. So, at 9:00 PM CST Friday, November 21, 2042, the public declaration was carried on all Texas networks and the three national networks. The national security advisor, Allen Jefferson had been at a party and didn't hear the news until two hours later. It was 12:15 AM EST before he was able to break away and find a private place to call the President with the news.

President Oren Campbell had told Jefferson before he left on Thursday that this was to be a working vacation, and that he was to be disturbed only due to the direst emergency, so it was with some trepidation that Jefferson placed the call.

It was 1:17 AM AST on a small unnamed island off the coast of northeast South America about ten miles from Georgetown Guiana, when Campbell answered gruffly. His phone was programmed to receive calls only from Jefferson, so he knew who it was immediately. "What is it, Allen, that you should be calling at such an ungodly hour?"

"Mr. President, I am terribly sorry, but I thought I had better let you know that Texas has seceded…"

Campbell interrupted, "I can't believe this. You call in the middle of the night to tell me that Texas has succeeded in doing what?"

"Mr. President, not succeeded, but seceded, as in breaking away from the Union!"

"What?!Campbell had been in the middle of some love making with his Secretary of the Interior, Nancy Larsen, on a moon lit beach; and to say that he was ill-prepared to deal with a situation of this kind would be the understatement of all time. Had Campbell instead been in the Oval Office and fully briefed on the possibilities, even then he was so inept he would have been unable to make any kind of meaningful decision. He was a successful politician because of his good looks, debonair manner, and golden tongue in speeches with the assist of a teleprompter. His handlers, which included Lester Parsons had selected him on the basis of those characteristics and not intelligence. In fact, his lack thereof was considered an additional plus, since it facilitated in "guiding" him.

Campbell responded, "Those 'Remember the Alamo' and Tea Party bastards have been talking about this for years, and as crazy as they are, I didn't think they would actually try to do it, but they are not going to goad me into some rash action. The proclamation means nothing without corresponding action, and nothing is going to happen over the holidays. I will put some thought to it, and in the meantime get word to the Cabinet for an emergency meeting at noon on January 1 and let Speaker Holmes and Majority Leader Grayson know this is to be the first item on their agenda on January 2. Also call Vice President Ramirez to have him nationalize the Texas National Guard and let him know I want him at the meeting also. "

Campbell had been married 34 years, and his wife, Dolores was well aware of her husband's sexual proclivities. He wasn't all that good in bed in any event, and she had long ago sought out other individuals, both male and female to satisfy her appetite. For appearance sake, Dolores had made the trip to Guiana with the President aboard Air Force One.

In Georgetown, he and the First Lady had gone their separate ways, each with a Secret Service entourage. Dolores headed to the local five-star Hyatt, where she was scheduled to rendezvous with one of her lovers, and Campbell travelled by helicopter to his private location on the secluded island. Larsen had travelled there with a couple of Secret Service females the previous day to ensure all was in order.

Larsen was at least as promiscuous as Campbell, but for a totally different reason. Nancy Larsen collected lovers like some people collect trading cards, but unlike the normal collector, she had no compunction in discarding, particularly if she could trade "up". Each of her lovers was a trophy and also a means to snare another. Despite Campbell being a poor lover, he was President of the country considered to be the fourth or fifth richest in the world. Her next target, although he appeared to be totally oblivious to her intent, was Igor Segurin, the President of the Russian Federation, which was generally considered to be the third wealthiest nation, closely behind Brazil and China. And who knows but that the Federation might soon ascend to first place, the way it was annexing territory. During the twenties, while the rest of the world was preoccupied with the Islamic terrorists, Russia was quietly rebuilding its empire to resemble the USSR of old. Its boundaries now extended from Poland in the west to Ukraine and Georgia in the south to Siberia in the east. Segurin had even joked at a White House dinner party a few months earlier that the U.S. was an "occupier" of Russian soil. This went over the head of the dull Oren Campbell, who merely laughed, but it was clear to

Alan Jefferson that Segurin was referring to Alaska and that the statement was not made in jest.

Nancy and Igor had met at that same White House party and shared a dance. Segurin was charming and important, and that was enough for Larsen. That he was widely known as a womanizer and seemed to have no particular interest in her did not deter her in the least. In fact it made it all the more exhilarating. She was a classic beauty and knew it, having heard it repeated continually over her thirty-eight years. She was confident that she could tame him. Campbell, on the other hand, had an inferiority complex about sex, and kept looking for the woman who would finally bring out his manhood.

When Ramirez called the Texas National Guard Commander, he was told that since Texas was now independent, the National Guard had been transformed into the Republic of Texas Militia, which no longer answered to the U.S.

Ramirez considered getting back to Jefferson or even trying to get through to the President directly, but decided against either since there was not much that could be done right now anyway. Campbell was known to have a nasty temper, and compounding the bad news in the middle of the President's vacation was thought not to be a wise move. Things would just have to wait till the New Year.

Chapter 15: Dominoes

Time and tide wait for no man. –Geoffrey Chaucer

As much as the President might have liked, the situation just wasn't going to stand still till the New Year or even for the next few days. On Monday November 25, all the Texas newspapers carried the declaration on their front page and announced a referendum for the following Tuesday for the citizens to decide if they agreed with the legislature. The referendum was almost moot, given the reaction of the citizenry over the weekend. There were a few protests, but they were drowned out by the shouts of approval from the population. The landslide confirmation came eight days later with 87% in favor.

Meanwhile, legislatures in at least a dozen states, were meeting and debating the subject. Despite widespread discontent and Texas' lead, support for outright secession, at least without some serious dialogue, was far from unanimous. The arguments varied from fear of war to being tried as traitors if secession failed, but the most prevalent argument was the dread of the unknown. Indeed, any state taking such a step would be venturing into a situation with little precedent as a guide and at that, not very encouraging.

Notwithstanding the above, there are thankfully always courageous individuals who despite the risks are willing to do what they perceive as right, so by the end of November, two other states, i.e., Alaska and Arizona, had declared their independence; and their legislatures were in discussion with that of Texas to form a protective alliance and possibly more. Moreover, West Virginia, despite strong Democrat leanings, was seriously considering secession, due primarily to EPA's war on the state's major industry. Virginia was contemplating dividing into two parts with the Washington metropolitan area remaining in the Union and the rest joining the secession ranks. Lon Whitt, a Virginia citizen, was encouraging talks with West Virginia in hopes of a merger.

When Jefferson called his boss the next time, he made sure it was daytime. Campbell was still in bed while Larsen was showering when he answered the phone at 10:00 AM AST on the second Monday after Thanksgiving. He did not sound like he was in a happy mood. "So what is it this time, Allen?"

"Mr. President, I am sorry to bother you again, but I felt you should know about developments since Texas' secession."

"Enough of the damn apologies. What is so fucking important that it can't wait for another month?"

"Sir, two other states have followed Texas' lead, and several others are discussing it."

After Jefferson filled in the details, Campbell asked him what he thought should be done. Campbell was a dimwit, but at least had picked a bright fellow as his advisor. "Mr. President, I have to say, I don't know. The Constitution is of no help since it has nothing to say about secession."

"What about martial law to deal with insurrection?"

"Sir, insurrection is generally defined as a violent attempt to overthrow a government."

"How about sending in troops to protect U.S. citizens and government property?"

"Pretty risky, Sir. Besides, at least so far, there have been no incidents that would call for a military response."

"Damn them! If it's a fight they want, why don't they come out swinging?"

"Sir, I don't believe they want a fight."

"Well, whether or not they want a fight, they are going to get one. They can't just decide they don't want to play anymore, pick up their marbles and go home."

"Mr. President, I fully understand. What would you like me to do between now and your Cabinet meeting on January 1?"

"Jefferson, (it's serious now since it is no longer first name basis.) You are my advisor, not the other way around."

"Yes, sir, Mr. President."

"I'm not finished. I didn't pick you because of your good looks. You are a Rhodes Scholar after all. I want you to use your brain and think. Go to the library and study. I want some specific recommendations at the meeting."

"Yes, Sir. Anything else?"

"Not that I can think of. Oh, keep me informed on any further developments."

"Of course, Mr. President!" Jefferson was hoping that there would be no further need for contact until his boss got back from vacation, but that was not to be.

A day after Christmas, Jefferson received a call from Lester Parsons, whom he had met and knew casually from several White House parties.

"Allen, this is Les Parsons. I need to get in touch with the President."

"Mr. Parsons, President Campbell is on vacation and is scheduled to be back in Washington on the 29th."

"Allen, I need to talk to him now!"

"Mr. Parsons, I am sorry, but he asked that he not be disturbed except for the most dire emergency."

"Dammit, Allen, this is an emergency and I need to speak to him immediately."

"OK, give me your number and I will ask the President to give you a call."

Campbell picked up on the first ring, "OK, Allen, what's the latest."

"Mr. President, I am very sorry to bother you again, but Lester Parsons insisted."

Campbell surprised Jefferson by telling him it was no problem and asking for Parson's number.

As soon as the call ended, Campbell was dialing Parsons.

"Hello, Oren."

"Hello, Les. How did you know it was me?"

"Just a strong hunch. "It had been less than five minutes since he had hung up on Jefferson. "Oren, we have a serious development on our hands. Virginia is talking about splitting in two with all but the area around Washington seceding. Not only that, but West Virginia may follow and then merge with Virginia."

"Yeah, I am aware several states are talking about seceding, but right now, it's only talk. What's so special about Virginia and West Virginia?"

"West Virginia just happens to be the state with the largest known coal reserves and Virginia since the discovery of the coal seam along the Shenandoah in 2019 may turn out to be the largest coal deposit in the world. If they join forces and secede, they will in all probability revive the coal industry, which would cause me an awful lot of financial discomfort."

"Well, what can we do?"

"Oren, you have no doubt heard about Lon Whitt. He is the key fellow behind this movement."

"So we have to eliminate him."

"Yes and no. If we kill him, someone will take his place. What we have to do is compromise him. I want you to find a gal for him. And not just any gal. She has to be cunning, charming, and of course a knockout looks wise."

"Got ya. I will get my people looking right away."

"Alright, Oren, but remember time is of the essence."

Campbell hung up and muttered, "Damn that Whitt!"

Larsen asked, "What was that all about?"

Campbell hurriedly explained and then called Jefferson back to get him looking for the right "gal".

Meanwhile, Larsen was thinking, "I know the gal for the job."

Chapter 16: Playtime over

Stephen Harvey, head of the Secret Service detail guarding the President on the remote island, dialed the number to the President's house phone. Campbell answered groggily.

"Mr. President, I hope I didn't disturb you, but you had requested me to call you two hours before your scheduled departure for the mainland to meet up with the First Lady for your trip back to Washington."

Campbell tried to sound Presidential, but his tongue was thick and dry, and he was suffering from a nasty hangover after a long night. His assurance that all was well probably didn't sound too sincere, but right now he couldn't care less. "Steve, I'll be ready."

It was December 29 and play time was over. Campbell was now regretting the scheduled New Year's Day White House meeting, but it was too late to reschedule. And, of course, it was time to get down to business, although Campbell had no clue as to what he should do.

Campbell might have been in rough shape, but remarkably, Larsen looked like she had just come from a day at the spa. "Orey, forgive me for saying so, but you look like something the cat dragged in. I thought since it was our last night here, I would make it a special night, but maybe I need to go a little easier on you."

"No way, Nan. I just had a bit too much to drink. By the way, you look fabulous."

"Thanks, Orey." And with that she gave the President one last juicy kiss as he headed out the door to meet his helicopter for the ride back to Guiana. The First Lady was already aboard Air Force One when the helicopter pulled up twenty minutes later. Campbell boarded and took a seat next to her for the quiet trip back to Washington. It was not that there was any animosity between them; they could as well have been strangers for all that they had in common for the last fifteen or twenty years. Not much was said as each pretty well knew what the primary activity consisted of during their respective vacations. The Secret Service was of course aware of the couple's extra-curricular activities, but they were the only ones privy to the secret.

A couple of hours later Nancy Larsen was on her way back to Washington aboard a small private charter. As soon as she had cellular service, she placed a call to Lester Parsons. "Les, it's Nancy. I understand you are looking for someone to deal with Lon Whitt.

"I am. Do you have someone in mind?"

"Come on, Les. Don't be coy."

"What will lover boy say?"

"He doesn't need to know. And even if he finds out, I can handle it."

"I have not a doubt, Nancy. I just want to keep him happy."

"That's my job, Les, and even if I say so myself, I think I'm pretty good at it. So, am I elected?"

"In a landslide, Nancy."

"So, how do I get in touch with this wanted man?" She smiled at the double entendre.

"Jonas O'Leary is a close friend and will know how to get in touch with him." Parsons gave her O'Leary's number and told her to leave a message for Whitt to call her.

Chapter 17: Merger proposal

On the same day that the President was headed back to Washington from his vacation on the South American island, Lon Whitt was in Charleston, West Virginia at invitation of several West Virginia leaders, preparing to speak to a joint session of the legislature. He now had a price on his head for "inciting insurrection", the same charge that his friend, Jonas O'Leary had been tried on two years earlier. Because of his wanted status, he now had to travel incognito, and appearing in public was a risk, but Whitt had never been one to back down in the face of a threat.

Secession had been a topic of conversation in West Virginia for the twenty years that the Federal Carbon Offset Surcharge had been in place, but it was one of those topics that people talk about but that few take seriously. After all, how could a small poor state surrounded by unsympathetic states and possessing few natural resources other than coal, which was being legislated into oblivion, hope to successfully become independent? Moreover, didn't the Civil War forever resolve the question of secession? But just perhaps what seems unfeasible at one point in time, suddenly becomes possible. Science is the eternal search for truth. If things are as they seem at the time, why continue the search? If true of science, why not of all things? Now with the secession of four states, it no longer appears to be a settled question. And with Virginia considering secession, the encirclement issue might also be resolved.

When Whitt was introduced and stood to speak, he received a standing ovation. He was well known and admired in West Virginia, not only for his military exploits during the Syrian War, but also for his stand against the EPA in their war against the industry that was the state's livelihood. The state had long been a Democratic stronghold, and the legislators certainly knew his political persuasion, but nevertheless, showed their admiration for someone they knew to be a true patriot.

He began, "Madame Speaker, Thank you for the gracious introduction. And Mr. Governor, Senators and Delegates, thank you for the warm greeting. I am humbled and proud for the opportunity to speak to you here today. As you know I am a citizen of your sister state of Virginia, but I will share something with you that I hope will remain here. I truly feel a closer kinship to your state than I do to the state I now call home. I was born and raised in West Virginia in a small town not very far from where I am standing today. I have coal in my blood. We lived in a town where probably eighty percent of the men worked in the mines. My own father worked in the mines and was severely injured in a mining accident that killed his best friend, who was my best friend's father. Dad, thankfully recovered, and despite Mom's pleas to the contrary, he went back to work in the mines and continued till he retired. Why? Some may ask. The work is hard and dangerous. Simple, because he loved…" Whitt paused and swallowed hard.

"…the work and had coal in his blood."

There was another standing ovation that lasted at least two minutes until he could quiet them down. Whitt continued, "Thank you, but enough about me. This is about you, your great state, and what has happened and is happening to the once greatest country in the world. You all are well aware of the momentous step that the State of Texas took shortly after the election. It was not done in haste or without extensive deliberation of other options and ramifications. What they concluded was that the masterpiece of government that the Founding Fathers had constructed had become so shattered that it was beyond repair and that the only recourse was to break off and from it attempt to reconstruct what our country had been and was meant to be. Since then, the states of Alaska and Arizona have followed Texas' lead.

"I know that you have been discussing your options and you should know that Virginia is doing the same thing. There is a slight difference, however, which is the primary reason I am here today. The area of Virginia considered to be the metropolitan Washington DC area is not wanting to secede, so there are discussions going on regarding Virginia breaking into two parts, similar to what happened at the start of the Civil War, which created the state of West Virginia. The sentiment in Virginia is to allow Northern Virginia to separate from Virginia to form a new state, followed by Virginia seceding from the U.S. We would like you to consider a merger of our states, which would strengthen each of us. With Northern Virginia gone, we have a strong common interest in the coal industry and we each have strategic advantages that will be complementary. Virginia has the coast, which gives us access to trade with Europe and South America. West Virginia has the Ohio River which would be another important trade conduit, assuming that other states along the Ohio secede, which appears likely. The mountains of both states provide excellent defensive advantages, if the U.S. decides to attack."

After Whitt's talk, there was a lively question and answer period, which indicated considerable interest in his proposal.

The session ended at 4:30 PM, and Whitt joined some close friends for cocktails and dinner. It was almost 8:00 PM before the dinner ended and Whitt was able to break away for his drive back to his new secret apartment in Georgetown. He pulled into his garage about 1:30 AM and was in his apartment and ready for bed twenty minutes later. He was exhausted and really not interested in any messages, but he couldn't resist to check before retiring. When he got the message, he was sorry he hadn't waited until morning, because he was now wide awake.

Chapter 18: The Message

The message was from his old friend, Jonas O'Leary. Nancy Larsen, Secretary of the Interior, had called him this evening to ask if he might be able to arrange a private meeting between herself and Whitt, who she had learned was a close friend of O'Leary. Larsen had provided her private number and asked that Whitt give her a call in the morning if he was so disposed. Since she had given O'Leary no other information, he was unable to give his friend much advice other than to be careful.. Lon was puzzled by the request. It could be a trap, but why use Nancy Larsen? He thought that he might have met her at some point, but could not recall when. What intrigued Whitt was the office she held. The EPA was part of the Department of the Interior, which meant that the EPA chief reported to Larsen! He spent the next hour trying to figure out what it meant, but one thing was for certain. He was going to call Nancy Larsen after he got some sleep.

He had set the alarm for 7:00, but when it went off, he decided he had better have a clear head for the phone call and reset the alarm for 9:00. He awoke, had a couple of cups of black coffee and then a quick shower. He dialed the number about 30 minutes later. Larsen must have anticipated it was Whitt as she answered in a sultry voice, "Hellooo."

"Secretary Larsen?"

"Yehhss?"

"Miss Larsen, This is Lon Whitt. You had left a message with Jonas O'Leary that you wanted me to call."

"Yes, Mr. Whitt. May I call you Lon? And please call me Nancy. Thanks for calling."

"OK, Nancy. What is it you wanted to discuss?"

"Lon, it's a bit sensitive. I think it best we meet to discuss."

"Can you at least give me a hint of what we will be talking about?"

"I'll bet you can guess."

"Not a chance, Nancy."

"OK, Lon, Let's just call it a secret until then."

"Miss Larsen…"

She corrected him, "Nancy."

"OK, Nancy, I don't think either of us has the time for games."

"Your time will not be wasted, I assure you, Lon."

"OK, Nancy. What time and where? It will have to be some out of the way place since, as you probably know, I'm a wanted man."

"Yes, I am aware. Let's make it at my apartment. It's in Georgetown, AND very private."

"O.K., What time, then?"

"I leave my office at 5:00. Give me a chance to get out of my work clothes, showered, and into something comfortable. How about 6:30?"

"That will work."

"And since I won't have had a chance to get something to eat, why don't we make it a dinner meeting? I can put something together pretty quickly, and I've been told I am not a bad cook."

"That sounds tempting since it's been a while since I've had home cooked meal, but I don't want to put you out."

"No problem at all. I am looking forward to it." She ended the conversation by giving him directions to her apartment.

Chapter 19: The Proposition

Larsen left her office early in anticipation of her dinner with Whitt and stopped by the grocery to pick up something quick and easy for dinner. She settled on the deli Cordon Bleu and some side casserole dishes which she would only have to pop in the oven. That and a pre-made salad, a loaf of fresh bread, a frozen dessert, and a couple of good bottles of Chardonnay, and she was set.

She got home at 5:30 with plenty of time to get ready. She used the time to tidy up the apartment and set the table. She also placed a well-worn copy of "Fifty Shades of Grey" on the coffee table in front of the sofa. That book had been published more than twenty years earlier, but was still a best seller in the erotica genre. Then she turned on the TV to watch ABC's 6:00 News. At 6:25 she turned off the TV, kicked off one of her high-heeled shoes, and awaited Whitt's arrival.

At 6:30 the doorbell rang, and Nancy greeted her guest, "My, but you are punctual. You will have to forgive me, but the traffic was terrible and I haven't even had time to change." Before Lon could respond, she continued. "I barely got in with time enough to set the table and get something in the oven."

Lon replied, "I like to be on time, Miss Larsen, and you needn't change on my account. ."

"Thanks Lon, but I will feel a lot more comfortable if I do." As she led him in, she thought to herself, "Now, here is a man. I may not even make it through dinner."

Nancy continued, "Give me just a few minutes to get out of my work clothes and freshen up. Just take a seat on the sofa and make yourself at home. There is some beer in the fridge or you can go ahead and get started on the wine. The remote to the TV is on the coffee table. And by the way, the name again is Nancy." She picked up her shoe, left the room, and closed the door.

Lon smiled and responded, "As you wish, Nancy."

Nancy called back through the closed door, "That's much better, Lon."

About twenty minutes later, Nancy reappeared in a sexy evening gown. "I'm sorry about that, but I hate those work clothes and I just had to take a shower."

"Nancy, you looked just fine before, but now maybe even better."

Nancy turned on a well- practiced blush, and said, "Thanks, Lon. Are you famished? I know I am."

Lon replied, "Absolutely. The aroma is a great appetizer."

"Thanks, I hope you like it. Just something I threw together. She began placing the food and asked Lon to take a seat at the table.

"Is there something I can do?"

"Sure, Lon. You can go ahead and open the wine."

They sat down and began eating. Lon complimented her on the food and Nancy thanked him.

As they were eating, Lon mentioned the book.

Again, that well practiced blush. Nancy asked, "Have you read it?"

"No, but I've heard about it."

"Good or bad?"

"I guess both."

"So what do you think?"

"I've never been much of a fan of vicarious experience."

She was not prepared for that response, and this time the blush was genuine. All she could come out with was, "Oh."

They were finishing the entree and had just about consumed the second bottle of Chardonnay when Lon said, "So Nancy, This has been very nice, but I still haven't learned the reason for the meeting."

"Lon, You know what you have been charged with and must have surmised why. You have been and continue to be a very influential voice in the secession movement."

"So are you going to read me my Miranda rights?"

"Nothing of the sort, Lon." I am prepared to make you a proposal."

"O.K. Nancy, I am listening."

"This comes not just from me, but from the President himself. What we would like is for you to give a nationally televised speech. The President's speech writer will help you with the wording. The gist will be that upon reconsideration, you are renouncing the secessionist movement. All you have to do is follow the teleprompter."

"So that's what you and the President want? What am I to get out of the bargain, the charge against me will be dropped?"

"Far better than that, Lon. If you agree, not only will the charge against you be dropped, but we've both had a bit too much wine and I would hate to be an accomplice to a DUI. You are welcome to spend the night here and we can get a little bit more acquainted."

"That is quite interesting. Would you consider a counter offer?"

"But, of course, Lon." She was thinking, "This is going to be easier than I thought."

"If you agree to have the EPA reverse their 'carbon dioxide-pollutant' declaration with either you or the head of the EPA, Alice Ridley, giving a nationally televised speech which I will prepare, acknowledging the grievous error made on the basis of faulty science, THEN I will take you to bed."

Chapter 20: White House Meeting

It was New Year's Day and the Cabinet members were almost all assembled. With considerable difficulty, in between library time, Allen Jefferson had been able to convey the message from the President to all concerned ,except for the Secretary of the Interior, Nancy Larsen. He had left her numerous messages with no response so was hoping that she had gotten the message, if not from him from one of her many paramours. (He was personally knowledgeable of her favorite hobby, but because of the closely guarded secret, unaware of her relationship with his boss).He did know that there would be no excuses if anyone missed the meeting because he had not contacted them and dreaded the thought. So it was with considerable relief when he saw her arrive just before noon. She nodded and smiled as she walked past Jefferson to her chair.

Jefferson, also smiling, greeted her, "Happy New Year, Madame Secretary. Good to see you. I kept trying to contact you about the meeting and was afraid you didn't get the message."

Larsen's smile turned into a grin as she replied, "Alan, I am sorry to have caused you any apprehension, but I had misplaced my phone and had to purchase a replacement. With the holidays and all, I just didn't think to get you the new number. I will text you the number after the meeting."

Jefferson wondered who had passed on the message, but thought better about asking. "No problem, Madame Secretary. Just glad to see you."

President Campbell called the Cabinet meeting to order at 12:00 noon,"Ladies and gentlemen, thank you all for coming out on a day when I know we would all much prefer to be relaxing in front of a roaring fire place and enjoying the days' festivities on TV. I know also that none of us has been able to enjoy our vacations, realizing that when we came back to work, we would be facing a far different and challenging situation than any of us could have imagined a few months before.

"As I am sure you are aware, three states have proclaimed that they have seceded from the Union, and numerous others are discussing the possibility. I have asked Congress to put this at the top of its agenda tomorrow, but I hope we will come up with some ideas today that we can pass along."

`Campbell asked Adrienne Pennington, Secretary of State and a retired history professor to begin by giving the group some historical perspective. She was a doughty old maid, but by far the brightest bulb in an otherwise pretty dim gathering except for Alan Jefferson and perhaps, Nancy Larsen. The rest of the Cabinet were primarily political appointees, and we can probably guess Larsen's primary qualification for her office.

Pennington began, "In April 1861 when the Civil War began…"

Larsen interrupted, "Are we going to have to listen to a history lesson on New Year's Day, when we have such a critical situa…"

Campbell interjected, "Shut up, Nancy! You will have the courtesy to allow Secretary Pennington to continue."

Although the President was known to have a short fuse of a temper in private meetings, this type of outburst was so unusual that it caught everyone by surprise and there were muffled gasps of astonishment. Larsen was even more surprised than anyone else in the room since it was she who called the shots when she and Campbell were alone in one of their lovemaking moments. She blushed a deep pink and said not a further word. She thought at the time, "He thinks he is king of the hill, but I am going to show him who is boss!"

Pennington continued, "As I was saying, in April 1861 when the Civil War began, there had been a period of peace for thirteen years after the Mexican American War, and the military had been downsized to a fraction of its former self. And although the North had an overwhelming industrial superiority, none of it was geared to the production of armaments. Moreover, there was no Constitutional provision to deal with the threat of secession or secession itself. On the plus side, the North was self -sustaining, where the South was dependent on trade with the North and Europe.

"So, comparing our situation today with that facing our nation almost two hundred years ago, we can see some remarkable similarities, but there are some big differences. In 1861, the seceding states were contiguous. Now, at least, they are widely separated. From a psychological standpoint there is also a big difference. Each side had strong unifying motivations:

For the South, contrary to popular belief, it was not the maintenance of slavery, except for a very small part of the population. The unifying forces were states' rights and defense of their homeland. For the North, Lincoln was able to make the cause, the abolition of slavery, although many Northerners prior to the War, wouldn't have placed a high priority on the issue. If Lincoln, instead, had made the issue the preservation of the Union, he never would have been able to rally enough support. One final point- most people believe that South Carolina and the other states seceded, maybe only a few days before the shots that were fired at Fort Sumter. In fact, South Carolina seceded on December 20, 1860, almost four months before the start of the War. Texas was the last to secede on February 1, 1861. What is the point of this little bit of history? Only that the War did not start with secession. The kindling was there, to be sure, but it took the match of the shelling of Fort Sumter to ignite it."

Campbell thanked Pennington and then asked Jefferson to speak. "Thank you, Mr. President. The main lesson from Secretary Pennington's presentation, I think we can come away with is that as much as we would like to respond quickly, it may be better to pause and consider very carefully the possibility that any action on our part may have unexpected consequences. One seriously complicating factor is that right now we have no idea of how many or which additional states are seceding. With negotiation, we may be able to head off any more secessions. On the other hand, if we press the issue, it may be the excuse some are waiting for to act."

The Vice President, Hector Ramirez next spoke, "I am reading an alternative Civil War history novel where the North blockades the South, and the war ends in six months after the Confederacy is forced to surrender for lack of food and supplies."

Secretary Pennington responded, "Indeed, General Winfield Scott recommended that very course of action, which according to historians would probably have brought a swift end to the War, but unfortunately was overruled by politicians."

Jefferson broke in, "The situation we are faced with is immensely more complex than the one facing the Union in 1861. We would have to have three separate blockades with each having a different set of problems. Texas shares a 1254 mile long border with Mexico, and while Mexico has no love lost with Texas, given its history, it is no friend of the United States either. And one might believe that Mexico would prefer an independent Texas, which would be vulnerable to an incursion to correct what they perceive as a historical injustice. Arizona borders the Mexican state of Sonora, which is controlled by the drug cartel, Ariel. Ariel certainly cannot be expected to assist us in a blockade, since it would be working against their self-interest. Alaska presents a totally different situation, but might be the easiest of the three, given our friendly relationship with Canada, although I doubt they would accept our troops on their soil…"

The Secretary of Defense, Warren Ledbetter, interjected, "We could certainly blockade Alaska's Canadian border with aircraft coming in from over the Pacific and staying on the Alaska side of the border."

Jefferson continued, "Thanks, Mr. Secretary, but as I was saying, wenwould still be confronted with a 6640 mile long shore line."

Several other of the Cabinet members offered suggestions ranging from economic sanctions such as tariffs or withholding funds from Federal programs.

The three seceding states had been careful to avoid any aggressive action to any Federal employee located in those states. Likewise, they had steered clear of Federal buildings and military installations to avoid any inference of trespassing that might have prompted a response from the Federal Government. True enough, they had declared their independence, but at this point it seemed a hollow ring. What the President and his advisors wanted to avoid at all costs was any action that might cause any more states to follow suit.

The White House meeting finally concluded at 4:00 PM after spirited discussion of the various recommendations but no consensus on a course of action. As Nancy Larsen was leaving the Oval Office along with her Cabinet colleagues, Campbell called after her, "Secretary Larsen, please remain a minute. I want to discuss some business." When everybody else had departed and the door was closed, Campbell continued, "Nan, I hope you are not upset, but I couldn't have you interrupting Adrienne that way."

"You were pretty nasty, Mr. President."

"I know and I'm sorry, Nan. I will try to make it up with you."

With that, Nancy opened the door and left.

Now the ball was in Congress' hands. Hector Ramirez in his role as Vice President of the U.S. and President of the Senate would fill his Senate colleagues in on what had transpired in the White House meeting and he would call Speaker Andrew Holmes to fill the House in as well.

Chapter 21: Congress- First day back

Typically, the first day back from Winter recess after a midterm election is a bit hectic although not nearly so much as after a Presidential year if there happens to be a change in Presidents. Nevertheless, there are new Senators and Congressmen and women to be seated, not to speak of all the new staff having to find their offices and learn the ropes.

But this was anything but a typical day. After all the organizing and preliminary protocol was finished, each chamber was ready to get down to business right after lunch. In the House, Speaker Holmes filled his colleagues in on what had transpired.

They reviewed the proposals from the day before, but hardly anything of real consequence was decided. It appeared that most members of the House were against secession, but feared doing anything drastic that would tip the balance in their respective states to secession. Whether their opposition to secession was based on principle or survival, as a member of one of the most elite clubs in the world, was open to question. After all, what other job had the fringe benefits of a member of Congressman?(Other than, of course, President and Vice President).

A Congresswoman from Massachusetts introduced a bill which would cut off Social Security, disability, and welfare benefits to any citizen of a state that had seceded. Her idea was that it would cause those receiving such benefits and those nearing retirement to pressure their legislatures to nullify their secession decree and rejoin the Union. Also, she believed it would be a strong incentive for those states that were only considering secession to drop the plan.

There were only two members willing to stand and speak in favor of the congresswoman's motion. The Speaker called for a vote and the bill was easily defeated. One bill that easily passed both chambers declared secession to be illegal. That it was probably unconstitutional was beside the point. At least Congress was doing something.

When the President got the report at the end of the day on what had happened, he was furious. He called Ramirez and Holmes into his office after dinner. "Hector, I understand the Senate wasted most of the day debating the immigration bill and you never even turned over the gavel to Majority Leader Grayson until the final minutes of the session. Didn't I make myself perfectly clear? We have a crisis on our hands. And you are discussing immigration?"

"Mr. President, I am sorry you are unhappy, but I have my constituency."

"Constituency?!Hector, let me remind you of a couple of things. You are the Vice President of the entire U.S., not from your home state or those of your heritage. Your constituency is each and every citizen of this country. A second point: You are the Vice President only because I picked you. You pull another stunt like this and you will be lucky to get a job selling burritos from a sidewalk stand! "

Hector tried to speak, "I—"

"No more excuses, Hector. I want action tomorrow and please give the gavel to the Majority Leader. And turning to the Speaker, Holmes, what the hell is going on with the House? The only bill you were able to pass all day is most likely unconstitutional, and even if it is constitutional, it means nothing without enforcement. I need something with some meat on it!"

"Mr. President, I understand, but I couldn't get my people to agree to anything else."

"YOUR PEOPLE? What you're saying is you couldn't lead your people. Come on, Holmes. You are the Speaker of the House, the third most powerful position in the country. Act like it. Let your people know what you want."

"With all due respect, Sir, what is it I want, or more correctly, what is it you want?"

"Holmes, What in the hell do you think I want? I want what Lincoln wanted in 1861. I want to hold the country together. These secessionists are trying to destroy our country. I want to put the hurt on them and make them sorry they ever thought of the word, secession."

"You don't want war, do you Mr. President?"

"Of course not, Holmes. If they start one, that's different. But for now, let's put the squeeze on them. We're into the weekend now, but I want some action on Monday."

"All right then. I will let our leadership know that's what you want, and I believe we can do it."

"That's the spirit, Holmes. Now what about the Senate, Hector?"

"I believe we will also do it."

"I don't want what you believe. I want you to do."

Chapter 22: Congress–Second day

The Vice President and Speaker had gotten their marching orders from the President, and it was now time for action. As they were headed out of the White House, Speaker Andrew Holmes was the first to speak, "Well, Hector, we got a butt whipping this evening, but that is nothing compared to what we will experience if we don't give Oren some kind of crackdown."

"I hear you, Andrew, so hopefully you have something in mind."

"With the military option out of consideration, the only thing left appears to be economic sanctions."

"Andrew, You're not saying you favor a military response?"

"No shooting, of course. Unless they start it, but I would like to see a blockade to teach these ass holes a lesson."

After leaving the White House, each got on the phone with his respective leaders that evening to fill them in on what was expected for the Monday's business.

When the House convened Monday morning, Speaker Holmes announced that the first order of business would be reconsideration of the bill proposed by the Congresswoman from Massachusetts regarding the cessation of Social Security and disability benefits.

A congressman from Wisconsin rose and shouted, "Point of order, Mr. Speaker. That bill was soundly defeated yesterday."

"Congressman Weber, due to time constraints there was no opportunity to offer amendments so I am asking for amendments at this time."

The House Whip rose and parroting the words he received from the Speaker the previous evening, "Mr. Speaker, I offer the following amendment to Congresswoman Kennedy's bill on cessation of Social Security, Disability, and Welfare benefits:

'The cessation of Social Security, Disability and Welfare benefits shall begin sixty days from today for any citizen of a seceding state, who doesn't renounce his state's secession and move to a non-seceding state. However, if the seceding state enters back into the Union prior to the sixty days, there shall be no cessation of benefits."

After a second to the amendment and time for discussion, the amendment was voted on and defeated by a margin of only four votes. Immediately thereafter another of the House leaders, Stuart Lindsay of California, rose to offer an amendment to the amendment.

The Wisconsin congressman rose again with a point of order.

The Speaker interrupted "Congressman Weber, I appreciate your attentiveness to protocol, but these are extraordinary times, and extraordinary times call for extraordinary measures. Therefore I will allow the amendment to the amendment. Mr. Lindsay, you may offer your amendment."

"Thank you, Mr. Speaker. My amendment will contain the same language as that offered by our House Whip, but in addition, any forfeitures of Social Security, Disability and Welfare payments shall remain in those respective funds with interest accruing to those currently on Social Security, Disability, and Welfare as well as those within five years of receiving benefits."

After a second and a brief discussion, it was voted on and passed by an overwhelming majority. The House then considered a bill to cut off food stamps with the same provisions as the SS and disability bill. That too passed with little dissent.

Congressman Weber of Wisconsin arose once more, "Mr. Speaker,.."

Speaker Holmes in an agitated voice interrupted, "Please, no more points of order!"

Weber responded, "No, Mr. Speaker. I just realized that what we just passed applies equally to the State of Hawaii. Was that intended?"

The Speaker was in a sweat now. He and most of the House must have forgotten about Hawaii, which was a totally different situation. That had been an amicable separation with world -wide approval. To apply those sanctions to Hawaii could have far reaching and undetermined global consequences. "Thank you, Congressman Weber, for bring this to our attention. May I have another amendment to the bill just passed exempting Hawaii and its citizens?"

The House Whip stood to offer the amendment, which was quickly seconded and passed.

Meanwhile, the Senate was attending to its duties as well. The Vice

President handed the gavel to Majority Leader Grayson. Bills for blockades as well as tariffs and cancellation of subsidies to the seceding states except Hawaii were all passed and sent to the House, Likewise the House bills were sent to the Senate for ratification. By the end of the day, all of the bills were passed and sent to the President for his signature.

When the Vice President and Speaker met with Campbell that evening, Campbell was ebullient. "That is more like it, boys. Campbell passed out a couple of his finest cigars and opened a bottle of vintage champagne. "Now let's see how those secessionists like playing hardball."

Chapter 23: Implementation

The next morning when Allen Jefferson reported in, Campbell asked him to join him in the Oval Office to discuss the bills that Campbell had signed into law the previous evening. After briefing him on the substance of the bills, Campbell asked Jefferson what he thought.

"Well, Mr. President, it is one thing to enact laws; it is something else to implement and enforce …"

Campbell interrupted, "Dammit, Allen, I don't need a lecture on the theory of law. I merely want to know if you think they will have the desired effect."

"Sorry, Mr. President. Of course, properly implemented, they should have the effect of pardon the language, 'pissing them off.'"

"So, Allen, how do we go about implementing?"

"Let's take them one by one. I suggest we put off the tariff for now. We would have to put in a lot of study to determine if we should cover all goods or exempt some and also the amount of the tariff."

"Why should any item be exempt?"

"I don't know, Mr. President, but there might be unforeseen adverse consequences from such a wide ranging action; besides without an effective blockade, tariffs are meaningless. The whole effort would result in a cross- border thriving black market."

"Well then, what about the blockade?"

Jefferson responded, "Again, a pretty complex situation. Three non-contiguous states with the likelihood of some others coming into play. I think the only practical approach would be to single out one state with the hope of getting that state to come back into the union and having the effect of getting the other states to follow. The easiest state would probably be Arizona, but I doubt that getting Arizona to come back would have much of an effect on the other states. On the other hand, since Texas has been the leader, I think if we can get them to relent, it might well have a favorable effect."

"That sounds good- a blockade coupled with the cut-off of Federal subsidies should have them begging to come back…"

"Sorry to interrupt, Mr. President, but the fact is that Texas sends far more to Washington than they get back in subsidies. Most studies only look at personal income tax and payroll tax as "state outgoes". When you throw in corporate and excise taxes, Texas gets back only about 40% of what it sends to us. Arizona, slightly more and Alaska, slightly less. Looking ahead at other states that may follow, almost all fall in the category of net payers to the Federal Government.

"Damn, damn. What a rotten coincidence."

"Not at all, Mr. President. The states that have the most favorable business climate are the ones that are averse to Federal Government expansion and erosion of personal liberty. And that position is what caused secession in the first place."

"So what do we do with respect to subsidies, Allen?"

"Sir, we have no choice. We have to stop the subsidies, but must recognize that it will be a net loss of revenue to Washington as those states stop paying Federal taxes."

"So, Allen, what I am hearing is that short of military action, a blockade is the only reasonable recourse we have."

"That seems to be the situation, Mr. President."

"Well, let us hope that the blockade is effective."

At this point, Alan Jefferson walked over to an easel he'd had brought in for this meeting. After flipping a few large pages up and over the easel, he came to a map of Texas. Using a laser pointer, he began to reveal his idea. "There are seven main highways that cross the Texas/United States border. Interstate 10 which leads into Houston, Interstate 20 at Shreveport, Interstate 30 at...."

"Okay, enough with the geography lesson, get on with it!" Campbell said in frustration. This whole debacle was going to ruin his legacy if he wasn't careful and all his advisors seemed capable of was collectively shrugging their shoulders.

"If we put a blockade at each one of those crossings and stopped all freight and supplies, then that would definitely hurt them, and do so in a timely fashion."

"What about the secondary roads and air supply?", Campbell asked.

"Sir, it would be impossible to shut off 100%, but we should be able to cut off 80 to 90% of ground supply by focusing on the interstates. No doubt that they will try to supplement by air, but that will be very costly and put a strain on them."

"You don't think that would provoke them to use their military?"

"No, for two reasons. First we just stop the freight, any passenger vehicles with Texas plates won't be detained. And secondly, even though our military has been scaled down - and now, it's actually about 40,000 troops less since they took over the Texas National Guard, we still vastly outnumber and outgun them, sir."

"What kind of numbers are we talking about, Allen?"

"Our troop levels were at about 250,000 before all this, but when Texas took over their National Guard, that dropped us to just over 200,000 troops."

"So what are we looking at as far as their capabilities are concerned?" asked Campbell.

"The Texas Air National Guard consists of a Fighter Wing, a Recon Wing, a Combat Communications Group, Engineering Squadron and their Security Forces Squadron. Their Recon Wing has in its inventory roughly 2/3 of our drone fleet, sir."

"Oh great, they've got most of our drones. Oh well, go ahead with the blockades, Congress sure as hell can't be relied on for any decisive action on this."

"Very well, sir" said Jefferson, "I'll get on it right away and notify the Joint Chiefs."

"Remember, I want no bloodshed, Allen."

"But what if our troops are fired upon? Texas truckers won't take kindly to having their cargoes confiscated."

"As a last resort they can fire back, but make it understood that this whole thing is a giant powder keg and I sure as hell don't want to be the one to ignite it."

"Yes sir" said Jefferson as he turned and started to leave the room.

"Hold on, Allen. We haven't talked about preventing other states from joining the rebellion."

"Mr. President, with all due respect, secession is not a rebellion."

"What the hell is it then? They are refusing to obey the Constitution."

"No, Sir. We've been over this before. There is nothing in the Constitution regarding secession."

"Are you sure about that? What about the Pledge of Allegiance- '..one nation. Indivisible'?"

At this point, Jefferson had to restrain himself from laughing. "Sir, the pledge was originally written by an American cleric, intended for use by all nations. The words, 'United States of America' were later inserted. The pledge has no force of law."

Campbell commented, "At times like these, I wish I had hired someone other than a Rhodes Scholar."

And Jefferson was thinking, "At times like these, I wish I was working for a President with some brain power."

"Okay, Allen. Let's hope the blockade works.

Jefferson replied as he left the office. "Yes, sir."

Chapter 24: Response

If the President and Congress thought they had their work cut out for them, it was nothing as compared to what the seceding states had on their respective plates. First and foremost, was the providing for the legitimate functions of government that heretofore been supplied by the Federal Government. Now, in addition, they had to deal with the punitive measures passed by Congress a day earlier. Since there was no formal communication between the United States and the seceding states, the media filled that function.

Houston and Collins were in the Texas President's office discussing what they had learned last night. Houston spoke first, "Well, we anticipated the blockade and tariffs, but I will admit, I did not think about Social Security or food stamps."

"Neither did I, Rich, but that may not be all bad."

"How so, Jerry?"

"Well, for one thing, we have 60 days, so we have some time, but more importantly, it strikes me as probably not in conformance with the Constitution. After all, unless the U.S. acknowledges that we are indeed separated, our citizens are still U.S. citizens, and even then, it will take some creative maneuvering to strip citizenship rights from an individual based on that person's address. And on the food stamp issue, they may be doing us a favor by incentivizing migration out of our state."

"Interesting point, Jerry, but what if they are able to cut off Social Security?

"The fact is, Rich, that with the inflation that has been going on and no concurrent growth in Social Security benefits, for a great many people, it is almost meaningless."

"That may be true, Jerry, but what about the greater number of people almost totally dependent on Social Security?"

"I think Texas could probably fund that with some of the corporate and high income personal tax savings."

"Sounds interesting, Jerry. Get with Jimmy and come back with a plan."

"You got it, boss."

"In the meantime, I am going to work on the blockade and tariff angle."

"Sounds good, Rich."

Chapter 25: Reaching out

That evening, Houston tried to think of various scenarios Campbell might employ for a blockade and/or tariff. "What if I were in Campbell's shoes? How would I approach it." He concluded that if a tariff were to succeed, there would have to be an effective blockade first, which simplified the problem only very slightly. With the three states that had seceded so far spread apart, how would a blockade work? The next morning, still mulling over possibilities, he sat at his desk in his office in the State Capitol Building in Austin and hit the intercom, requesting his secretary to get Jerry Collins in his office ASAP.

"He's in a meeting with Jimmy Phelps, the Treasury Secretary. Do you want me to break in?" Juanita replied.

"No, Juanita. Just get me the Governor of Alaska on the phone."

"Right away, sir."

Alaska has a storied past with America and was once considered

"Seward's Folly," and "Andrew Johnson's Polar Bear Garden" following its purchase from Russia in 1867 for about two cents per acre. The total price of $7.2 million was a tough pill for many Americans to swallow as being a good investment at the time. But then when gold and oil were discovered, Alaska began to look like the smart investment that it turned out to be. Natural resources are an integral part of the history of its statehood with the United States; so much so that their state constitution mandates that natural resources are to be managed as a "public trust."

Alaska is also the only state that is nearly completely dependent on oil, gas and coal revenues to fund governmental functions. Those revenues comprise a full 90% of the state budget and the insane restrictions placed on coal production and use, along with the rumored coming gas regulations prompted Alaska to take the same action that Texas did and draw up Articles of Secession.

It was less a function of defiance, but more a function of survival. By detaching themselves from the Union, Alaska could allow the production of their precious natural resources without the strangulation placed on them by the EPA. The 2042 mid-term elections that gave rise to Texas seceding from the Union prompted Alaska to do likewise. Anticipating the result, Governor Bill Hubbard, a month earlier had asked his legislature to draw up and vote on Articles of Secession, which would become active in the event that Democrats gained a super majority in the Senate. Like Texas, it passed nearly unanimously in the Alaskan House of Representatives by 39 to 1 and completely unanimously in the state Senate, getting all 20 votes.

After the results of the elections came in, it was clear to Gov. Hubbard that they would have to follow through with the Articles of

Secession and put it to a special referendum so the 1,394,676 Alaskan citizens could voice their opinion on the matter. With the rampant inflation caused by the EPA regulations, the citizenry voted for secession in near landslide numbers with 94% saying yes to the creation of the sovereign nation of Alaska. Bill Hubbard was only the third governor of Alaska to be born in the state. The other two were Alaska's first governor once statehood was conferred onto it, William Egan and Bill Walker who was elected in 2014.

Hubbard was a pragmatic man, not afraid to work with the opposing Party, but he also firmly believed in the Constitution and the principles that founded the United States of America. On those bedrock ideals, he never wavered. And the direction his country was going for the last few decades not only troubled him, but made him wonder if the US could even be saved. The way he saw it, since President Woodrow Wilson introduced Fabian Socialism to America early in the 20th century, America had been spiraling down the drain.

He'd considered running for President, but with nearly 60% of the populace relying on the government for some type of assistance, he knew that the numbers were stacked against him, or anyone else that was espousing the end of the nanny state. "Oh well", he thought. "Now that we've seceded, I guess I'll have to give up my aspirations for the White House. But the flip side of that coin is that I'm President of the sovereign nation of Alaska."

During his reverie on this matter, his intercom buzzed and his secretary announced that President Houston was calling from the Republic of Texas.

"Thanks, Dolly. I'll pick up. Hello, Richard, as if I didn't know, what prompts your call?"

"Bill, I just wanted to call to welcome you to the party. Seriously, as you know it's just our three states, I mean nations against the mean old Republic and I think it would be prudent to do some joint planning for various contingencies."

"Richard, I couldn't agree more, but with that imbecile in the White House, how can we begin to predict what he may do?"

"Point well made, Bill. As you know, a couple of days ago, Campbell signed several bills that Congress passed designed to pressure us into submission."

"No way we are coming back, Richard. That damn EPA was sucking us dry. The loss of Social Security will be a small loss as compared to getting our fossil fuels going again."

"I hear you, Bill. I've got my Chief of Staff and Treasury Secretary working on something right now to replace the SS checks with corporate tax revenue, since home based corporations will not be paying Federal tax any longer."

"OK, let me know when you have something worked out."

"Will do, Bill. Have you given any thought to the blockade threat?"

"Not much, Richard. With our vast shore line, I think they will have quite a problem trying to enforce it."

"I think you are right and given that there are three of us and maybe more joining in the near future, it does seem impossible, but as you say, there is no predicting what that SOB might do. We don't think he wants war, but we are ramping up our forces just in case, and I would advise you to do the same. You've got not only Campbell to worry about, but that nutjob Segurin at your back door, too."

"Yeah, I know. Our intelligence says he's got his eye on the Aleutians, but so far he hasn't made a move on them yet. Along those lines, what about a treaty of alliance?"

"Bill, I would love to say yes, but I think it might be a hard sell right now, given our respective geographies. Maybe at some point in the future after more states have joined our cause."

"I understand, Richard. I appreciate your candor."

"Certainly, Bill. But how will you respond to that if he does?"

"I'm not sure," Hubbard sighed. "What would you do?"

"Can't say, but I do know that Segurin is afraid of all-out war because he thinks it would mean nukes."

"What gives you that idea?"

"Last year in Dallas at that summit for world leaders we hosted for the Federal government, Segurin and I ended up at the bar. His security was pretty unhappy about him being in such a public place as the hotel bar. They looked as nervous as a bunch of long tailed cats in a room full of rockers, but Segurin was intent on getting drunk and he invited me to sit down. During the course of our conversation, he let slip how he would do almost anything to avoid a nuclear confrontation with the West."

"Well, well. That's a nice little tidbit of information to have. Thanks Richard. But there is still little I can do to thwart him if he does advance on the Aleutians. We don't have near the military capability you do. Our only Naval ships are ice breakers, tenders and patrol boats, and they're barely armed at all."

"What are your troop numbers, Bill?"

"Well, with the Army National Guard and the Air Guard, I've got about 22,000 troops. How about you?"

"I'm just shy of 40,000. But that's part of why I called you, Bill. I'm expanding my military and upping my troop numbers. My goal is 150,000 troops. I don't want to go to war with Campbell, I just want to make him blink. After you and I and Zimmerman over in Arizona seceded and took over our state National Guards, it dropped him from over a quarter of a million to about 175,000."

Chapter 26: Financial planning

When Governor Houston hung up from his call with the Alaska governor, he saw that he had received a call from Jerry Collins. "Yeah, Jerry, whatcha got?

"Rich, as you know, I've been in a meeting with Jimmy Phelps discussing options we may have in responding to the cutoff of Social Security and welfare payments. He concurs that we will benefit substantially from the trade-off of Social Security versus Federal corporate and personal income tax. Last year, we had just short of twelve million citizens receiving social security benefits with an average benefit check of $7,212 for a total of about eighty-six billion dollars. Federal personal and corporate taxes totaled over two hundred twenty billion dollars."

"That part sounds good, Jerry, but what about the people on welfare?"

"Jimmy tells me that for last year, there were 13.2 million of the population receiving welfare of some kind, averaging $7550 for a total of slightly less than one hundred billion dollars."

"You are telling me that welfare recipients are getting more than social security beneficiaries?"

"Yep, boss. I knew you wouldn't be tickled to hear that!"

"Damn right!"

"But there is something else that has positive ramifications, Rich."

"I'm all ears, Jerry."

"You know we have been working against Washington for years to do something about the illegals. Well, of our current six and a half million, slightly more than four million are receiving Federal assistance."

"Well, I'll be damned!"

"Absolutely, Rich. Washington has finally decided to do something about the problem, but I doubt that is what they had in mind. One more thing- of the remaining nine plus million, we estimate more than half are able-bodied, who would rather receive assistance than work. What it all boils down to is that we probably get rid of four million illegals without having to do anything and maybe two or three million more of folks who prefer welfare over work. So we can substantially reduce corporate and personal income tax and still have enough left over to fund social security and welfare for those in true need."

"That is great news, Jerry. Tell Jimmy I appreciate the job he is doing. Now if we can only solve this threatened blockade as easily. And by the way, I was talking to the Alaska governor to see if he had heard anything from Washington when you called. He hadn't, but I think it would be a good idea to touch base with your friend, Governor Zimmerman."

"Be glad to."

Chapter 27: Arizona

When Collins left Houston's office, he put in a call to his old high school sweetheart, Florence Levin Zimmerman, who was now governor of Arizona. They had gone on to find other loves, but had gotten back in touch at their twenty year high school reunion in Scottsdale twelve years ago and found after all those years they still had a lot of interests in common, including politics. They were both strong conservatives although Collins tended more to the libertarian side, while Zimmerman was the typical conservative except in the area of religion. They both were avid and accomplished athletes, having lettered in sports in high school and going on to varsity sports in college. Collins had been the starting quarterback for the Arizona state champion Saguaro Sabercats and his school's leading golfer in his senior year. At only five feet eight inches and170 pounds, he knew he was way too small for major collegiate football, but he did win a substantial scholarship to The University of

Texas in golf. Until he arrived in Austin, he had envisioned himself as a winner on the PGA circuit, but those dreams quickly vanished when he started playing with other members of his team. He was an excellent golfer, but so were his teammates and players at competing schools. Compared to them he was just an average golfer, so he realized he had better apply himself in academics if he was ever able to achieve any success in life. Fortunately, he was sharp mentally and enjoyed learning so that when he focused on his studies, he did quite well. He could have done even better, but there was the social life to attend to.

He and Florence had been in love, or at least they thought they were, but Florence's parents put an end to the budding romance. Not that her parents were all that religious, but they were determined that their only daughter not marry a "shaygetz".

When Collins headed off to Texas, Florence was devastated, but her parents were delighted.

Florence was every bit the athlete that Jerry was, earning letters in swimming and diving for all four years of high school. She was a very proficient swimmer, but her forte was diving, and her favorite was the "swan dive", which fit her physique perfectly.

At five feet nine inches (one inch taller than her boyfriend) and a classic model figure, her execution of the dive was every bit as graceful as the swan it was named for. Her plain face and oversized nose prevented her from being considered beautiful, but they were more than made up for by her winning smile and personality.

In addition to her athletic prowess, she was no slouch in the classroom. Even with all the time in the pool and on the diving boards, student council, and a very active social life, she was able to maintain a 3.8

average. Based on her grade point average, ACT score, numerous activities, and aquatic skills she had full paid scholarship offers from no less than eight prestigious universities, but opted to stay close to home at her mother's alma mater the University of Arizona in Tucson. Given her athletic and academic credentials, she was sought after by a number of sororities, but her parents wanted her to be in a Jewish sorority so that she would meet and marry a nice and well-connected Jewish boy. Following her parents' wishes, she joined her mother's sorority, Sigma Delta Tau. As her parents hoped and predicted, she met and dated a number of Jewish students and in her sophomore year met the fellow who she would marry a few years later, Josh Zimmerman.

He was four years her senior and a second year law student. He definitely fit the profile Florence's parents had hoped for. His father was the senior partner in a prestigious Phoenix law firm and his mother, a professor of creative writing at nearby Wilkes College. Josh was an only child, and slightly introvertive, but the other qualifiers were in place. He was bright and Jewish.

Florence apparently had her sights set on politics as she had majored in government and minored in public speaking. After graduation she interned for a congressman for a while then returned home to run for Phoenix city council when she was only twenty five, with Josh, her new husband, as campaign manager. She narrowly lost but she and Josh learned enough in the process that two years later she won with 70% of the vote. She was a strong proponent of smaller government and lower taxes and was consistent in her voting on those issues. In fact, her constituents learned early that when she promised something in her campaigns, she delivered. She didn't always get her way, but there was never any question where she stood. She was elected mayor when she was only thirty-one and dealt skillfully and decisively with the riots of 2026. She could easily have won re-election as mayor but opted to run for Congress and won handily.

She and Josh briefly discussed moving to Washington, but Josh was firmly established in his father's law firm, and a move would mean starting over. They agreed that Florence would fly home on weekends when Congress was in session, which she did initially. But as time passed, the flights home became spaced further apart due to the hassle of flying, and the time apart began taking its toll on the marriage. Florence caught wind of rumors regarding her husband's philandering and it wasn't long before she started getting even.

When she advocated for term limits and stepped down after two terms as a congresswoman nobody was surprised, but it made it that much easier for her to beat a long entrenched and shady senator the next election. Now governor at 50 she was still swimming although she had given up diving several years ago. She had maintained that school girl figure and looked closer to 30 than 50.

"Hi, Jer. I had been meaning to call you, but as you can imagine, I've been a little tied up."

Collins chuckled, "Yeah Flo, just a little. Seriously, Houston and I are well aware of your share of domestic problems, but he thought, and I agree, that it would behoove us to start doing some joint planning for various scenarios." Collins ran through the possible scenarios that he and his boss had discussed.

Arizona, by most measures, may be one of the least likely states to think about secession. It is landlocked and unlike Texas, it is dependent on the outside for most of its needs. It does have a thriving agriculture, but lettuce is the main crop with very little grain. The one big plus is uranium, due to the discovery of an immense uranium deposit just outside the Fort Apache Indian Reservation in 2026. Uranium had been mined in the Grand Canyon area for more than a hundred years, but not until the price of uranium began its steep assent in 2023, concurrent with the Federal Carbon Offset Surcharge, had it attracted the interest of prospectors. In ten years, its price had gone up by ten times to $200 per ounce and now, a decade later, to $1750.While the extent of the deposit had not been determined, it was thought to possibly be the largest such deposit on earth, which would make the new nation of Arizona the richest in the world.

Chapter 28: Ghost Storm

January was almost gone with Les Parsons and Bradley Sims growing more uneasy with each passing day of no effective response to secession. Their gains from shorting Atlas Energy stock were rapidly shrinking as its stock price began to rise from its low of 25 cents a share to its current 83 cents. "Les, I think we had better cash out while we still have some profit left."

"Nonsense, Brad. Coal is on its last legs and it won't be long till Atlas is history."

However, what Parsons didn't tell Sims is that he would cash out that day if not for the fact that Stephens was cornering the market on his own stock. He gobbled up every little offering as soon as it became available, driving up the price still more. Atlas Energy had actually turned the corner on profitability and was once again in the black, albeit slightly, owing to his international sales from Australia and reduced overhead in the U.S.

Parsons knew that Stephens was depending on the secessionist movement growing until he was able to bring back his extensive coal production from West Virginia.

To top it off, Atlas had declared a dividend of 20 cents a share, so Parsons and his partner were not only having to pay interest on their short interest, but now would have to pay the dividend to shareholders, which for all practical purposes was one man, Robert J. Stephens III.

"What we do have to do, Brad is stop the secessionist movement."

"Isn't that what that legislation of three weeks ago was all about?"

"Brad, tell me please, what has happened since then?"

"Not much, I guess."

Pounding his fist on his desk, Parsons yelled, "Not much? A farce of a blockade and other than that not a fucking thing! Putting that dumbbell in the White House may be the stupidest thing I ever did in my life. I knew he wasn't a genius, but I had hoped he had some common sense."

"So, what's the plan, Les?"

"Texas is the key. If Texas backs down, Alaska and Arizona will fold faster than a bad poker hand. If Campbell doesn't understand how to do a blockade, then I will have to show him."

So it was with that in mind that he dialed the President.

Campbell picked it up on the first ring. "What's on your mind, my friend?"

"What's on my mind! What the fuck is on your mind?"

"Whoa Les, first let me remind you that you are speaking to the President. Did someone put some itching powder in your jock?"

"Oren, let's not forget who put you there in the first place. Now what in hell are you doing about secession?"

"Well, just for your information, we are in the process of putting together a blockade."

"Oh, that is just dandy. And how long until the blockade is complete?"

"Les, it's not as easy as that. You know our military ranks are depleted, so we have to have time to gather the personnel. Besides that I've got a lot on my plate. It's easy to sit back and be a rear seat driver, but you don't have three states trying to poke you in the eye on the world stage. If I don't get these assholes to stop this foolishness, I'll be going down in history as the President that killed America."

"Three states? You know we had talked earlier about Virginia and West Virginia. It appears now that they are ready to do it."

"How in the hell did you hear that? I haven't heard that!"

"Oren, with all the coal in those states, don't you think I'd have my finger on the pulse of those people?"

"Well what in the hell are we supposed to do to stop all this? I sure as hell don't want to use the military and start the Second American Civil War."

"Why not? You've got the entire military at your disposal?"

"First of all, I'm not firing on US citizens, even if they have seceded and secondly I don't exactly have the 'entire' US Military."

"What do you mean?"

"Texas declared ownership and control of the Texas National Guard, and this prompted Arizona and Alaska to follow suit. So now the US military sits at under 200,000 troops. With all our overseas bases and deployments, that leaves me with a skeleton force back here at home."

"I see what you mean, Oren. You're in a world of hurt here. But I may have a suggestion."

"Oh?" said Campbell, "And what would that be?"

"I have connections to a very capable, discreet private security company that could be of use to us in this situation. The company, called Geistersturm, is made up of former KSK or Kommando Spezialkräfte members.

"Les, if you don't mind, speak English.

"Sorry, Oren. They are German terms. Geistersturm means Ghost Storm and Kommando Spezialkräfte means Special Forces commandos.

"So what do you have in mind for these special forces storm troopers?"

"I was thinking that they could be useful in being a bit more forceful in the blockades you are trying to set up."

"How so? So far none of the Texas truckers have given us any problems to speak of."

"Yes well, I took the liberty of having Geistersturm look into these blockades and it seems that the only trucks crossing your borders are fleet vehicles. Virtually all the independent truckers left operating have moved their licenses to the states surrounding Texas. That way, they're not molested at the border, either going in or coming out of Texas. Geistersturm has composed a list of these truckers and can effectively stop their end run around your blockades."

"I don't know Les, I can't afford any blowback. And what if a situation escalates out there? How do I know your Ghost Stormers won't unleash hell?"

"They're professionals. They understand limits and they understand parameters."

"Hmmm, okay" mulled Campbell, "but only on US 10 leading into the city of Houston. It's a port city and we'll definitely grab their attention, letting them know we can do it at every major crossing."

"Okay, I'll get right on it. I assume you'll be arranging their pay via the usual methods for black ops private contractors such as this?"

"Yes, of course Les and you'll get your cut too."

Chapter 29: New Virginia

After Campbell, hung up from the call with Parsons, he thought about calling in Allen Jefferson, but decided against it. He was mulling over the conversation, mainly the part about Virginia breaking apart and joining forces with West Virginia in seceding. "I can nip this in the bud. Jefferson is just too timid; it's always '...you can do this, but on the other hand...' Parsons is always trying to boss me around; I will show him I am able to be decisive..."

It had been almost a month since Lon Whitt's speech in Charleston. Although he had received a warm reception, there was by no means a consensus regarding secession. Nobody argued that West Virginia had not been severely injured by the regulations against coal, but the strongest argument against secession was the question of what would happen to the state on its own. West Virginia, in contrast to Texas, Arizona, and Alaska, was very dependent on Federal support. Even before the war against coal, the state was relatively poor, but now even more of the population was below poverty level and reliant on Medicaid and food stamps. Robert Stephens had kept his mines going, even while they were losing money; so although there was strong support for secession in both West Virginia and Virginia, there was equally strong support for staying in the union. The kindling was there; all that was needed was a spark to sway at least some of the population to secession.

Campbell dialed his Secretary of Defense and Ledbetter picked up, "Yes, Mr. President."

"Warren, there is word that Virginia may be splitting off from the DC suburbs to join with West Virginia in secession. We need to head this off. I want to nationalize the National Guard of Virginia and West Virginia, and I will be imposing martial law in both states. Any vocal proponent of secession is to be arrested and detained until this powder keg cools down."

"Yes, Sir, Mr. President. I will get word to the adjutant generals in the two states to advise them of the nationalization. And I assume you will be contacting the Attorney General and the FBI for implementation of martial law."

"Yes, of course." The fact of the matter was that Oren Campbell was in water out of his depth and he had better call in Allen Jefferson.

That night Campbell went on national TV to announce the steps he had taken.

Lon Whitt was watching national news and heard the announcement. He thought to himself, "Well. Mr. President, I think you have just done us a favor."

This was the second time this century that martial law had been declared in the United States by Presidential order. The only previous instance was Abraham Lincoln's declaration during the Civil War. In 2026 President Markham had declared martial law to deal with widespread rioting and arson due to the depression, but this was very different. There had been no widespread lawlessness, rioting or arson. The justification of potential secession seemed flimsy at best and pressure to retract martial law began to build immediately. There was even talk in the Senate about starting impeachment hearings. Finally, after four weeks of countless arrests, and searches, President Campbell relented and ended martial law. He also released the National Guards of both states.

But it was too late; the kindling had needed the spark, and Oren Campbell had graciously responded. During the four weeks of martial law, there were secret meetings of legislators from both states and legislation drawn up so that upon cessation of martial law, the state legislatures went into action. Two days after martial law was lifted, the commonwealth of Virginia declared its independence. The three counties comprising the suburbs of the District of Columbia quickly responded by seceding from Virginia to remain in the Union and calling their state North Virginia. A week later, West Virginia seceded and merged with Virginia to form the new nation of New Virginia. There were some slight details to be worked out, including which governor would be in charge. The decision was made by a coin flip with Governor Graham of Virginia winning the flip to become President with Governor Singer of West Virginia his Vice President. It had been agreed that after two years the roles would be reversed and a Presidential election would follow two years later.

Chapter 30: Alaska

Campbell had thought Igor Segurin was cracking a joke when he remarked about Alaska being occupied Russian soil, but he was dead serious and now with Alaska on its own and no match militarily with his country, Segurin was ready to seize the opportunity to right the wrong of 1867.He knew Oren Campbell and knew him to be an ineffectual and weak president. But he also knew him to be prideful and not too smart.

Although Russia was more powerful than the U.S., he did not want to start World War III, since the next world conflict would almost certainly involve nuclear weapons and it might be difficult to differentiate between the winners and the losers.

Segurin decided that his most prudent gambit was to move into the Aleutians. Russia already owned the westernmost of the islands and could make the case that Seward's purchase did not include the Aleutians.

Under cover of darkness on the morning of January 20, 2043, Segurin made his move with 20,000 elite light infantry from the Russian owned Commander Islands onto Atu and eastward occupying each of the 69 Island chain. Some of the islands were so small that detachments of five men were stationed, more as a symbolic gesture than consequential, but by the end of the day, the Russian tricolor flew on each of the island chain. It had been a bloodless conquest with hardly a shot fired.

The Aleutians had been important militarily one hundred years earlier during the war referred to as World War II, but since then all of the military installations except for that of Kodiak had been closed. Even the base at Kodiak was more of a show piece than functional. The 800 marines stationed there considered the assignment a vacation. The only problem was the lack of female companionship. Of the 800 marines, only 38 were female, and even with the six female civilian office staff, it was hardly a good working ratio.

The Russian force had landed on Kodiak Island at 3:00 AM, and although there were twelve guards on duty, they were quickly overwhelmed by the superior force. With the guards taken care of, the remainder of the marine contingent was taken by surprise in their sleep. It was a bloodless surrender.

Segurin got the news when he awoke later that morning and was delighted. He was ready to follow up that coup with the bigger one of Alaska and would have done so except for some domestic problems he had to attend to in a number of his western European satellite countries. Perhaps inspired by the U.S. secession, concurrent uprisings had begun.

Chapter 31: Christina St. James

Christina St. James was on top of her game and her game was being a movie star. She had come from humble beginnings, although with a noble pedigree as a direct descendant of Sam Houston, like the governor. She couldn't recall ever meeting Richard Houston, but might have bumped into him at one of the two or three Houston family reunions she had attended as a child. Only a mediocre student, the one subject that she loved was history- no, make that Texas history. She had read every account of the Texas War of Independence that she could find in the El Paso Library and had seen the movie, "The Alamo " at least three or four times.

Perhaps, that is what had inspired her to go for an acting career. She had been in two high school plays and when she learned that UTEP offered a degree in drama, that was a natural since she could save money by staying at home. Another lure was the women's rifle team.

After college, with a recommendation from her faculty advisor, she landed a spot on a crime drama which aired on the FX television channel. Playing a beautiful, but hard as nails detective in Chicago, Christina found her audience and her audience had discovered her. It was mere coincidence that her great grandfather on her mother's side had been a famous actor by the name of Clint Eastwood, who gained fame playing the same sort of role. The ratings for the show went through the roof and it was still going strong four seasons in. But before the start of the fifth season, Christina knew she had to break away from it, or run the risk that she'd be typecast into that role forever more. So, despite having the best rated TV show in the history of the Nielsen ratings, she turned down the studio's unheard of offer of $5 million per episode or $120 million for twenty-four episodes, over the course of a year. Christina left the show and headed out to Hollywood and the uncertainty of that vocation called "movie star."

Staying in sync with her meteoric rise on the small screen, she found the same success on the big screen. Her first two movies demonstrated her star power. The first was a drama where she played an emergency room nurse that gets caught in the middle of a hostage crisis, where she has to make a choice between her patient and her life. And the second was an action flick, in which she played an FBI agent left for dead, who seeks revenge on the bad guys responsible for the deaths of her husband and children. Both were blockbusters and proof that America accepted her no matter what role she chose.

After that, the movie offers came pouring in. Christina found herself in a place to reach out and push the boundaries of her acting talent. She took roles that other Hollywood stars shied away from and she nailed about 95% of what she tried. Sure there were a couple of "bombs." But a St. James bomb that cleared $300 million dollars was considered a dud, while anyone else making that amount on a movie would call it a "box office bonanza!"

As with all actors, St. James started to get a bit bored with the same old, same old. And that is how she found herself with her agent and bodyguard in San Antonio, Texas doing research for her upcoming film portraying her as a time-traveling CIA agent who finds herself in the Alamo back in the year 1836. With her skills, and foreknowledge of the tactics taken by Santa Anna, she could turn the tide for Texas and avoid the deaths of many of America's icons of that era.

So after a long week of taking in the sites at the Alamo Shrine, and reviewing what she already knew of the history, she was ready for a breather. Looking forward to seeing her sister in Baton Rouge, it had been over four years since she'd been able to visit Charlene. A good old fashioned sisterly visit of sipping hot tea late at night while gossiping about, well anyone, was long overdue. She would take her custom SUV for a leisurely drive across Texas and into Louisiana. It would take her two days, but there was no rush.

Her new agent, Ken Tomlinson, asked Eduardo, her long time bodyguard, "Wouldn't it make a lot more sense for us to fly to Baton Rouge? After her family visit, we can fly back here, get in her SUV and drive home. A lot shorter trip and easier on all of us."

Eduardo laughed and said, "Ken, you've got a lot to learn about Miss Tina. When she makes up her mind, there is no turning back. Besides that trunk of hers would have created a bit of a problem."

"Yep, I recall when the two of us loaded it, it was a bit on the heavy side, but that shouldn't be a problem."

"It's not the weight, it's the contents."

"Her private stock of gold?"

"Nope, her armory."

About that time, Christina reappeared from having excused herself for some freshening up. "Guys, hop in and I'll drop you at the airport."

Contrary to his own advice, Eduardo responded, "Miss Tina, I really think we should go with you".

"Thanks, Eduardo, but there is no need. Besides you haven't had a day off in at least a couple of years."

Despite Eduardo's words of advice, Ken chimed in, "Come on, Christina. This is a bad idea. Yeah, you should go see your sister, but not alone. You're too recognizable. You won't have any security at all."

"Oh please, Ken. I'm from Texas; I learned to shoot before I learned to ride a bike, for cryin' out loud."

Eduardo added, "That doesn't mean you're not in danger without me, Miss Tina. And besides, what about...you know who?"

"My stalker?! He's in Los Angeles, not here in Texas."

"Do we know that for sure? He could be right her in San Antonio."

"How would he even know that? I just changed our plans!"

"I agree with Eduardo, Christina. We are concerned about your safety, particularly now with Texas having seceded. It's a powder keg just waiting to blow."

"I know you are Ken, but I'm a big girl and I can take care of myself. And besides, I'm a Texan and glad they finally did it. Now that that's settled, if you'll get on the phone and book the two of you back to LA. I'll drop y'all at the airport and be on my way."

Chapter 32: Trouble at the border

On the way to the San Antonio airport, Christina had a change of mind. She knew Eduardo too well and decided to make sure they had boarded the plane before leaving them. The flight to LA was to depart in about an hour so they would have time for a quick lunch together at the Alamo Bar and Grill in the terminal. She dropped them in front and went to park. When they entered, Eduardo told Ken to purchase the tickets while he went down to rent a car and get his luggage in.

Ken was waiting at the restaurant when Christina arrived twenty minutes later. She asked, "Where's Ken?

"He'll be along. Just a trip to the restroom."

About that time, Eduardo joined them, and they had their quick lunch. When they finished, they headed to security.

After Eduardo and Ken had passed through, the officer spoke to Christina, "Sorry, Ma'am. You will have to turn over your weapon."

"Over your dead body!"

Eduardo couldn't help a wide smile, but he kept his back turned so that Christina was unable to see.

Now the officer was a little less polite. "Ma'am, You WILL turn over your weapon!"

"And I say, NO way! I have a legal open carry permit and I am a Texan."

"Sorry, Lady. That permit does not work past this security station. You either give up your weapon or turn around. You will not enter carrying a weapon."

Eduardo interjected at this point, "Officer, she was unaware of the rule." And then to Christina, "Miss Tina, you head on to your sister and stay safe. We'll be fine. We're ticketed and our baggage is checked." A little white lie, but all in the line of duty.

"All right, Eduardo, but no shenanigans."

"Yes, Ma'am."

She went back into the terminal and waited thirty minutes at the end of the concourse. When they didn't appear, she felt relieved that they had taken off and were on their way to LA. She retrieved her car and headed out of town on I-10. It was about a three hour drive to Houston where she would spend the night.

As sharp as she was, Eduardo had outguessed her. About fifteen minutes after she had left the terminal, he and Ken exited the concourse and went to the car Eduardo had rented. Ken asked, "With her head start and the way she drives, how do you figure we're going to catch up without getting a ticket? More important when she turns off for gas or a rest stop, how are we going to find her?"

"Ken, just relax. I can tell you exactly where she is right now with this little device." As he spoke, he showed Ken a small electronic monitor that he had turned on. It read, 'Interstate 10, mile marker 491'.

"Ingenious!"

"Nope, just a GPS tracking device that I planted under her SUV for just such occasions."

"She's unaware?"

"Absolutely."

About three hours later, Christina exited the interstate, got some gas, and then checked into a motel. A bit later, she left the motel for a nearby restaurant, had supper and then went back to the motel for the evening. All the while Eduardo and Ken were no further away than a couple of blocks. They checked into their motel and gassed up after supper. Eduardo knew that she would be up bright and early so he set the alarm.

The next morning after breakfast and checking out they waited in their car. The wait wasn't that long since she was back on the road at 7:30.

As Christina got back underway to her sister's house in Louisiana, she reflected on the relationship between herself and her older sister, Charlene. Charlene was the stereotypical first- born, never causing any trouble and always the sweet young lady. Christina, on the other hand, was the rebel and tomboy. She wasn't a bad girl, but just mischievous. As different as they were, they were very close and considered each other their best friend. Charlene had married right out of college and settled down. A few years ago, she lost her husband to cancer and had been living alone ever since. Christina felt bad that her career kept her from her sister for such long stretches of time, but was determined to make it up to her this trip.

And so went her thoughts as she pulled up to a line of cars at the checkpoint set up on the I-10 bridge out of Texas. Seems there was something different about this checkpoint. There were military men sitting in some sort of armored vehicles. But the colors weren't right. The US Army didn't wear black camouflage and berets. They had to be mercenaries.

On her right hip was a holster holding the pistol that had caused the trouble at airport security the day before. A gift from her father, it was a Remington 1911 R11 45 caliber, which she carried everywhere. Just in case, she decided to pop open her trunk and retrieve a second holster and two additional weapons. The first was a Smith and Wesson M&P pistol, also a 45, and the second a Sterling 30 caliber carbine. Before she closed the trunk she removed several clips of ammunition for each weapon.

"There now, we'll see what this is all about. A gal can't be too careful these days," she said to herself as she buckled the second holster on her left hip and tucked the pistol in and got out of her car. Eduardo had pulled up to within three or four cars behind. When he saw her get out, he reached into the back seat of the sedan they had rented and got his pistol, rifle and several clips of ammo for each.

"You expecting a war, amigo?" Ken asked Eduardo.

"Not necessarily, but we all know how trouble seems to follow Miss Tina."

Remembering the encounter at airport security yesterday, Ken responded, "That it does, my friend. That it does."

As Christine moved stealthily around the line of cars toward the bridge, she thought to herself, "Just like Campbell to hire out his dirty work. Glad I didn't vote for the jackass." As she drew closer, she noticed a semi- truck which had to be at least 30 years old pulled over on the side of the bridge which spanned between the two states. The tractor was so old, it seemed to be an old International 1700 series like her dad had used on their farm. Standing in front of the truck, an elderly man and woman appeared to be arguing with some of the men in the black camouflage. Both the mercenaries were wielding what appeared to be semi-auto rifles, but that didn't seem to faze the older couple at all.

As Christina continued up to the bridge and approached the older couple's truck she could hear the argument. One of the mercenaries was speaking with a thick German accent.

"I said get back in your truck and turn around. You will NOT cross into this country!"

"What you don't understand, sonny, is that everything we got is tied up in this load of watermelons, and we've got to get through to the refrigerated warehouse in Lake Charles or they will rot. Is that what you want?" asked the by now, irate old man.

"What I want, is for you and your wife to get in your truck and turn around, because you are NOT entering the United States of America carrying commerce and having Texas plates."

"Well then, we've got ourselves a stalemate, sonny. You talk real big with those black uniforms and automatic weapons. My grandfather fought you Krauts at Normandy and the Battle of the Bulge. You guys had the high ground at Normandy and had us outnumbered and out gunned, but we still beat you. You don't scare me one bit, No sir! We'll just wait for some REAL authorities to come and hear our case.

At that point, the man who had been doing all the talking merely glanced at the man standing next to him. Upon that silent order, the second man raised his rifle and put the muzzle right up against the old woman's head.

"Now if you don't move, I will make you a widower and then with the next shot a dead one."

"Wait! Wait! Don't hurt Martha, please! PLEASE!"

Pulling the pistols out of their holsters, Christina crossed underneath the trailer of the older couple's truck and approached them from the passenger side of the truck. At this angle, she had a clear shot of the head of the German who was threatening the old woman.

"I'd put it down, if I were you!" Christina yelled. "Otherwise your boy that is so brave he has to pick on old women here is going to get an extra couple of holes in his head."

Immediately both of the mercenaries reacted. The leader took a step back to communicate with the men in the armored vehicle while the man holding the gun on the old woman's head grabbed her upper arm and pulled her in front of him. The old man turned and ran back to his truck, trying to reach the shotgun he carried in the cab. Or at least he tried.

The man holding his wife turned his gun and shot the old man in the back, three times. Before the older man's body could even hit the ground, Christina opened fire on the shooter and killed him with a single shot to the head. Then his leader made the fatal mistake of trying to draw on Christina. This time it was two shots, but the first had done the trick..

Chapter 33: White House reaction

In Washington DC, President Oren Campbell was in his Oval Office going over a speech he was to give later in the week at a fundraiser. "Dammit all," he thought, "Not only do I have this secession business to deal with, but I've still got to worry about getting re-elected."

Allen Jefferson rushed into the Oval Office without knocking.

"What in the hell??!!" thundered Campbell, "You damn well better have a good reason to burst in here, Allen!"

"I do sir! The mercenaries have opened fire at the checkpoint on I-10 at the Louisiana/Texas border."

"Opened fire? On who?"

"As near as my sources can tell, they've killed a trucker and are in a firefight with…with…"

"Spit it out, man! With WHO??!!"

"Christina St. James, the movie star, sir."

Campbell's jaw fell open at this point, and he was, for once, speechless. "The…the movie star? How in the hell are they…Why are they?"

"I don't know sir, but they're taking heavy fire from Ghost Storm, evidently."

Pounding the button on his intercom, Campbell bellowed to his secretary, "Get me Les Parsons, NOW! And I don't want to hear that he'll 'get back to me' either!!"

Campbell sure as hell didn't need this kind of crap at all, and certainly NOT with an election year coming up, dammit all!

"Mr. President, Mr. Parsons is on the line."

"Parsons! You guaranteed me that your Ghost Stormers wouldn't embarrass me!! So explain to me why they shot and killed a Texas citizen and are trying their damnedest to kill Christina St. James!!?"Campbell shouted.

"Oren, I just got apprised of the situation, myself. Let me reach out to my contacts and find out what happened. As soon as I know, you'll know!" and with that, Les Parsons hung up on the President of the United States.

To say that didn't sit well with President Campbell would be an understatement. Fuming and so filled with anger that he feared he might have a heart attack, Campbell called Jefferson back in.

"Yes sir?" said Jefferson as he re-entered the Oval Office.

"I need you to dig up everything we have on Lester Parsons."

"Lester Parsons, sir?"

"Yes, I have the feeling I'm going to need leverage on him so dig deep."

Chapter 34: Pandemonium on the bridge

At the sound of gun shots, panicked people began fleeing from their cars and pandemonium broke loose on the bridge. Christina darted forward and grabbed the old woman bringing her back under the passenger side of the truck. At least there, they had some cover. Christina then got her phone and gave it to the woman, telling her to dial 911, which the woman did, who then said, "Honey, keep those SOB's busy while I get up in the cab to get Frank's shotgun."

Surprised, Christina asked, "Ma'am, can you shoot?"

Sobbing, she replied," Honey, are you kidding? They killed my husband and those sons of bitches are going to pay. I'm Texas born and bred, and yes, I can shoot."

"In that case, take this", as Christina handed her the carbine and some ammunition."

Both Ken and Eduardo looked on in astonishment as Christina had interjected herself into the altercation taking place.

"What in the hell is she doing??!!" shouted Tomlinson.

"I don't know, but I'm going to protect her."

"You do that, I'm calling the authorities."

So while Eduardo worked his way up to the truck, Ken Tomlinson put in a call directly to the Governor's mansion. "Oh yeah? Well I don't care how busy he is. Tell him that if he doesn't get on the line with me pronto, he will be having to attend the funeral of one of Texas' national treasures!!"

"Christina St. James!!! That's who!!"

In less than 30 seconds, the phone clicked and Governor Houston was on the line. "What is it, Ken? What is so all fired important?"

"I'll tell you what. I'm down here on the 10 as it crosses into Louisiana and there are mercenaries – armed mercenaries in armored vehicles that just killed a Texas citizen and have now drawn down on Chris!"

"Oh my God! He's done it!"

"Who has done what?"

"My Intel told me that Campbell was going to put mercenaries at one or more of the federal highways that leave Texas. I didn't believe that Campbell would be that dim, but evidently I underestimated his capacity for stupidity."

"The question now is, 'what are you going to do about it?'" asked Tomlinson.

"I'll launch a drone from Ellington right away. It'll be overhead in no time."

"A drone?!! How about some actual man power??"

"Calm down, a drone will give us eyes on the scene and I can also scramble a helicopter with some Rangers."

"Okay," Tomlinson said, "but hurry, Christina is pinned down right now, taking fire."

Chapter 35 Reinforcements

When the call came in from Ken Tomlinson, Houston was in a conference with Jerry Collins and Adjutant General Rafael Hernandez, discussing how the recruitment effort was coming along. Houston briefed the two on the confrontation at the border and then turned on the video to be able to have a live update when the drone arrived on the scene. Hernandez immediately got on the horn to scramble a drone and an Osprey helicopter with a unit from the 8th Texas Regiment, called Terry's Texas Rangers, who were the 'cream of the crop'.

Once the drone got over the area, it was easy to see that, unbelievably, Christina St. James was holding her own. As if it had been lifted right out of one of her movies, she and an old woman were keeping the members of Geistersturm at bay. All the backed up cars on the bridge were preventing the armored vehicles from advancing, but it was only a matter of time before the heavily armed storm troopers found the pair of women who were creating such havoc. The Osprey had landed about a half a mile from the checkpoint, and the Rangers were making their way easterly, towards the firefight, but were being delayed by the panicked civilians.

Using the empty cars for cover, Eduardo made his way to the older couples' semi-truck, and found her and the old woman in a fire fight with the mercenaries.

"Eduardo, under normal circumstances, I would be asking what the hell you are doing here, but these are not exactly normal circumstances."

"No, Miss Tina, but are you all right?" Eduardo frantically asked her.

"I'm fine, Eduardo. But this woman's husband is out there on the ground in front of this truck."

"He's dead, though."

"No, we saw him moving. He's still alive, but needs medical attention ASAP!"

"Here, take my AR-15. You lay down cover fire for me and I'll get him."

While Christina and the woman laid down a barrage, Eduardo darted out, grabbed the old man by the collar and began to drag him back to safety under the semi.

"Scramble two Black Hawk helicopters armed with rockets ASAP! And get those Rangers out there to that bridge. I want this contained and those sons of bitches turned into buzzard bait!!" thundered Hernandez. "And make damn sure those civilians pinned down under that semi are kept alive!"

Houston interjected, "General, have the Rangers do what they have to do, but let's try to capture as many of the mercenaries as we can so that

President Campbell will have to continue to pay for his idiocy."

"Right, Sir." Hernandez responded and then relayed the order to the commander of the unit.

Back on the bridge, Eduardo was doing his best to drag the old man back to the safety of the far side of the semi amid all the gunfire when a hatch opened on the Ghost Stormers' armored vehicle and a grenade sailed out towards him.

Christina rushed forward to grab the grenade, but it rolled under the semi. So, immediately she grabbed the old man along with Eduardo and yelled out to the wife, who was still blazing away to join them under the trailer, as far towards the back as they could and lay flat on the ground. Seconds later, the grenade detonated, destroying the cab of the rig with it and igniting the fuel tanks under the cab. The explosion rocked the entire bridge and some people thought the roadway might give out right from under them. Huddled underneath the box trailer of the rig, miraculously, the four had not been injured by the blast, and the blaze and flying shrapnel had slowed the advancing mercenaries.

Back in Austin, Houston, Collins, and Hernandez watched the real-time video feed from the drone circling overhead with a mixture of Texas pride and anxiety. They were thankful, that someone had dragged that trucker to safety before his rig exploded. But they couldn't see Ms. St. James, the movie star or the older couple. And President Houston also realized that they might well be the first casualties of Texas' secession from the United States. "General, how soon till the Rangers reach the bridge?"

Hernandez had just gotten off the radio with the commander of the unit. "Sir, our Rangers are approaching the bridge now. When the drone makes its next pass, you'll see them."

"Are you in direct radio contact with them, General?"

"Yes Sir."

"I want to know whether Christina St. James is still alive, along with the owners of that semi-truck that's on fire on that bridge."

"Okay, just one minute Sir while I verify that."

General Hernandez then relayed President Houston's concerns to the unit commander who reported back that the smoke was obscuring their vision, but as soon as they had visual contact, they would verify.

The video was now showing that with the blaze subsiding, the mercenaries were advancing up the bridge with a tank followed by three armored cars. As the tank moved forward, it was pushing the cars over the side of the bridge as if they were toys. The Black Hawks had now arrived, and Hernandez gave the order to attack. In short order, the planes had turned the armored vehicles into charred twisted metal. The attack had momentarily halted the twenty or so surviving mercenaries that were on foot, but now they were on the move again with vengeance in mind.

The second in command, who became the leader after that meddlesome woman killed his Captain, saw her and three others hiding under the rear of the trailer of that insufferable old couple's truck. If they had just turned around, none of this would have happened.

"Hey, Bauer! You and Weber make your way to the back of that truck. Under the trailer there is the woman who killed our Captain. We MUST avenge his death. Go! Kill the woman!"

"Jawohl!"

Under the trailer, Christina saw that she was out of ammunition and said they needed to retreat. Eduardo was in agreement.

"Go" he said, "I will hold them off for as long as I can."

At that moment, the two mercenaries came up upon them from the rear with their automatic weapons pointed at the group. Bauer spoke, "Lay your weapons down and hands high."

Eduardo lowered his weapon and while raising his hands slipped a Bowie knife from the sheath in his boot. He leapt at Bauer, who shot him in the chest in mid-air, but as Eduardo landed, the knife found its mark in Bauer's heart. It was probably not needed, but Weber finished the job with two shots to the body guard's head. Weber now spoke, "I hope that no one else tries something foolish, or I will kill you all. Now who was the one that killed our captain?"

Uncharacteristically of Christina, she was sobbing hysterically, not at danger to herself, but for the loss of her dear friend. She raised her hand to answer Weber's question. Weber now pointed his weapon at Christina and said, "Danke, Fraulein. Auf wiedersehen."

Two quick shots rang out and Weber went down. The first had knocked the weapon from Weber's hand and the other had mangled his knee. The Ranger who had done the shooting said, "Sorry, folks. We would have been here sooner except for the traffic." It would have been funny except for the dead Eduardo.

Christine had stopped crying long enough to tell the Ranger about the severely wounded old man and the need for immediate medical attention. He relayed word to the medic who was in the detachment just coming up behind him. She then asked if she could borrow his rifle to finish the mercenary off. "Sorry, Ma'am. General's orders to take as many prisoners as possible."

Christine was now back in character, "What's one more or less son of a bitch gonna make a difference?" It may have sounded funny, but Christine was in full seriousness. By now the unit of Rangers had rounded up the last of the mercenaries, seventeen in all, most of them with non-lethal wounds.

The old woman had been crying convulsively during the ordeal but now paused to say to the medic, "Sonny, you've GOT to save my Frank. He's my whole life and I'd be lost without him. Please don't let him die out here on this bridge." And with that outburst, the woman began to sob again.

The medic replied, "He's lost a lot of blood, but I've stopped the flow with a pressure bandage. We're going to evacuate him to the nearest hospital and we'll do our best."

Chapter 36: Retribution

Back in Austin, Houston, Collins, and Hernandez breathed a collective sigh of relief. Collins spoke first, "It certainly ended a lot smoother than I had anticipated."

Houston responded, "True enough, thanks to our Rangers, but we can't let this go unanswered. They've killed one of our citizens, and it may turn out that another will die. General, many thanks for your assistance today. Continue to work with Kristen Walker to increase our numbers and tell her we are pleased that she has us up to 60,000, but remind her the goal is 150,000, which we may need sooner than later. In the meantime, Jerry and I are going to come up with a response to this incident."

After Hernandez left the room, Collins spoke, "Rich, I hope your comment of 'sooner than later" was not totally serious."

"Jer, I sure hope we will not need them, but with that idiot in the

White House, who can tell? What we need to do is send a strong message to let him know we will not stand by and have our citizens attacked."

"Rich, you know I agree, but at the same time we have to let the asshole save some kind of face."

"Do you have anything in mind?"

"Yes, as you know we are in great shape energy wise since we became independent and got free of EPA's restrictions on coal burning. Actually the U.S. has benefitted from the use of our power."

"So you are suggesting we cut off our power to them?"

"Only for a while, Rich, to teach Campbell a lesson. As cold as it is right now, I figure a month without our power should create enough discomfort that the message will be understood. If we cut off power too long, it will antagonize our neighbors, who we are hoping will join us in secession. It also might trigger a military response."

"Sounds good, Jer. Draft a letter, let me see it, and then we will transmit it to Dimwit."

"Right, boss."

The next morning at the White House, Allen Jefferson brought the following letter to the President, which had been sent by overnight mail.:

February 1, 2043, from the office of the President of the Republic of Texas

President Campbell,

As I am sure you are aware, a group of mercenaries employed by your office attempted to blockade Interstate 10 leading from Texas into Louisiana. In addition to creating a major disruption of one of our economic lifelines, your hoodlums killed one of our citizens and severely wounded another who is currently on life support. All of this was without provocation on our part. We had hoped that our separation would be peaceful and that our nations could remain on friendly terms. We certainly have no differences with the individual states and no intention of causing anyone harm, however, you have left us little choice in the matter. If we did nothing and just ignored the incident, it would imply that we accept the matter and most likely encourage further incursions on our territory, likely of an escalating manner. Therefore, as of 12;00 noon central standard time on February 2, 2043, our power grid will be closed from connection to the U.S. The duration of this closure will be thirty days, ending on March 4 at 12:00 noon, provided there are no further provocations.

Sincerely,

Richard Anderson Houston, President, Republic of Texas

"That son of a bitch! If he thinks he can intimidate me, he is sorely wrong. "Jefferson, how will that power closure affect us?"

"Mr. President, I will have to check with the National Power Board for exact numbers, but I can tell you that we will feel the effects immediately. Our utilities cannot begin to supply all our power needs since so many have been changed over to 'alternative energy sources'. A fair number of utilities have converted over to solar and wind power because of the subsidies and tax incentives. Since these are interruptible sources they have to be backed up with gas powered generators, creating huge inefficiencies…"

"Whoa, Allen. Can you slow down and speak English? What in the heck are 'interruptible' sources?"

"Certainly, Sir. Interruptible refers to sources that are dependent on weather conditions. Solar cells need sunlight and wind mills need wind. In the absence of sunlight or wind those sources can provide power only to the extent that they have charged batteries. Since in most cases, there is no excess power to charge batteries, those sources are interrupted when conditions aren't right."

"But we still have nuclear and natural gas powered utilities?"

"Yes, sir, but not nearly the capacity to satisfy demand, and the cold weather exacerbates the situation."

"So what do you recommend?"

"My recommendation is to' hunker down' and conserve energy for thirty days and not do anything more to antagonize them."

"You are telling me to give in?!!"

"No, Mr. President. You asked for my recommendation and I gave it to you. If you wanted me to tell you what you wanted to hear, you should have told me."

"Enough of your sass, Jefferson. Remember who you are speaking to."

"Yes, Mr. President. Sorry, Sir."

Chapter 37: Mass migration

Jerry Collins' prediction of migration as a result of the act signed into law by President Campbell on January 6 was apparently taking place. Cessation of Federal benefits to recipients, residing in seceding states was to begin on March 6. By February 28, an estimated two million undocumented immigrants had fled Texas for the neighboring states of Arkansas, Louisiana, New Mexico, and Oklahoma, and many more were preparing to move. In addition, an estimated one million U.S. citizens had left Texas for those states as well.

However, a migration of that magnitude doesn't occur without consequences. All but New Mexico had already been discussing secession, and it wouldn't take much to make it happen . By early March all four states had set up roadblocks on major thoroughfares leading out of Texas and refused entry to anyone who could not prove U.S. citizenship, but it was impossible to patrol every dirt road, so that tens of thousands continued to cross into their states.

New Mexico was being hit from two sides since people were leaving Arizona as well, but the numbers from Arizona did not begin to approach those of Texas due to Arizona's crackdown on illegal immigrants months before secession. And Alaska was pretty much unaffected by the law. Yes, there were citizens that would be losing their Social Security, but like Texas, the savings from Federal corporate, personal and excise taxes would more than offset the loss.

Finally, the citizens of Louisiana had had enough. They had just suffered through the coldest February on record compounded by the power shortage, resulting from the cut off of power from Texas. Now there were all those immigrants, mostly illegal, without jobs living on the streets and creating havoc. To add insult to injury, Louisiana's neighbor to the west was doing quite well. On Sunday, March 12 there was a mass march of an estimated fifty thousand into Baton Rouge to demand the legislature pass a bill of secession. Of course, the legislature was not in session that day, but the message was clear. On Monday, the first and only item on the agenda was secession. By mid-day both houses had passed the legislation and it was sent to the Governor's office for ratification, only needing confirmation by popular vote. He signed and a special election was scheduled for the following Saturday to allow as many citizens as possible to vote. On March 18, a record turn-out of 79% of registered voters voted three to one in favor of secession.

Arkansas and Oklahoma quickly followed Louisiana's lead over the next two weeks, so by April 1, The United States of America was down to forty one states with others likely to follow in secession. The law cutting off Federal benefits to seceding states could be likened to a nuclear chain reaction, where splitting nuclei result in ever increasing numbers of nuclei. So too, with the cessation of Federal benefits, putting pressure on adjoining states to follow in secession. Anticipating this, the neighboring states of Arkansas, Louisiana, and Oklahoma erected blockades and passed deportation laws against illegal immigrants. This halted the migration as well as further secessions for now.

Chapter 38: Blackmail

The Governor's office receives large volumes of mail, mostly inconsequential, but even the least of these requires some sort of polite response. Her secretary was quite proficient at handling all but the more sensitive issues and this freed up Governor Zimmerman for the more important issues of the day. On this Thursday a letter to the Governor with no postage arrived, which was marked PERSONAL in large capital letters and the secretary came in, placed it on Zimmerman's desk, and left the room. Zimmerman called back to her secretary, "Sheila, this letter has no postage. Did it come through the mail?"

"No, Governor. Brad, my assistant brought it in to me and said that it was at the top of his in- basket when he had gotten back from a trip to the restroom." She opened the letter and began reading.

Hello Governor,

You probably don't remember me, but I sure remember you. Let me refresh your memory. It was a dreary Wednesday night thirteen years ago in a small out of the way suburb of Washington where we met. It was a honkytonk kind of bar with loud country music. I bought you a drink at the bar and after a dance we sat down at a table, had a few more drinks and then left the place for a nearby motel. You told me your name was something like Mary Smith, but I remember at the time figuring that you had made up that name, because you sure didn't act like any Mary Smith I ever knew at the bar or in the motel room that night. My name, by the way is Rex Morgan, not that you might recall, but I think it best that we get to know one another a little bit more.

As she read, she tried to recall. Thirteen years ago – the time was right, but how could it be? There had been a few, but probably no more than five or six; and she had been extra careful. Always a different bar in a different town where nobody knew her or would even recognize her. In each case she would take the additional precaution of parking in a different place and taking a taxi to the designated spot for the evening.

In retrospect you might have been better advised to use a pseudonym like Dolores McCutcheon or Agnes Weyerhauser, which would not have been so obvious. I do compliment you, however. You definitely made the chase difficult, which made it all the more exhilarating. In any event, I want to congratulate you. You have made a real name for yourself, and I certainly have no intention of hurting you or your career. Au contraire, I want to be your friend. Ha, I will bet that you had no idea I or one of your other one nighters *even know how to spell* au contraire, *let alone know the meaning. You see, I, too, am a pretty educated person, with degrees in philosophy and psychology.*

"Where in hell is he going with this?", she thought. She wanted to stop reading and shred the letter, but resisted the impulse and continued to read.

Unfortunately, I have a bit of a problem and am reaching out to you as a friend to help me out. As smart as I am, I made a huge mistake in getting involved with a gambling syndicate controlled by the mafia. I want out, but they have threatened to kill me. I need $10,000 to pay them off and another $10,000 to get out of the country and restart my life. I assure you that I will repay your generosity by never asking for another dime and never trying to contact you again. You can let me know by e-mail within 24 hours at rexalonglostfriend@vmail.com. Just write OK and I will be back in touch to tell you where to wire the funds.

With deepest regards,

Rex

Zimmerman started to shred the letter and paused. "What if I don't respond?" she thought. She copied the e-mail address and shredded the letter. For the next hour, she was unable to get her mind off the letter. She told her secretary that she was feeling ill and was taking the afternoon off. "I'm sure it will wear off and I will be back in the next day." Zimmerman would have preferred to take a long weekend at a spa and try to clear her mind, but she had too much to do, what with secession and normal business.

She was at one of her favorite lunchtime restaurants and ordered her normal quiche, but today instead of her customary iced tea, she ordered a martini. She considered ordering a second but thought better of it since she had an eight mile drive home through the city.

Chapter 39: Blackmail (part two)

It was 11:30 AM on Friday, approximately 25 hours after Governor Zimmerman had received the ominous letter. She had finally been able to put the letter out of mind and focus on business at hand. An automated voice emanated from her computer, "You have e-mail." When she opened it, all the memories of yesterday came flooding back.

Good morning, Governor. I am disappointed that I hadn't heard from you. Perhaps, you thought I was playing games. I assure you I am dead serious. Now that the deadline has passed, I regret to inform you that there will be a nominal penalty of 20%. The new deadline is tomorrow at 11:30 AM. I probably do not need to tell you, but any further delays will be costly. Looking forward to a favorable reply,
Your good friend, Rex

Zimmerman normally had the presence of mind to deal

unemotionally with problems, but this was something that she had never faced before and she had no idea how to handle it. If she consented to his demand it would probably only encourage him to continue to come back for more.

On the other hand, what was he likely to do if she continued to ignore his demands? Increase the penalties? Expose her infidelities and probably ruin her? Increasing the penalties would do him no good if she never gave in, and exposing her would end his hold on her without him benefitting, other than the satisfaction of revenge for her rejection.

But wait, he could probably make some money by selling the story to a tabloid, but what proof did he have? She could threaten to inform the authorities to go after him for extortion, but then the story would certainly come out. Again, what proof could he possibly have? Upon reflection, she decided the best course of action was to reply in such a way that he could not use her reply against her.

Dear Mr. Morgan,11:53 AM January 28, 2043

Thank you for your request. As you must know I am deluged with requests for various worthwhile causes, and while I would love to be able to respond in a timely manner, my duties preclude me from doing so. I would be happy to donate $1000 to the charity of your choosing and trust that will be acceptable. Again, the large number of requests that come into my office just will not permit me to go beyond that amount. I feel sure you understand.

Sincerely,

F.L. Zimmerman, Governor of the State of Arizona

Dear Florence, 11:55 AM January 28,2043

I think we can dispense with the formalities, given our past close relationship, and

I also think we can stop wasting each other's time. I had been prepared to accept $24,000 to let bygones to be bygones, but now with the aggravation, the price is now $30,000. You have until 11:30AM to say we have a deal. By the way, you are probably. wondering how I tracked you down after all these many years.

As cagey as you were, you made three mistakes. 1)Wearing that very expensive Rolex that night…"

"The Rolex- Oh, no!" Memories of that night came streaming back. She recalled that the guy had been so gentlemanly to let her shower first, but when she finished and came out of the shower, he was gone and so was her Rolex. She had considered contacting the authorities to be on the lookout at pawn shops for such an identifiable item but thought better of it when she realized the ramifications.

…That told me you were a woman of means and I knew you weren't just an expensive prostitute, since they don't give their merchandise away. If it had been a Timex or some cheap costume jewelry, I wouldn't have bothered wasting my time trying to find you.2) Having your three initials inscribed on the backside. Just two initials would have made the job colossally more difficult, and again, I probably would not have wanted to spend the time. By the way, your last initial of "Z" narrowed the field significantly. I have a good friend who happens to be a detective in D.C. and with my assumption that you were a highly paid employee in either government or the private sector helped him narrow the search. 3)Your final mistake and clincher was your e-mail to me, telling me that you would "donate" $1000…

"How could I have been that stupid?", shethought. She was already thinking of ways to extract herself from this predicament, but read on.

....I had narrowed the list to four women, having the initials F.L.Z., living and working in Washington at the time, who were between ages 21 and 45. Two of them just ignored my messages. The other said I obviously had the wrong individual and threatened me with alerting the authorities for harassment if I persisted.

So, Florence, you now know that I know you were the one. You are probably thinking, "O.K., He knows, but what proof does he have?" Good question. You probably think I pawned that expensive watch, but you don't give me enough credit. I realized that the value of that Rolex was far more than I could ever get by selling it...

"Oh, my God!" She knew then that he had all the proof he needed. There was more to the e-mail, but she quit reading and looked up a phone number. Florence dialed the number.

Chapter 40 Pre-empt

After a couple of rings, a recorded voice came on, "Good day, you have reached the voice mail of Jared Hardigan Live, America's top rated conservative talk show host. Please leave a message and phone number, and we will get back to you as soon as possible."

Florence began, "This is Florence Zimmerman, Governor of Arizona. I have something to tell you that I feel will be of great interest to your viewers, not only my supporters but my detractors as well." She left a number to her private line and awaited a return call.

A short time thereafter, a call came back from one of Hardigan's female assistants. Florence thanked her for the return call, but insisted that she speak to Hardigan. The young assistant began, "I understand, Governor, but Mr. Hardigan…"

Florence interrupted her, "Miss, I don't want to hear about policy or protocol. I will be expecting a personal call from Mr. Hardigan within ten minutes. If it turns out he is too busy, I will be calling Mr. Floyd Jensen, his main competitor." With that, she hung up.

Five minutes later, Florence's phone rang and displayed the caller ID of Jared Hardigan. Florence answered, "Mr. Hardigan, thank you for calling."

"No problem, Governor. And I apologize for my young assistant. She needs to learn that there are exceptions to rules."

"No apology necessary, Mr. Hardigan. I completely understand. I know you are a busy fellow, so I will get right to the point." With that she laid out the entire story. When she got to the end, she told him, " I am asking $100,000 to be donated to my favorite charity, 'The Association to Aid Abused Women', for exclusive rights to my story provided you give me the full hour to come onto your show this evening so that my constituents can hear the story first hand."

Hardigan, replied, "Governor, I will say it is a bit unusual to change my scheduled interviews at the last minute, but under the circumstances I shall be happy to grant you the time. Can you be at the studio at 6:30 tonight, which would give us thirty minutes to get ready?"

"Absolutely and thank you!"

At 7:00 that night after a brief introduction by Hardigan, Florence began, "Good Evening, my fellow Arizonans. I have always tried to be straight with you and conduct myself befitting of the high honor you have bestowed on me. What I am about to tell you I certainly am not proud of, and that it happened many years ago does not begin to absolve me of the guilt I feel." She then related the story and finished with the words, "I am truly sorry. I will have my office send out an electronic referendum to all Arizona registered voters on Monday submitting my continued tenure to a vote. The Secretary of State will tally the vote on Wednesday and if you feel I should vacate the office, I shall do so. It has been an honor and privilege to serve you. Good night."

The referendum was not even close. 82% of Arizonans supported the Governor.

When Rex Morgan heard about the broadcast, he was furious. "That bitch, who the hell does she think she is dealing with? If she thinks she can outsmart me she has another think coming. I will show her who is calling the shots." Morgan dialed his detective buddy in Washington, "Derrick, you did a great job in helping me nail down my "date" thirteen years ago. Unfortunately, she pre-empted us by going public with her confession. Our information now is worthless. What I need you to do now is to go after her close friends and associates to see what kind of dirt we can come up with. I don't need to tell you that the juicier the details and the more prestigious the individual, the greater the value."

Chapter 41: The calm before the storm

It was late September and President Oren Campbell was in good humor. It had been almost five months since the last secession and his approval ratings, although still below 50%, had been on a dramatic upswing, possibly helped in part by the dividend checks received by Social Security and welfare recipients resulting from forfeitures from those who had elected to remain in the seceding states. The climate was also cooperating and, EPA was claiming credit for the mildest summer on record. The agency put out a statement that its efforts to reduce carbon dioxide emissions were paying off. There was, of course, no mention of the fact that while the rate of increase had subsided, atmospheric carbon dioxide levels were still going up, and the cooling that was taking place had long been predicted by scientists, who knew that solar cycles, not carbon dioxide, had been the reason for the earlier warming and were the cause of the current cooling.

Campbell called Jefferson in for a meeting. "Allen, I have been so distracted by this secession crap, I hadn't even thought about getting a replacement on the Supreme Court."

"Mr. President, I totally understand. I've thought about it, but I think it might be best to just hold off for now."

"What's the problem, Allen?"

"It's just that there is no need at this time. If an issue arises where we need that additional vote, you can get that justice in with no delay. On the other hand, things have calmed down and we don't want to do something that might cause any other state to think about seceding."

"Damn, Allen. I'm President and I can't even do what I want,"

"Sir, it's your decision to make. I am just giving my opinion."

"All right, Allen. I'll hold off for now."

Whatever the cause of the mild summer, Lester Parsons and his buddy, Bradley Sims, were not in a happy mood. The coal industry had come back to life, and with it, Atlas Coal stock, which was now up to $1.40 per share. "Les, I'm going to cover my short on Atlas. I figure I am just about at break-even."

"Brad, good luck on that."

"What do you mean by that?"

"Brad, you're a big boy. You certainly know what a 'short squeeze' is?"

"So what are we going to do about it, Les?"

"I think we may have to up the bid price significantly to shake loose some of that stock."

"Take a loss?"

"You got it, Brad. That S.O.B., Stephens has us over a barrel and he knows it."

"So how much are you thinking?"

"$3.00- maybe as much as $5.00 a share."

"Damn, Lester. $5.00 would wipe me out."

"The alternative is declaring bankruptcy and letting the courts decide."

"OK. Let's try $3.00."

Chapter 42: El Diablo

Javier Suarez, aptly nick-named El Diablo, was as ruthless as his namesake. Sometimes, appearances can be deceiving, but not so with El Diablo. Just looking at this short stocky ugly man, missing one of his tobacco stained upper front teeth with pock marks on his face and piercing mean brown eyes that were all the more menacing because they were out of alignment, would scare most people. Deep scars on his left cheek and arms were evidence of a lot of knife fights over his forty two years and one could guess that as a child he was the target of a lot of teasing about his looks, but probably not a second time by the same individual. He had a quick temper and his associates learned early that El Diablo was not someone to cross.

His cartel, Ariel, was the one remaining drug cartel in all of Mexico after twenty-four years of intense drug wars between competing cartels and the Mexican government. In the early years, the various cartels were the governing agencies in much of Mexico with only slightly less power where the legitimate government ruled. But even to refer to the government in those areas as legitimate is a stretch with all of the corruption going on. The drug trade was so profitable that the drug lords had little problem in offering enough of a bribe that even the more honest individuals had a difficult time resisting the temptation and for the few who tried, they were either persuaded by threats on their families or eliminated.

Finally along came a fearless charismatic leader, Juan de Carlo Montalban, with probably no more scruples than the drug lords he was campaigning against, but he was promising to rid the country of the drug trade and make Mexico great again. Up to that time, when a drug king pin was arrested, it was rare for the individual to even be convicted, but when occasionally, one was found guilty and imprisoned, an escape quickly followed. One month after Montalban came to power he showed that things would be different. The very first drug lord to be arrested after a record breaking reward was posted was mysteriously assassinated one day before his trial. There were rumors that the government had been responsible, but since the assassin was never apprehended, there was no proof. The Church and a reformist coalition rallied behind him, and with the elimination of and imprisonment of drug lords one after another, his power fed on itself until like an avalanche it was unstoppable. By 2042, the government had eliminated all but one of the cartels and pushed it westward until it controlled only the state of Sonaro and the Baja peninsula.

It was not for the lack of trying, but Montalban had been unable to break Ariel's hold on Sonaro and Baja. The officials had been so corrupted and committed so much evil, including murder and sex trade, that they feared life imprisonment or execution, if the Mexican government ever regained control.

Until Florence Zimmerman became governor of Arizona in 2040, Ariel had been enjoying a lucrative and pretty much unchallenged drug trade across the border, but she had promised in her campaign for governor that she would rid Arizona of illegal drugs and characteristically, she was following through on her promise.

During the summer of 2043, there were increasing numbers of arrests and drug confiscations, and El Diablo was growing restless for some means of curbing Arizona's interference in his business.

Chapter 43: Ransom

" Jefe, what do you want us to do with him, finish him off pronto or slowly,"

"No, Pancho", replied El Diablo, "Not yet. I want to send his Senora a ransom note."

"Ahha, Jefe, how much?"

"$10,000," El Diablo answered.

"So little?"

"I want her to be able to afford it, so that she will come to us. You have this gringo's driver's license. Send her a message that we have her husband, and that if she wants to see him alive, she will say nothing to the authorities and bring the money to us." El Diablo was illiterate, but not stupid. His lieutenant, Pancho was born to an educated family and had learned English as a child.

"Si, Jefe. I will take care of it."

"Muy bien, Pancho."

September 21, 2043

Dear Senora Brockton,

As you have probably learned by now, we are holding your husband. He has not been harmed and will not be so long as you follow our instructions to the letter. Do not be tempted to contact the authorities if you wish to ever see your husband alive again. We have paid informers throughout the state of Arizona and will know if you even try. You are to bring $10,000 in unmarked $100 dollar bills ...."

The Arizona Border Patrol, like all the border patrols until secession, was an arm of the Federal Homeland Security Agency. There were 4200 agents assigned to Arizona, and when secession occurred, Arizona offered them the choice of leaving Federal service and joining the newly formed border patrol reporting to the state or taking their chances on obtaining employment in some other capacity with the Federal government. Many were natives of Arizona, but even more coming from other states had made their homes in Arizona and did not want to uproot their households. There was also the consideration that they might not have jobs if they left the state. With inflation and budgetary cutbacks throughout the Federal government, civil service was highly uncertain. Over three thousand of them accepted the offer despite the fact that salaries had to be reduced substantially to keep them in line with state troopers' salaries.

Sergeant Brett Brockton had been an Arizona border patrol agent for eight years after four years as a Tucson city policeman. He had a degree in criminology from The University of Arizona where he had met his wife, who was in pre-law. Brett had aspired to the FBI, but there were no openings at the time of his graduation so he joined the Tucson police force. He and Lenore were married shortly thereafter and then when Lenore became pregnant, she dropped out of school with the thought of caring for her infant until the child was school age. Unfortunately, she had a miscarriage in her eighth month and Lenore rather than going back to school, took a job as a paralegal to supplement their income.

During the short time Brett was a cop, he had had several run-ins with drug gangs and distinguished himself as a courageous and selfless cop. He was on the "fast track" for promotion, but when the opening for border patrol came up, Brett didn't hesitate to apply, and it wasn't only the difference in salary and benefits that made the decision easy. It was the fact that he would be fighting the real war against drugs not the skirmishes he had been involved in as a policeman. There were fifty-one applicants for the single position and the screening was intense. There were of course the interviews and background checks, but there were also psychological and lie detector testing and then physical and endurance testing. The entire process took seven days, and by the last day, the field had been winnowed down to three candidates. The other two were excellent candidates, but did not have the on the job experience Brett had. He continued to distinguish himself as a border patrolman and in short order had been promoted to the rank of sergeant.

Now he was in the hands of his sworn enemy after being captured in a gun fight on the border about 20 miles east of the Lukeville border crossing station four days earlier. Brett had not gone down easily. His right knee had been shattered by a high caliber bullet, but the clincher was a bullet wound to his right temple that knocked him out. The bullet had entered just above his brow and exited at the top of his ear. A centimeter or so further in and Brett would have joined his two dead colleagues. His team of three had been overtaken by twelve drug runners, and when the battle was over, Brett and four bad guys were the only survivors. El Diablo had certainly heard about this fearless border agent and was determined to take revenge, but also use him as an example to his compatriots.

Lenore Brockton had been contacted by the border patrol about the gun fight later that evening. The fact that Brett was not found meant that he had not been killed in the shooting. It was not certain that he was still alive, but she held out hope. When she picked up her mail after returning from work, she was sure the unstamped envelope addressed to Mrs. Brockton and marked urgent was from his captors. After reading the note, she was aware of the danger, but knew that she had to follow the directions explicitly if there was any hope of seeing her husband alive. The only question was how to raise the $10,000 quickly without drawing any attention to her. It was not that much money since she and her husband brought in more than that after taxes every month, but it was a week away from payday and they had only $4200 in their checking account. She remembered the $20 gold coin that Brett had made into a necklace and given to her for their tenth wedding anniversary that, given the current price of gold, the coin alone should bring at least $6000.She hated to part with it, but hopefully, she would be able to redeem it after this was all over. She called her work number and left a message that she thought that she had caught a stomach virus and would not be in. Before going to bed she made her plan for the next day. Time would be crucial since she had a long drive to meet the kidnapper at 2:00 PM. She checked for pawn shops close to their bank. Unfortunately, there were no pawn shops close to where they normally banked, but there was a branch only two blocks away from a number of pawn shops. First she would need to get filled up at a nearby gas station, then to a pawn shop at 8:00 AM. Even if they were busy she should be able to complete her transaction in forty five minutes. Then to the bank for the withdrawal by around 9:00 and out by maybe 9:20 and on her way out of Tucson by 9:30, which should give her plenty of time for unexpected contingencies.

Chapter 44: Payoff

The next morning bright and early she was at one of the many Tucson pawn shops with an oversized purse just after it had opened for the day. She took the necklace out of her purse and handed it to the clerk. He examined it, wrote a price on a slip of paper and pushed it over the counter to her. When she saw the offer she was so devastated and angry that she could barely register a response. "You've got to be kidding or think I'm an idiot. Gold is over $6500 an ounce."

"OK, Miss, I'll go $4,750, but not a cent more."

"All right then; I'll take my business elsewhere." With that she picked up her necklace, put it back in her purse stormed out of the shop and entered a shop two doors down. After having a similar experience at that shop and two or three more, her anger had mutated into a feeling of panic. She was fast running out of time. It was now 9:10 and she still had to go by the bank and then drive to the appointed rendezvous in Yuma,

242 miles away. She had figured that the trip on Interstate 8 would take about three and three quarter hours, allowing for a fifteen minute rest stop. This was based on sticking to the speed limit, since she didn't dare allow herself to be stopped for speeding, which would screw up her timetable, not to mention the possibility the trooper might want to search her car after noticing that she was in panic mode and find the $10,000 all in the instructed $100 dollar bills in her purse.

She entered another pawn shop when a bearded bald headed man presented himself and asked what he could do for her. She screamed, "Are you the proprietor?"

"Yes, Lady. Whatdaya have?"

"What are you paying for gold?"

"It all depends. Can I take a look at whatcha got?"

She again took the necklace out of her purse and put it on the counter.

He picked it up, looked closely at it and asked, "Whatcha asking?"

Lenore was getting close to losing it again, but restrained herself. She responded angrily, "No sir! You tell me what you will pay or I will take my business where a customer is appreciated."

The man chuckled, "OK, Lady. How 'bout $4600?"

Lenore thought about leaving this shop as well, but time was an issue. She replied, "That's ridiculous. You know that coin is worth at least $6500."

"No Lady. If that coin din't have a hole in it, it would be worth more, but 'cuz I'm a good guy, I'll go $5000."

She didn't like this fellow at all. She would much rather have dealt with one of the others who at least were polite, but she didn't have time to quibble. "If you can go $5800, we have a deal."

"Lady, it's 'gainst my better judgment, but I'll go $5250."

"What if I throw in the necklace?"

"Lady, that was my offer, $5250 for the coin and necklace."

"I need $5800!"

"Let me look at that diamond." He was pointing to her ring finger.

"Absolutely not!", she said.

"Look, Lady. Ya wanna do business or not. I've got lots of other stuff I could be doing."

Lenore couldn't believe she was apologizing to this crude bastard, but the words just came flowing out. "OK, I'm sorry, but that's my engagement ring."

"Lady, I don't care for history. I just want to see if it's real or fake."

She slid the two rings off her finger, replaced her wedding ring, and laid the engagement ring on the counter. "I assure you it's real. I had it appraised last year for insurance, and it was valued at $2500."

He examined the diamond through a magnifying glass. "I see a black speck. I can offer ya $850."

She screamed, "You are a thief!"

"No, Lady. I'm a businessman. You said you needed $5800. The coin, necklace, and ring give you $6100, so you will have $300 to spend wherever you like. So do we have a deal?"

"How long will you give me to redeem them?"

"One week. After that they are fair game for anyone who wants them."

Lenore asked, "How much to redeem them?"

He replied, "Only $7500."

At this point, she was so angry and worn down she could not even muster a word.

"So it's a deal then?", he asked.

She nodded weakly and was able to softly request it to be in $100 dollar bills. She counted the money and walked out of the pawn shop feeling light headed after that ordeal, but she needed to focus. The time now was 9:43.

She walked into the bank at 9:55 and up to a teller's cage. She identified herself with her driver's license and told the teller she wanted to make a withdrawal of $3900 from her checking account. After verifying Lenore's account, the teller asked if a cashier's check would be acceptable. Lenore said, "No thanks, I would prefer cash and all in $100bills to make it easier to count."

The teller responded, "Certainly, Mrs. Brockton. Just give me a minute, please."

The minute turned into five minutes and Lenore was going into panic mode when a bank officer appeared with the teller. He said, "Mrs. Brockton, that is quite a sum to be carrying around. If you don't mind my asking, is this for some kind of emergency?"

She was totally unprepared for this. She responded in a loud shrill voice and several customers looked over to see what was going on. "I can't believe this. We have done business with this bank for years with no problem and now I want to make a withdrawal of some of our money and you are acting like it's your money!"

The bank officer replied, "Mrs. Brockton, please calm down. You will get your money, but these days we need to be especially careful." He then instructed the teller to grant her request.

After counting the money and putting it in her purse with the proceeds from the pawn shop, she left the bank. By the time she got to her car it was 10:22 and all her careful planning had apparently been for naught. Her forty-five minute leeway had disappeared and she was now in a time deficit. She was going to have to take a chance on going just a little above the speed limit and hope that she wouldn't encounter an overzealous cop. And she didn't want to even think about any other unexpected delays.

Chapter 45: Payoff (part two)

Lenore arrived in Yuma with ten minutes to spare. Thankfully, she was acquainted with the town and the courthouse due to several trips here for her boss. The letter had instructed her to park at one of the visitor's slots at the court house and sit down at a bench across the street at 2:00 PM. There were a few people on the courthouse side of the street, but none at or near the bench. She awaited the clock striking 2:00 and took a seat. It was two or three minutes later that a neatly dressed Hispanic man appeared and took a seat beside her. He said, "Crazy weather we've been having, wouldn't you say?"

This was Lenore's cue. She followed with, "Yes, but weather is always a little crazy."

"Mrs. Brockton, I presume?"

"Yes."

"And may I presume that your purse contains the agreed amount?"

"Yes."

"Good. Just follow my directions and there will be a happy outcome for all concerned."

"Where is my husband?"

"He is waiting for you. Now go to your car and stop here to pick me up. When I get into the car I will tell you where to go."

When they were about ten miles out of town on a country road with no one in sight, the man told her to pull over to the side of the road. After she had done so, he got out and told her to move over to the passenger side. He then instructed her to put her hands behind her back whereupon he proceeded to tie her hands together and blindfold her. This was so uncharacteristic of Lenore Brockton to be so compliant, but with all the frustrations of the day, compounded with the fear of the unknown she had been worn down to the point of exhaustion.

After they had driven for about twenty minutes, he pulled to a stop, got out, opened the door and led her out. They were in the middle of a desert. Lenore, of course, could not see, but she could sense the dry heat even in late afternoon coming up through her low heeled shoes. They walked a few yards and then proceeded down a shady incline, and Lenore sensed they were in a tunnel from the lack of headspace and the relative coolness. The incline leveled out after a few more yards and then it was level for the length of two or three football fields, before it ascended again and then out the other side. They then got into another car and drove an hour or so. When they stopped, the man untied Lenore's hands and removed the blindfold.

"Welcome to Mexico and the principality of Ariel."

What she saw rivaled the grandest movie set she had ever seen. It was a massive hacienda with statuary, fountains, trees and flowers all pristinely landscaped. "Where is my husband?", she screamed.

"Be patient, Senora. You will see him very soon."

Lenore noticed the change of address from "Mrs. Brockton" to "Senora", which she took to reinforce the idea that she was no longer under the protection of her home country or state.

He led her up the white marble steps to the entrance of the palace and down an elaborate hallway. At the end of the hall was a heavy door, which the man opened, and they descended a stairway. At the foot of the stairs was another heavy doorway and as soon as she entered she shivered, not so much because of the temperature difference, although it was cold, but because of a menacing apprehension. The large windowless room had no resemblance to the palatial surroundings they had just left. It was dank and dark. The walls and floor were all concrete grey and a single large round florescent light hung from the similarly colored ceiling. The only furnishings were a table with black straps and several crude straight back wooden chairs. She shuddered and screamed, "Oh, my God!", when she examined the table. One of the courses she had taken in her pre-law studies was the Inquisition. She recognized the table as not a table at all, but a medieval torture device, known as the "Rack". As she was trying to put the thought out her mind, she caught sight of her husband, being led into the dungeon through an opposite door, accompanied by two heavy set guards and then followed by the ugliest man she had ever seen. Her husband was bound with his hands tied behind his back and steel ankle bracelets secured by a six inch chain, severely restricting his range of movement. She, on the other hand, was no longer bound and ran to him, hugged and kissed him. "Darling, what have they done to you?" She had seen the large bandage covering the right side of his face and the bruises and bloody wounds on his naked upper body.

Brett did not answer her question, but only responded with, "Honey, you should not have come."

"How can you say that? They threatened to kill you if I did not follow their instructions."

"They will do that anyway, and now you are in danger."

Pancho interjected, "No, Senor and Senora. Everything will be fine if you follow our instructions."

Lenore responded in a shrill voice, "I have done everything you asked."

Pancho replied, "Unfortunately, Senora, the situation has changed. We have learned that one of our people is a traitor, working with the Arizona Border Patrol, informing them of our every move into your state. Regrettably also, your husband has refused to cooperate, so we thought that you might be able to convince him that both of you would be better off if he only gives us the name of this traitor."

Brett spoke up, "I have told you I know nothing of a traitor; not that I would give you his name if I knew."

"You see, Senora Brockton. You have a very stubborn husband."

"What do you want me to do? Anything, so long as you let me and my husband go."

Pancho licked his lips. "Well now, maybe we are getting somewhere." Pancho gave the order and the guards led Brett over to the Rack and lifted him onto it. When they had him strapped down with his arms extended as far above his head and legs straight and extended as far as possible, one of them pressed a button, which caused the Rack to tilt partially upright so that he was able to view his wife.

Pancho spoke, "Now, Senor Brockton, I ask you again, who is the traitor working against us?"

"Ass hole, I have told you already, I do not know."

Pancho gave an arm signal, and one of the guards turned the ratcheted wheel one notch, which caused the table to part one centimeter. Brett could feel the increased tension in his arms and legs, but wasn't about to give his captors the enjoyment of his discomfort as long as he could stand it.

Lenore spoke, "Please stop! I will bring more money, whatever you want, but just stop."

Pancho replied, "Senora, we do not want any more of your money; we just want the name of the traitor."

"He told you he doesn't know."

"Yes, Senora, but we don't believe him. Perhaps you can convince him to cooperate."

"If he doesn't know, how do you expect me to be able to convince him?"

The ugly man said something to Pancho in Spanish.

"Senora, we have learned that failed memories are many times brought back to life, using the right kind of persuasion. Let me demonstrate. Senora, please remove your shoes."

"I don't understand. Why?, she asked.

The ugly man gave a hand signal and the guard operating the rack tightened it another notch.

Brett grimaced and Lenore saw that Brett was in pain. She quickly removed her shoes. "OK, now what?"

Pancho replied to Brett, "Senor, we can end this very quickly if you will just cooperate. Who is the traitor?"

"You damned son of a whore, go ahead and kill me; I don't know."

"No, Senor, your memory will come back. Now, Senora, please remove your stockings and no more questions if you wish to not inflict more pain on your husband."

Lenore slowly removed her stockings as Brett strained at his bindings and cursed his tormentors.

"Senora, you are a quick learner. I must say also that your legs are far too beautiful to be covered."

Lenore now understood and she trembled with what she knew was to come. She prayed that lightning would strike the hacienda, consuming them all in fire but at least ending the torment.

Each time Pancho repeated the question and Brett refused to answer, Pancho would instruct Lenore to remove another article of clothing. If she paused even for a few seconds, the rack was further tightened until Lenore continued to undress without additional prompting.

Brett had already heard the dual pop of the ball and socket of his shoulders separating and felt the excruciating pain, but restrained himself as best he could from exhibiting any pain so as not to cause his wife any additional anguish or let his tormentors know that they were succeeding in inflicting pain.

However, the men in the room were paying far more attention to his wife, enjoying the spectacle and yelling.

Lenore understood only a few words of basic Spanish, but most of what they were yelling she was unable to translate. However, she had a pretty good idea of what they were saying and the thought made her shudder in disgust. By now, she was naked except for her panties and Brett had thankfully lost consciousness due to pain.

But the tormentors were not about to let Brett miss the rest of the show. The ugly one said something and the guard operating the rack let up the tension a couple of notches and another splashed Brett with a bucket of cold water.

"Senor Brockton, wake up. The best is yet to come."

As Brett regained consciousness he heard Pancho speaking.

"It is unfortunate that your husband is not as cooperative as you, but because of your cooperation, you may just earn a reprieve for you and your husband."

She heard the words and tried to believe.

And then as Pancho was giving her another command, Bret was saying, "No, No! Please Lenore, don't do it."

Pancho had introduced Lenore to the ugly man. "Senora Brockton, Let me have the pleasure of introducing you to our leader, El Diablo. You will be happy to know that he has been admiring your beauty and wishes for you to come sit on his lap."

Chapter 46: The Report

It had seemed like days, but it was scarcely twenty-four hours before Lenore was back in Arizona after having been led back through the tunnel with her quadriplegic husband on a stretcher. They had both been blindfolded with Lenore again having had her hands tied behind her. There had been no such need for Brett since he had been stretched so far that neither his arms nor his legs were functional. Once out of the tunnel, Pancho drove the two in Lenore's car an hour or so, removed the blindfolds and Lenore's bindings and gave her directions back to Yuma. Pancho got in the car that had been following and drove off.

Brett had been in and out of consciousness the entire time and had begged to be put to death. Now he was pleading with Lenore to end his misery. She wanted to commit suicide as well, but she needed to stay alive for Brett and to be able to bear witness against those savages. Between retching and sobbing she could hardly drive. She and her clothes stank from bodily fluids, her own and those of her tormentors. "How many were there? Four or six or more? It mattered less but she could not keep it out of her mind. And then the women!" She would have liked to pull over, disrobe, and burn her clothes except that she had nothing else to wear; besides she had two urgent tasks before anything else. She had to get Brett into a hospital as she was sure he was bleeding internally and might be close to death. Secondly, she had to get to a pharmacy where she could purchase something to head off pregnancy. Although she had no cash, thankfully, they had let her leave with her purse and credit cards. They wanted to make sure she could get back home to let the authorities know what was in store for them if they tangled with Ariel.

Two days later, when Florence Zimmerman received the report from Andrea Shackelford, the assistant director of the Arizona Border Patrol, she was outraged.

"Those bastards! If they think they can intimidate us, they are sadly mistaken." She called for her secretary. "Sheila, get word to the Lieutenant Governor, Cabinet and the legislature leaders that there will be an emergency meeting in the Capitol meeting room at 9:00 AM tomorrow. No excuses from anybody." She then turned back to Shackelford. "Andrea, the 'traitor' whose name they were trying to extract from Brockton can be very valuable in our fight against Ariel. His identity must be protected at all costs."

Shackelford responded, "Governor, I wish it were so, but we have no one from Ariel working for us."

"So it was all a ruse to justify the torture?"

"Apparently so, Governor."

"OK, Andrea. Nothing that group of degenerates would do, surprises me. So, now tell me about Brett and his wife. Whatever we can do to try to put their lives back together, I will do my darndest."

The next morning when all were assembled, Florence began. "Thank you all for coming on such short notice. I know each of you has a list of priorities, but what I am about to discuss must take top priority." She then related what she had learned about Brett Brockton's torture and maiming, and the gang rape of Lenore. She left out their names to protect their privacy, but did not leave out any of the sordid details. She told them that in her college days, the girls in her sorority brought porno films in from time to time for a Sunday evening's entertainment, and at the time thought they were the most depraved behavior possible, but in retrospect they were tame as compared to what went on with the Brocktons. "This low life El Diablo and his gang think that we will be intimidated by their actions; on the contrary, we are going to respond as probably we should have a long time ago against this insidious attack on our values. I am asking for a declaration of war." She instructed her press secretary to call a news conference for 2:00 PM where she would make the public announcement.

Chapter 47: Whatever it takes

There had been very little notice, but all of Arizona's big city media as well as that from many of the smaller towns were represented for the 2:00 news conference. Florence began, "Thank you all for coming on such short notice. Had I not considered the matter of utmost urgency, I would have given you more time. As you may recall, when I was running for governor, I pledged to eradicate illegal drugs. Although we are not there yet, most objective observers would agree that we have made excellent progress in the two years I have been governor. The leader of Ariel, El Diablo, knows this and believes by his actions, which I will now describe, that we will be intimidated into easing our fight." After describing in detail the atrocity, she continued. "What he fails to understand is that we are not about to be bullied; he has in essence declared war on us and we will answer his declaration with one of our own. Both houses of our legislature will be meeting in emergency session this evening and I fully expect them to follow through on my request for a declaration of war against Ariel.!"

There was a flurry of questions from the press over the next fifteen minutes. The first question taken came from Sherry McClellan an outspoken liberal reporter from The Phoenix Sun, one of the few liberal newspapers in the state. "Governor, what exactly do you mean by a declaration of war?"

McClellan and Florence had tangled frequently since she had been Governor and before that when she was in Washington. There was no love lost between the two and Florence was fully prepared for some sort of challenge. She had intentionally chosen McClellan for the first question so that she could get her out of the way and allow some more substantive questions from the press. "Sherry, what part of 'declaration of war' do you not understand?"

"Governor, I think you know what I am asking. Are you saying this is to be all out war with no holds barred?"

"Sherry, war is an armed conflict between parties, the purpose of which is to defeat the other for territorial, economic, or other reasons. In our case it is our security that is at stake and what we will be fighting for. So long as Ariel exists, our security is threatened. Our goal then is the eradication of Ariel and the prevention of another drug cartel taking its place."

"So you are calling for all- out war?"

"Whatever it takes, Sherry. Whatever it takes. Next question, Frank."

"Governor, do you anticipate a ground invasion into Mexico?"

"Frank, I will be conferring with Major General Scott of the Army National Guard and Brigadier General O'Hara of the Air National Guard and listening to their recommendations."

"And if they say go?"

"If they say go, I will think on it, but whether or not, I am not about to give our enemy any advance notice of our intentions or strategy."

"Next question, Ginger."

"Governor, how many troops do you intend to call into active duty?"

"Ginger, same answer as I just gave to Frank."

The press conference concluded about ten minutes later with no one the wiser on how this declared war was to proceed, which is exactly the way Florence Zimmerman wanted it. If anything, it confirmed what most people already knew. Arizona had a no nonsense governor, who had no fear of taking decisive actions.

Meanwhile in Mexico City, President Montalban had been watching developments north of the border with keen interest. He had noted that there had been no response from Campbell when the three states had seceded and none also when Russia had taken the Aleutians. Now it appeared that the independent state of Arizona would be invading the Mexican state of Sonaro. Although Sonaro was under the control of El Diablo, it remained part of the sovereign nation of Mexico.

For all of Montalban's failings, he was a Mexican patriot. He considered the loss of Texas in 1836 a blot on Mexican history and saw now the possible opportunity to rectify that wrong. If Texas joined Arizona in the fight against Ariel, in Mexican territory, this could be the justification he needed to declare war on the two states. He realized that Mexico couldn't win a war with the U.S., but he was confident that in a military confrontation with just Texas and Arizona, Mexico would be the victor; and to the victor belongs the spoils.

Word of Arizona's declaration of war had also reached Ariel. When El Diablo was told, he laughed. "Apparently La Gobernadora does not know who she is dealing with. We will capture more of her border guards and subject them to the same treatment we delivered to Senor Brockton. It will not be long before she has no more men willing to serve, and she will be begging for mercy."

Chapter 48: Conference

Two hours after the press conference concluded, the two generals were seated across from Florence Zimmerman in her office. Florence spoke first, "Thank you, gentlemen for meeting at such short notice."

The two nodded and spoke almost in unison, "No problem, Governor."

Florence smiled and said, "You fellows may have missed your calling. Perhaps a duet." They all laughed.

"Seriously, as you probably know, I have no background in military matters, and I need your best advice."

As the ranking officer, General Scott replied, "Governor, we appreciate your bringing us in. Tim and I have been talking since we heard the news. As you know, President Montalban had been decimating the drug cartels until he ran into Ariel...'

Florence interrupted, " General, you don't mean that we can't defeat those SOB's?"

"No Governor, not at all. We just like to have as much intel as we can get before we engage an enemy and we have very little on Ariel. As you know, the border patrol has captured a number of drug runners and interrogated them, but they are low level flunkies and know very little. The Mexican military is not a powerhouse, but one would think that they would have had the strength to crush Ariel. We have no idea of their numbers or if the population supports the cartel or not. The mission would be a lot easier if the population is not in bed with the cartel. But then we would have to be careful to not turn them against us due to collateral damage. The main problem however, is that this issue has an economic aspect that the military has no response for…"

Florence thought she knew what the general was referring to, but let him continue.

"That aspect is supply and demand." We can handle the supply aspect alright, but there is nothing we can do about the demand side."

Florence responded, "That's what I thought you were referring to. I have some thoughts on that. You handle the supply issue and I will work on the demand side. So what do you recommend we do right now?"

Scott answered, "We have one company of Special Forces, most of whom are fluent in Mexican Spanish. We would like to send a three man detachment to reconnoiter Ariel's headquarters and capture one of the guards for intensive interrogation. It is likely that he will know more than we have been able to glean so far. Once we have the intelligence we need, we will come back to you with further recommendations."

"Then do it."

"Governor, you have no problem with our crossing over into

Mexican territory?"

"None, whatsoever."

"Thank you, Governor." The generals saluted and left the room.

Unbeknownst to the generals or practically anyone else, since it was top secret, Florence had anticipated the economic issue of demand. In accordance with her promise to eliminate illegal drugs from the state, she had her old sorority friend, Professor Annette Katz at work on the problem since the early days of her administration. Katz, who had been married and divorced numerous times had early on gone back to her maiden name, since it was a lot easier than changing names each time she remarried. She was a brilliant biochemist in charge of the chemistry department at the University of Arizona and had been delighted to hear from her old friend and help her with a problem that had plagued drug enforcement authorities for decades, i.e., how to reduce demand for drugs.

Two drugs, cocaine and heroin accounted for almost all of the illegal drugs coming into the country. In their first meeting on the issue, Florence outlined the problem and an idea she had. "Annie, this is kind of wild, but I wonder if it would be possible to synthesize substances that would look, taste, and smell like the drugs, but instead of giving a 'high" would cause extreme nausea.?"

"Flo, what a terrific idea! Yes, I think it is possible. It might be as simple as substituting one atom for another in the molecule as for example substituting a sulfur atom for an oxygen atom."

"That's great, Annie. You've lost me since I did not even take first year chemistry, but I figured if anyone could do it, you could."

That meeting was two years earlier and since then they had met two or three times to review progress. To maintain secrecy they had agreed that they would have no discussions on the subject other than in personal meetings. As soon as the generals had left her office, Florence called her old friend to see if she was free for an update. Katz said she was and that she had some good news. Florence could hardly wait but told her that she would be right over.

About thirty minutes later, Florence rushed into Katz's office and said, "So Annie, what's the good news?"

"Flo, we have been able to do exactly what you had asked for. Compound H and compound C look, smell, and taste so much like their real counterparts that not even an expert would be able to tell them apart until, of course, they experienced the adverse effects about five minutes later."

"What about the 'high'?"

"Flo, these substitutes give the same 'high", but that effect is overwhelmed by the extreme nausea that follows."

Florence inquired, "So Annie, I assume you have tested these drug substitutes on human subjects?"

"Absolutely, Flo. We used ten prisoner volunteers each for the mock cocaine and heroin."

"And all of them became nauseated shortly after taking the drug?"

"Yes, violently so, but that's not all Flo. Two days after they had recovered from their nausea, we administered the real stuff, and the convicts exhibited the same symptoms!"

"That's incredible, Annie, but is it possible that this is only a short term effect?"

"That we don't know for sure yet, but my guess is that we have altered the body chemistry so that it now rejects the real thing. It may be a reaction similar to Pavlov's experiment. We plan to do some more experimentation over a longer term and that's why I had held off calling you. By the way, I heard what those bastards did to your border agent and his wife."

" Yes, Annie and we are going to make them pay!"

" Men! There ought to be a subst…"Katz broke out in laughter before she finished and Florence joined her.

Chapter 49: Recon

Six days after the generals' conference with Florence, and waiting for a moonless night the three man Special Forces detachment entered one of the many tunnels used by the drug carriers and crossed over the border about thirty miles from Yuma. The border patrol's interrogations had not yielded much, but at least they had learned the location of several of the tunnels and El Diablo's hacienda, which was about seventy miles from the border. Their orders were to remain undetected, proceed to the hacienda, capture one of the guards and bring him back to Phoenix for interrogation.

As with any mission, a number of parameters needed to be taken in account for successful completion. The distance involved and the need to carry a person back dictated some type of vehicle. The vehicle had to be small enough to go through the tunnel, and the lack of concealing vegetation necessitated a silent running vehicle. Tesla battery powered bicycles fit the bill. They had the range, speed and power to enable them to traverse the distance and back in two hours with plenty of battery power left. A small wagon pulled by one of the bicycles would be used to carry the captive. Each of them also carried an ultra-violet flashlight.

Just as one of the three Special Forces detachment emerged from the tunnel, an elderly man came around from the back of a small farm truck, parked at the side of a wide curve in the road, maybe not more than twenty yards to the right of the tunnel. The soldier quickly ducked back into the tunnel, "Damn!", he whispered.

"What's the problem, Chuck?"

"Sarge, there's an old guy next to a truck, parked about fifty feet from us and with his headlights on and aimed right in our direction."

"Did he see you?"

"I think so, Sarge, but I'm not sure."

Vinny chimed in, "We've got to eliminate him. We can't take a chance on our cover being blown."

Sarge responded, "No, that would only complicate matters. Chuck, you go and see if he is alone. Then we'll come out and question him."

After a few minutes, Chuck came back and confirmed that he was alone. "Sarge, I think he is harmless. The poor guy is probably seventy years old or so, has his arm in a sling, and is trying to change a tire."

Vinny responded, "No time to get sentimental, we've got a missi…"

Sarge cut him off, "That's enough, Vinny. Yes, we have a mission, but we have an unanticipated problem and have to deal with it."

The three emerged from the tunnel and approached the old man. Sarge greeted him in Spanish, "Como esta?"

"No tan bien", answered the old man.

Sarge continued in Spanish, "I can see. May we help?"

"Si. Mucho gracias.

The three set to work and had the job done in minutes.

The old man was beside himself with gratitude and had tears in his eyes. Sarge had told him they were border patrolmen chasing a bad guy. The old man let it be known that there was no love lost between him and the cartel. This sentiment was also shared by his fellow countrymen. "They poison our ninos and make them slaves."

Sarge empathized, "They do the same thing in our country."

This was some useful information. At least Arizona wouldn't be at war with the whole population and may well have some allies in the fight.

They bid him goodbye and he responded as he headed down the road, "Adios y mucho gracias."

Vinny asked Sarge, "What if he tells them about us?"

"Vinny, I don't think he will, but if he does it will be about some border patrol agents that crossed the border to chase after a drug carrier."

After the truck was a safe distance away, the three mounted their bicycles and headed off in the direction of La Hacienda staying just far enough off the road to be able to follow it but not be detected by any traffic. It was about 11:00 PM when they arrived. There had been only two other vehicles that they had encountered and they had had enough time to get even further off the road when they saw the approaching lights.

At the hacienda there was no need for the UV flashlights since it was so lit up. They surveyed the scene. An eight foot stone wall surrounded the mansion with a heavy wooden gate at the entrance. The gate was probably about twelve feet across so as to allow two cars to pass through with ease. There were two guards outside the closed gate and perhaps two or more just inside.

Sarge reviewed their orders for Chuck and Vinny, "We are to remain undetected and leave no trace that we were here. We are to capture one of the guards and bring him back for interrogation."

Vinny remarked, "It would be one hell of a lot easier if we just killed one of those guards at the gate and brought the other back."

Sarge responded, "Yeah, Vinny, that would be a lot easier, but that wouldn't be following orders. What we're going to do is scale the wall, find a guard by his lonesome, subdue him quietly, and carry him back over the wall."

Vinny responded, "Sure hope he's a light one."

All three laughed.

Chapter 50: Interrogation

At La Hacienda a little after eight the next morning, the call went out, "Where is Ronaldo?" He was one of the guards stationed along the interior of the wall and was nowhere to be found. His twelve hour shift had ended at eight and his replacement was to have been briefed on any developments, of which there were generally none.

At the same time at Military Headquarters in Phoenix, an interrogation was underway. Major Underwood of Army Intelligence repeated the question, "Ronaldo, how many guards are located at La Hacienda?"

Ronaldo had been ignoring the questions and pleading for some heroin. The major finally replied, "OK, Ronaldo, I will make you a deal. You answer a question and I will give you a little heroin. You answer another question and I will give you some more, but I warn you, if it turns out that the information you have provided is false, you will be locked in a cell with no drugs."

Back at La Hacienda, word had just reached El Diablo about the missing guard. El Diablo was enraged. "Find him and when you do, I want him placed in a dungeon with no drugs for two days. And what about the guards at the gate? What did they say?"

Pancho replied, "Jefe, they swear that no one went through that gate last night."

"Then search again, and when you find him, bring him to me first."

"Si, Jefe."

"And if he is found outside the villa, the two gate guards are to be imprisoned along with Ronaldo with no drugs."

The interrogation continued at Military Headquarters. "Now we are getting somewhere." The major directed the Lieutenant to administer a minute dose of heroin to Ronaldo. The dose was just enough to relieve the withdrawal symptoms for about five minutes. "You see, you give us some information and we give you some heroin. Now, where are the drugs stored?" After two more hours of questioning, it was clear that there was no more information that could be extracted from this low level flunky.

But they had gained some valuable intelligence. An airfield located about ten to twenty miles southeast of the villa held numerous aircraft, the number and type of which he did not know. Since the airfield was not his responsibility he also did not know about security there, but almost certainly, there were guards around the clock. There were two anti-aircraft guns at the villa and possibly others at other locations. Twenty guards were stationed around the villa at any time on twelve hour shifts, two at the gate, six more around the perimeter, ten on the interior wall, and two personal bodyguards for El Diablo within the palace. A transformer was located just outside the wall to the rear of the villa. There was a dungeon and a secure room in the basement where the drugs were stored and a back-up generator was located. It was not clear what the total number employed by Ariel was, but probably less than two hundred. This did not take into account all the police and other government officials taking bribes. And then there was an unknown number of children who had become addicted and acted like a sort of secret police of informers.

After the generals had been briefed on the results of the interrogation, General Scott called Florence to set up a meeting, to fill her in and make recommendations.

Chapter 51: Strategy planning

"So, Generals, did you get the information you needed?"

Scott replied, "Governor, we didn't get all the intelligence we would have liked, but we got enough to give us the confidence that we can dispose of Ariel in short order." He then spelled out the strategy that he and O'Hara had devised. It would be a joint air-ground operation.

"That's certainly good news, but I admit I am a bit puzzled. If Ariel can be eliminated so easily, why wasn't the Mexican Army able to do it."

Scott answered, "Good question, Governor, but the answer has to do with the difference in objective. Montalban certainly wanted to destroy Ariel, but his main objective was to bring the states of Sonaro and Baja back under Mexican rule. We learn in military training that there must be a primary objective that cannot be compromised by secondary objectives. In Montalban's case, he expended so many resources in attempting to capture territory, that he didn't have the remaining resources available to do the job of eradicating Ariel."

"But Montalban is a military man. Surely, he was aware of that."

"Yes, Governor, but he also knew what we had pointed out in our first meeting, i.e., that destroying Ariel would not do away with the drug problem. As the old saying goes, 'nature abhors a vacuum'."

"So, General O'Hara, do you concur with the strategy?"

"I will defer to General Scott, Ma'am."

"General, do I detect a note of disagreement?"

O'Hara replied, "General Scott outranks me, Governor, so I defer to his judgment."

Until then, Florence had had a faint smile, but it had faded and changed into a stern look as she responded, "May I remind you gentlemen that I outrank both of you. General O'Hara, what is your judgment on the matter? "

"I find no fault with the plan in general, but I would prefer a bit more intelligence before we proceed."

"What would you suggest then, General?"

O'Hara replied, "I would like another recon mission with more planes over a wider area, Ma'am."

Florence responded, "I see, and what say you, General Scott?"

Scott replied, "Governor, one can never have too much intelligence, but we risk jeopardizing our surprise factor with more recon flights."

"That makes sense to me, General, and how about you, General O'Hara."

"It does, but I've just got a gut feeling that we need more intel."

"Well, gentlemen, I guess that leaves it to me to decide. I'm afraid I need more justification than "gut feeling" for a delay." Florence then went on to tell them of Professor Annette Katz's work. The generals were intrigued and delighted.

It was agreed that the strategy would be three pronged. 1)First a recon mission to locate the airfield. 2) Then destruction of La Hacienda with the killing or capture of as many of Ariel's operatives as possible. 3)Planting of the heroin substitute through undercover drug distributors.

The recon mission would take place at night using four unmanned MQ-1 predators equipped with UV sensors and cameras for night time use. The La Hacienda operation was code named Swift Sword and would be accomplished by a coordinated air/ ground attack 48 hours after the reconnaissance data from the predators was analyzed. Planting of the heroin substitute might well be the most difficult aspect of the strategy, but the generals were confident that they could come up with a way.

The next night, the predators had returned from their three hour recon mission with the airfield pinpointed. The informer had been close in his estimation. It was 12.2 miles east southeast of the villa. The predators had spotted six fighter aircraft, two helicopters and several smaller planes, probably for the transport of drugs. There was also a hangar, which possibly held additional aircraft.

Chapter 52: Operation Swift Sword

Fifty-eight hours later, Operation Swift Sword was underway. The air portion of the operation was to begin as soon as the ground force was in position surrounding the villa, with the major portion of the force facing the gate about 750 yards away. Lt. Col. Hager commanded a task force of two hundred troops equipped with machine guns, flame throwers, and bazookas.

At 1:08 AM, when they were in position, Hager had his radio man contact Major Simmons, the commander of the air operation who had a force of three F-16A Fighting Falcons armed with conventional and napalm fitted rockets as well as their normal rapid fire cannons. "Eagle 1, this is Batman, come in, please."

"Batman, this is Eagle 1."

"Eagle 1, we are seated and waiting for the party to begin." The planes were already in the air on the Arizona side of the border when the order was given. In less than ten minutes they were over the target airfield. Another couple of minutes and the airfield was ablaze, but Simmons quickly realized that the airfield was fake since there were no explosions which would have occurred from burning gasoline tanks. He informed the other two pilots and radioed back to the ground force. "Batman, this is Eagle 1, it appears that the program will have to be changed. I think we may have some uninvited guests."

Col. Hager's radio man immediately gave Hager the message. The colonel wasn't sure what had precipitated the change in plans, but it was fairly clear that Simmons was anticipating some enemy aircraft in short order.

Generals Scott and O'Hara were in Phoenix headquarters listening in on developments. They too had come to the same conclusion as Simmons. General O'Hara asked his superior, "Phil, don't you think we need to get some more aircraft on the way?"

"Tim, I don't think we know enough at this point to be committing additional resources. Let's wait to see what Hager and Simmons have to say."

Simmons ordered his task force to move on as quickly as possible to La Hacienda and be alert for opposing aircraft. Simmons' squadron was over La Hacienda when Ariel's fighters approached, at least five and maybe more. Almost immediately, Simmons saw a rocket coming down directly at his plane from his left. Just before impact, Simmons turned sharply up and to the left causing the rocket to narrowly miss his plane, but before he could signal his executive officer whose plane had been on the same course at a slightly lower altitude and about thirty yards to his right the rocket entered the rear of the plane's single jet and there was a fierce explosion. The exec officer had not seen the on-coming missile till it was too late because his vision had been obstructed by Simmons' plane. He managed to eject, but he and his parachute were on fire as he fell to his death. Now it was just Simmons and a young pilot in the other remaining plane. Lieutenant Richard Stennard, who had no previous combat experience, had begged Major Simmons to permit him to go on this mission, and Simmons, against his better judgment, had relented at the last minute. Stennard's older brother had been one of the border guards with Brockton on that ill- fated mission, and Stennard was out for revenge. Since it was believed that the mission would be a low risk situation, Simmons had allowed Stennard to be part of the mission. He now had regrets, but it was obviously too late. As he was thinking, he saw a missile headed in Stennard's direction, "Eagle 3, take evas…"Simmons was cut off in mid-sentence by another explosion, this one his own plane. An anti-aircraft blast from the villa had found its target. His engine afire, he was able to eject safely before his plane was consumed by the flames. As his parachute slowly lowered him, he could see that Stennard's plane had also been hit and was on fire. He could not see a parachute so it appeared Stennard had not even had time to eject. As he looked down on the scene, spot lights from the villa had illuminated the area around Hager's ground force, which was being decimated by bombs and rockets from the enemy planes as well as machine gun fire from the villa. Hager ordered a retreat, but the Tesla bikes were no match for Ariel's armored vehicles.

When the battle was over two hours later, all but eight of the ground force had been either killed or captured. Simmons, too, had been captured as soon as his parachute had landed, and as he was the ranking survivor by far, he was the prize catch for El Diablo.

Radio contact had been lost at a little after midnight, but enough had come through for the Generals back in Phoenix to realize that the situation had deteriorated beyond anything to salvage. Since the word they were listening for from either Hager or Simmons never came they agreed that sending in additional forces blind could end up compounding a bad situation.

Chapter 53 Aftermath

The next morning as El Diablo surveyed the damage to his villa, he spoke, "So La Gobernadora thinks she can mess with El Diablo? We need to teach her a lesson."

"Si, Jefe.", Pancho responded.

"How many gringos are we holding, Pancho?

"Jefe, it is difficult to say. A large number have died and several more are near death."

"Find out how many are healthy enough to travel and let me know."

"Si, Jefe, but may I ask where we will be taking them?"

"We will be sending them back home after we feed them some of our best caballo for a few days. They will then become some of our best customers and I am sure can be persuaded to join our marketing force.

"Fantastico, Jefe. And what about the pilot, Simmons?"

"Simmons, we will hold for ransom"

And at the Governor's office in Phoenix, meeting with her two generals, Florence had just been apprised of the disaster, since she had spent the evening meeting with her military intelligence people discussing how to plant the fake drugs. Her face reflected her anger. "Well, gentlemen, what do you have to say about our mission last night?"

General Scott spoke first, "Governor, no one can deny it was an unmitigated disaster."

"And what do you say, General O'Hara?"

"I totally agree, Governor."

"Would you say the disaster could have been avoided?" Florence asked.

Scott again, "If we knew then what we know now, of course. But hindsight is always 20/20."

"I see, so what do you recommend be our next step?" Florence asked.

Scott replied, "Ariel obviously has a much greater military capability than any of us could have imagined. We need a lot more intelligence on their resources before we commit to another attack."

"General Scott, is that not what General O'Hara had recommended in our meeting three days ago?"

"Well, Governor, yes, but I am sure General O'Hara would agree that even two or three more recon flights may not have gained us enough additional information to have avoided this."

"So General Scott, I suppose it is up to me to decide where we go from here. Therefore, as of this moment, you are hereby relieved of command and discharged from Arizona's army. You are also demoted to the rank of Brigadier General and will receive your pension on that basis.

Scott was flabbergasted, but said nothing, saluted and left the office.

"Now, General O'Hara, as of now, you are in command of the Army as well as the Airforce."

"Thank you, Governor. I will do my best to live up to your confidence in me."

"Of that, I have no doubt, General, but I am guessing that you are expecting a promotion in rank. Unfortunately, I regret to inform you that will not be the case.

You should have followed your 'gut feeling' and held firm for additional reconnaissance. Now show me that my confidence in you is not misplaced. Give it some thought and then come back to me within a week with some specific recommendations."

"Yes, Ma'am." With that, O'Hara saluted and left the office.

As soon as the door was shut, Florence had dialed her old friend and lover. Collins had caller ID so knew immediately who was calling. "Hey Flo, good to hear from you. What's up?"

"Jer, I've got problems. As you know, we have declared war on Ariel, and my generals had led me to believe that it would be an easy and quick victory. Unfortunately, they were off by a long shot. I recall when I was in Washington, I met a college pal of yours who was with the CIA. Since he was a Texan, I am wondering if he had joined Texas in your secession. His name was Butch… ".

"Sure, Flo. Butch Fleming did join us and brought along two of his subordinates who were also Texans. He heads up our military intelligence team. By the way, how is it that you met Butch in as big a place as Washington?"

"When I was in Congress, I was assigned to the House Intelligence Committee and Butch was briefing us on some mis-use of classified documents. I don't remember the details, but it struck me at the time as bit of a waste of time and resources."

Collins responded, "Yeah, business as usual for D.C., but Butch has come up in the world since you knew him as a low level operative. When he left early this year, he was Assistant Director."

"Of the CIA?"

"Absolutely, Flo, and now we have him."

"Wow, Jer! I guess the three of us have done pretty well for ourselves."

"Indeed, Flo, but you most of all since you are now a president."

"No, Jer. I was elected Governor and will remain Governor until the people say I am President, but back to the reason I called. I could sure use some better intelligence than I have access to right now, and I am using the term with both its meanings."

Collins laughed, "One of the things that attracted me to you early on was your sense of humor. Let me talk to Houston and see if we can do without Butch's services for a short while."

Thanks, Jer. Just let me know.

An hour later, Florence picked up the call from Collins, who informed her that Butch Fleming was on indefinite TDY to Arizona. "Thanks Jer, but that was quick."

"Quick and easy, Flo. Houston feels as I do that we are in a drug war too. It may not be all Ariel, but there is little doubt that Ariel's sphere of influence extends way beyond its official borders into Texas. If we can help you knock out Ariel, it should significantly reduce our drug problem, that is, until some drug lord comes in to take Ariel's place."

"Well, Jer, I believe we have an answer to that." Florence then went on to explain what Annie Katz had come up with. When she hung up from Jerry Collins, she dialed General O'Hara to inform him of their new intelligence asset. "I will meet with him in a couple of days and then get the three of us together for a strategy session, but in the meantime I want you to continue to think about the situation and be prepared with some questions in view of the new intelligence."

"Yes, Ma'am. I am looking forward to meeting Mr. Fleming to hear what if anything he knows about Ariel."

Chapter 54: Butch Fleming

Early in the morning two days later, Butch Fleming had stepped in Florence's office after being announced by her secretary. "Butch, great to see you again after all these years."

"Likewise, Governor. Although you have moved up a bit in the world since those House Intelligence days."

"As you have, Butch." They both laughed. "But please call me Florence."

"As you wish, Gov..,I mean Florence."

"Butch, as you are aware, we have a problem. Ariel obviously has military assets beyond what we had knowledge of. I am hoping you can help us fill in some blanks."

"Florence, it so happens that we know quite a lot about El Diablo and Ariel. The CIA has been tracking El Diablo for years in his dealings with the Taliban in Afghanistan and the Russian Mafia."

"That's intriguing."

"Absolutely, Florence. I could go on and on with stories about El Diablo, but what you need to know is that Ariel has some first class weaponry, obtained mainly from Russia, including at last count fourteen MIG-31 jet fighters, numerous fixed wing aircraft and a bunch of late model heavy duty tanks. I do have an inventory of specifics dating from 2041 that I can pull up."

"So that explains Mexico's inability to defeat Ariel?"

"Absolutely, Florence. Mexico's military was no match for Ariel's."

"And that idiot, General Scott tried to tell me that the reason was strategy or some such nonsense. When I demoted him, I shouldn't have stopped at Brigadier General; I should have made him a corporal."

"Don't be too hard on the guy, Florence. After all he was operating on limited intelligence."

"You got that right!" They both laughed.

Florence dialed General O'Hara to confirm that his calendar was open for a strategy session that afternoon.

"Governor, I had a meeting scheduled with a couple of my subordinates to discuss strategy ideas, but that can wait."

Chapter 55: New strategy session

After the introductions, Florence spoke. "General O'Hara, you may recall in a meeting a couple of weeks ago, I had asked General Scott that if Ariel was to be such an easy push over, why hadn't Mexico been able to defeat Ariel?"

"Yes, Ma'am. I recall the conversation very clearly."

"Well, Mr. Fleming has a very different explanation. Mr. Fleming, if you will, give General O'Hara your slant on this."

"Certainly, Governor. General, very simply, Mexico's military was no match for Ariel's. Although Mexico's numbers far outweigh Ariel's, its equipment for the most part is way outdated, and their air capability does not even come close to that of Ariel's."

"Let me interrupt, Mr. Fleming. Since my career has been spent in the Air Force, that is the field of my expertise. Do you have specifics on Ariel's air capability?"

"Indeed, I do, General." Fleming then continued by informing the general of what he had told Florence in their earlier meeting.

"MIG-31's?Our F-16 Falcons wouldn't have a chance."

Fleming responded, "Nor did Mexico's F-5's."

General O'Hara countered, "Our only chance is to catch those MIG-31's on the ground."

"Absolutely, General, and Governor Zimmerman informed me of the effort to do just that with the ill-fated attack on an airfield that turned out to be fake." The concept was sound, but the attack failed due to faulty intelligence. Unfortunately, I do not know the location of their airfield, but I am aware of their use of the tactic that the British used against the Nazis in World War II to great advantage. The fake airfields diverted the attackers from the true target and had the additional advantage of giving the British time to get their aircraft in the air and confront the attackers."

O'Hara responded, "If we could lure their planes into the air without taking large losses, we could maybe track them back to their airfield."

Florence's serious countenance till then changed into a wide smile. "That sounds like a winner, General. Draw up a plan and let's get together again at 1:00. Mr. Fleming, if you will join me for lunch, I have something else to discuss."

O'Hara saluted and left the office.

"Butch, Hopefully, this new strategy will destroy Ariel's military capability, but we have an issue that may be even more difficult." Florence then filled him in on the ersatz drugs and the need to have them planted.

"Florence, we will need an inside man for that. I think I have a candidate, but let me think on it."

"Fine, Butch. How are you for a sandwich lunch? I know a great delicatessen just up the street."

"Sounds good to me."

After lunch they got back to the office and O'Hara was waiting just outside the door.

"So General, what do you have for us?"

"Governor, my plan is based on using our unmanned predators as a gambit to draw out the MIG's."

"General, 'gambit' implies to me sacrificing our predators. Is that a correct interpretation?"

"Probably, Governor. We don't have many predators, but losing some of them beats losing even one of our Falcons and pilots."

Florence nodded. "I certainly agree with that, but how many predators do we have and how many do you figure we could lose?"

"We have twenty-two in operating condition and three more needing some maintenance. As for the number we could lose, there is no way to know for sure, but I think it is safe to say we might lose 50% or more. I think you would agree that if that would eliminate their air superiority, it would be worth it."

Florence responded, "If that kind of loss would lead to the destruction of Ariel, I would certainly agree."

"Governor, unfortunately, certainty in military affairs is impossible. There are too many imponderable variables that may come into play."

"General, I recognize that certainty in life itself is impossible, but being in the position of having to make the final decision and not having the military background, I want to make sure that I am making a decision based on the best information available."

"I totally understand, Governor. Let me say this. If we can eliminate their air superiority, which I think we can, I feel confident that we can then destroy Ariel itself in short order."

"Would you agree, Mr. Fleming?"

"Governor, I don't have the training in military strategy and tactics that General O'Hara possesses, but it makes sense to me that if we have air superiority, we should be able to knock out Ariel."

"O.K. then, General. What's the plan?"

"Based on the fact that it was less than ten minutes between our air attack on the fake air field and the appearance of the enemy aircraft, we calculate that their base has to be within fifty miles of La Hacienda. We send three of our unmanned predators to attack La Hacienda and have our remaining nineteen spaced along the 314 mile circumference. The predators will be spaced roughly sixteen miles apart, meaning that they will have to view a slice of the pie of about 400 square miles. When the MIG's come after our attack, we should be able to determine fairly closely where they came from. At that point the remaining predators scatter for home. A few days later we send up three more predators to pin-point the base location and then follow with an attack from our Falcons while the MIG's are on the ground."

"All right, General. Let me think on that and I will get back to you."

"Yes, Ma'am. The general saluted and departed.

"So Butch, what do you think of the plan?"

"Florence, I think there may be another explanation for the short time span between the attack on the fake airfield and the appearance of the enemy fighters. You have to consider the possibility that you have a mole in your organization."

Chapter 56: Finding the mole

"Do you really think so, Butch?"

"Florence, I am not sure, but my instinct tells me it is so."

"I've heard that kind of reasoning before. Can you give me any facts that would help me come to the same conclusion."

"Certainly, Florence. From the radio transmissions, we know the attack on the fake airfield began at 1:17AM and the enemy jets appeared at La Hacienda at 1:29AM. If their base was right next door, would you think it reasonable for the pilots to get ready at that hour and have their aircraft in the air in that short of a time-span?"

"Butch, all I can say is that I am glad I have a CIA fellow on our side".

"Correction, Florence. It is TIA now."

"Right, so what do you recommend we do now?"

"Before any further offensive action, we screen every person that had access to 'Swift Sword'. Do you have a competent and trustworthy individual to administer lie detector testing?"

"I do. Julianne Weber was with the FBI prior to secession, and her specialty was interrogation and lie detection."

"Did she have any prior knowledge of 'Swift Sword'?"

"No, she is not attached to the military. She is head of homeland security reporting directly to me."

"Is there a room in this building that would be suitable for testing?

"Yes, just down the hall second door to the right is a sound-proof room we use just for that in screening new employees."

"Excellent. We want to keep this interrogation completely under wraps. At this stage we cannot trust anyone that had advance knowledge of the operation. Call General O'Hara and let him know that we think there may be a spy in the organization and that he should have all the people that knew about 'Swift Sword' together tomorrow morning in your office for lie detector testing. He is not to inform them the reason for the gathering."

Florence first dialed Weber, "Julianne, we think we may have a spy in our midst. I would like you to administer lie detection tests to a few individuals at 9:00 AM tomorrow if that suits your schedule."

"Governor, you know your priorities are mine as well. I will see you tomorrow morning at 8:45."

"Thanks, Julianne"

She then called General O'Hara to advise him of Butch's suspicion and the interrogation.

At 8:45 the next morning, a group of seven were assembled in Florence's office. Florence spoke first, "Thank you all for coming on such short notice and being prompt. General O'Hara, you have already met Butch Fleming, formerly of the CIA and now heading up the Texas Intelligence Agency." Pointing to Weber, she continued, "This is Julianne Weber, formerly with the FBI and now heading up Arizona Homeland Security. Would you introduce your three subordinates?"

After the General introduced the three, Florence spoke again, "Thank you General. Now let me explain why we are here. We have reason to believe that there is a spy in our organization working for Ariel. Please do not take this personally, but we are asking every person that had previous knowledge of operation 'Swift Sword' to undergo a lie detector test, which will be administered by Julianne Weber. We will begin immediately. Who wants to be first?"

General O'Hara raised his hand.

"Fine, General. Just follow Ms. Weber down the hall to the second door on the right. The rest of you will remain here till the General gets back and then the next person will be tested."

An hour and a half later, Julianne returned with the last of the subordinates and spoke, "Governor, you will be happy to know that everybody tested truthful and you have no spies here."

Fleming spoke, "Are you all sure that there was no one else that had prior knowledge or maybe overheard the plan?"

General O'Hara responded. "The only other person was General Scott."

Florence asked, "General, would you have any idea where Scott is?"

"I would guess on the golf course, but if not I think I can get in touch with him."

"Please do, but tell him that I need to see him about his pension."

"Yes, Ma'am. Do you want me to call him now?"

"Absolutely,"

Chapter 57 General Scott

Florence was at lunch with Butch Fleming, when her cell phone rang. Her caller ID showed that it was General Scott. "Hello General, thanks for getting back."

"Certainly, Governor. O'Hara told me you wanted to see me about my pension.

What's the problem?"

"No problem, General. Just a minor detail we need to clear up."

"What's the detail? We can probably clear it up over the phone."

"No, General. It shouldn't take that long, but you really need to be here."

"All right then. How about nine tomorrow morning?"

"General, how about 1:30 this afternoon?"

"Governor, I have a tee time in thirty minutes."

"General, I suggest you cancel it. This is important."

"Governor Zimmerman, with all due respect, may I remind you that I am a civilian now and no longer take orders from you."

"General Scott, you should know me better than that. I would not have requested you to come in the first place if I did not think the matter urgent and in your best interest to clear up as soon as possible."

"OK, Governor. I hope this is short so that I can get back to something worthwhile."

"I assure you, General. Your time will not be wasted." After hanging up, Florence exclaimed, "That pompous ass; I should have made him a corporal!" She then dialed Julianne Weber and advised her to be ready for an additional test at 1:30.

"General, thanks for coming and being prompt. I know how important golf is to you, but as you will see this matter is of utmost importance. We have reason to believe that we have a mole in our organization and have been doing extensive lie detector testing."

"So, what's that got to do with me, Governor?

"We are asking you to undergo testing, General."

"What?? This is an outrage! You humiliate me by discharging and demoting me. Then you bring me here under false pretenses to undergo lie detection."

"General O'Hara submitted with no problem."

"Governor, O'Hara reports to you; I do not.

"We cannot force you to take the test, General; but if you don't, we will assume you are guilty and have you indicted for treason."

Scott's face reddened and after a pause, he spoke. "Governor, may we speak privately?"

"Of course, General. Butch, if you would excuse us for a few minutes, but please stick around."

"Certainly, Governor."

After he had closed the door behind him, Florence spoke. "O.K., General, what's on your mind?"

"I am being blackmailed…"

"Yes..?"

"I am a happily married man…"

"General, we're wasting your time as well as mine. Please get on with it."

"I am trying. What I am about to tell you must be held in strictest confidence."

"General, I will agree to confidentiality only if it is not Arizona's business."

"Fair enough. An old friend of yours had contacted me two months ago, telling me he had personal information about me that he knew I would prefer to keep confidential."

"A friend of mine?"

"Yes, a Mr. Morgan..Rex Morgan. Somehow, he found out about a friend .."

"General, Rex Morgan is no friend of mine, but I gather you have been cheating on your wife. Not that I condone that, but I couldn't care less. What I want to know is what the hell does this have to do with the issue at hand?"

"No, no. It's nothing like that; my friend is..he is.."

"O.K., General. You are gay, but you were still cheating on your wife. Again I don't give a damn if you had been having sex with a goat. Please get to the point."

"Morgan was blackmailing me for outrageous sums. I told him I could not afford and he put me in touch with Ariel."

"So, Ariel has been paying you to spy on us. General, you know that you are confessing to treason, and you also know what the penalty for treason in wartime is."

"Yes, I am fully aware. I only ask that my secret go to the grave with me to protect my wife from further humiliation."

"General, you should have thought of that long before now, but I have no interest in exposing your secret. Unfortunately, I cannot speak for Rex Morgan."

"I understand. I am hoping that when he sees I have no way of continuing the payments, he will forget the matter."

"Good luck on that, General, but I do have a proposition for you. If you work for us against Ariel, I will get your sentence commuted to life."

"What do I have to do?"

"Let me bring Mr. Fleming back in and we will discuss it."

Chapter 58: The Plant

"Jefe, we have just received a message delivered by our courier from General Scott."

"So what does it say?"

"The truckload of drugs intercepted at the border near Nogales last week is being transported to Phoenix as evidence against several of our compadres. The driver and assistant can be bought."

"What was the quantity of drugs taken from us?"

"Twelve thousand kilos of cocaine and eight thousand kilos of heroin."

"And how much is our dear general asking?"

"Two hundred thousand U.S. dollars."

El Diablo laughed, "A bargain! Wholesale value is fifty times that, but tell him we will give him $100,000 and 500 kilos of cocaine for his men."

When Scott, who was under house arrest, so as not to alert the public, received the message, he passed it on to Zimmerman who told him to OK the deal. He was to tell them that the contraband was to be moved from a warehouse in Yuma at 2:00 PM on Thursday, two days from now, and that he would await instructions to pass on to the men. The message came back from Ariel by secure e-mail and hour later. "Have your truck head out of Yuma on Interstate 8 as if headed to Phoenix with the driver's assistant following in a car so they will have transportation back to Yuma. Pull over at the first rest stop where you will see a red 2030 model Ford parked on the side of the road. As soon as we are in possession of the truck, your money will be wired to your Swiss bank account. The cover story for your men will be that a car disguised as a police vehicle with flashing blue light had them pull over at the rest stop where the truck was taken over and the men tied up until they were found several hours later by some travelers who had untied and taken them back to Yuma."

Scott replied, "Message received. Intercept will be arranged."

Two days later, all went as planned. The fake drugs had been planted in the same cartons of the original drugs and the State Police had been ordered to not interfere. There would have been no need for the non-interference order since Ariel had transferred the drugs to a stolen UPS truck which had gone back to Yuma and was on its way to Las Vegas via US 95. The remnants of the original truck was found days later as a burned out hulk in a ravine a few miles out of Yuma.

The shipment arrived at a warehouse on the outskirts of Las Vegas at a little after eight that night. Two workers assisted the driver and his assistant in unloading the merchandise and when the truck was unloaded and sent back, one of the workers called,

"Antonio, the truck arrived in good shape and we just finished unloading the merchandise. We are headed home for a good night's sleep."

"Good, I'll tell the boss." The boss was Al Gorgonzola, head of the Las Vegas mafia, which controlled all of Nevada. Over the next few days the merchandise was broken down into one ounce bags for distribution throughout the northwest.

Chapter 59: Repercussions

Within two weeks of the delivery of the "merchandise" to the Las Vegas warehouse, there was a flood of related headlines from Northwest newspapers. Tacoma Daily News- "Doctors are at a loss to explain the rash of addict applicants for drug treatment in the last few days." Sacramento Courier – "Heroin addicts setting all -time records for entering drug treatment" Boise News- "An inexplicable surge in suicides by drug addicts. Reno Tribune- "A spike in drug treatment registration". Portland Gazette- "Gangland shootings related to drugs on the rise". Seattle Morning News- "Drug related crimes hitting new records". Television and radio news and talk shows were echoing the news.

Although it was all happening in the Northwest, the news was being broadcast all over the country and it had not escaped Washington's attention. When Campbell saw it on one of his favorite talk shows, he was ecstatic. He called Allen Jefferson in for a meeting. "Allen, this is the first good news we've had since last November. It's perfectly clear that our anti- drug campaign is finally working. I want this broadcast on all the networks and in all the newspapers. Maybe this will get people's minds off the damned secession movement."

Gorgonzola and his counterparts throughout the Northwest were not so happy. In fact they were in a rage. The bosses were accusing Gorgonzola of poisoning the shipment so as to move in on their territories. They were threatening retaliation and even assassination. Finally, he was able to calm them down a little by pointing out that his area had been affected as well, so now the focus was on Ariel.

When El Diablo got the news, he too was full of rage, but he knew who was responsible. General Scott had double crossed him and El Diablo would make him pay.

He had Pancho send the following message by e-mail to Governor Zimmerman.

Dear Gobernadora Zimmerman, you must know by now that your General Scott had been engaging in some 'after hours' work for us, and I would like to make you a proposal. We can save you a lot of time, trouble, and embarrassment of a trial for one of your closest advisors if you will turn him over to us. I can assure you he will not escape punishment. In return we will send back your Major Simmons, who has a few physical problems, but is otherwise in good health.

Sincerely,

El Diablo.

Florence was in conference with Fleming, when she received the message. "Can you believe the gall of that bastard? I would like to personally castrate the SOB."

"I hear you, Florence, but he has a point. You don't need any more unfavorable publicity after that failed attack. And besides we get Simmons back."

"You're right, Butch, but it kills me to have to give in to that shit head."

"Florence, all this discussion may be academic. After all, legalities may be a bit of a problem with someone that has been indicted for treason, being released without a trial. I think we have to get Scott's agreement."

Chapter 60: Repentance

Florence summoned Scott to be at her office in one hour. When he arrived, Florence told him about El Diablo's offer. "General Scott, the 'plant' worked perfectly, and your assistance in carrying it out will undoubtedly be used as a mitigating factor by your attorney in your defense for trial of treason. You might just get away with life in prison. Nevertheless, you and your family will be disgraced, and what you did to our troops will have to remain on your conscience for the rest of your life. Your alternative is to avoid the trial and face the wrath and punishment of El Diablo. . I want you to go back to your apartment, think about it overnight and give me a call in the morning with your response."

"Governor, I don't need to think about it. I will take you up on the alternative."

"General, you know what they did to that border guard and his wife. They are utterly ruthless."

"Yes, Governor. I am well aware. I had no idea that so many of our soldiers would die. I thought there would be a retreat and it would just go down as a failed attack."

"Sure, General. It's amazing the rationalizations that the human mind is capable of, but we won't belabor the point. Your decision is firm then that you are willing to offer yourself in trade for Major Simmons?"

"Absolutely."

"All right then. I will contact El Diablo and we will set up the exchange."

Chapter 61: The Exchange

The exchange was to take place at the Yuma Border Crossing and had been planned to be a quiet unpublicized event at 11:00 on a Sunday morning when most people are in church. But it was not to be. Mrs. Scott had spread the word to all her friends, who in turn contacted the media as well as all of their friends, and so shortly it seemed that all of Arizona knew about their heroic general. Florence for her part did nothing to stifle the publicity since after all, her state could use a morale booster. One would have thought that when Mrs. Scott heard about the planned exchange, she would have tried to talk her husband out of it. On the contrary, she was all for it, as now in addition to being the wife of a retired general, she would be the wife of a patriotic hero who was willing to sacrifice his life for that of a fellow officer. They had been married fifteen years shortly before he had received his first star, and she of course became aware of his sexual preference early in their marriage. She was, however, not going to let that minor issue prevent her from the prestige of being a general's wife, and was perfectly content to let him have his fun while she enjoyed her paramours. She contacted Jared Hardigan who was delighted to have her on his talk show to talk about her heroic husband. It was prime time Saturday night only hours away from the scheduled exchange the next morning, and with all the publicity, a record setting number of viewers were tuned in. After Hardigan introduced his guest, he got right to the point. "So, Mrs. Scott, can you tell us why your husband is willing to engage in such a selfless act?"

"Jared, very simply, he is a good and courageous man. Since the attack on Ariel under his command had failed, he felt personally responsible, and feels this is the least he can do to try to make up for all those young men who lost their lives".

The next morning the exchange site was full of well- dressed men and women with children and sometimes babies in carriages. Everybody, it seemed, was carrying a picnic basket, somewhat reminiscent of a picnic gathering on a Sunday almost two hundred years ago at a village in Virginia named Manasas, where a bloody battle ensued. The people at this gathering seemed also oblivious to the danger of being so close to what was to take place.

The Arizona Border Patrol had cordoned off the area one hundred yards from the gate, but cautioned the onlookers that even at that distance there was danger if Ariel began shooting. El Diablo had made it clear in his acceptance of the exchange that La Gobernadora would regret it if any tricks were to be pulled. Zimmerman replied that she would stand behind the agreement, but if Ariel had any tricks in mind, they too would regret it.

At the appointed time, the two opposing forces were in parallel lines on opposite sides of the gate much like they would have been in battles of old. There were maybe fifty of Ariel's men in full battle dress armed with automatic weapons and bazookas. On the Arizona side, there were only twenty heavily armed soldiers, but hundreds more in reserve in the event they were needed. Major Simmons was wheelchair bound and was brought to the gate. General Scott walked up, returned Simmons' salute, both sides withdrew, and as quickly as that the drama was over.

Chapter 62: Attack plans

General O'Hara, Butch Fleming, and Florence were in a conference to decide the next military step. It was clear that O'Hara's plan to track the MIG's back to their airfield would have to be revised. It had been based on the assumption that the airfield was very close to La Hacienda. While that possibility could not be ruled out, it was probably more likely that the airfield was a considerable distance away. The drones are all propeller driven and could not begin to follow the MIG's. Even the F-17 Falcons would not be able to keep up with the MIG's, so a different strategy would be needed.

Fleming suggested a ground attack on La Hacienda to "cut off the head of the snake".

O'Hara disagreed, "Without air superiority, the ground force would be destroyed, same as before."

Fleming responded, "General, I admit that I am no military strategist, but what if the MIG's didn't show up?

"Mr. Fleming, how are you going to keep the MIG's on the ground?"

"Well, General, if they had not been alerted, why would they be in the air?"

"Mr. Fleming, if you have a plan to keep them from being alerted, would you care to share it with us?"

Before Fleming could respond, Florence noted that General O'Hara had a sardonic tone in his voice and was becoming annoyed with this outsider questioning his judgment on military matters. She broke in, "Gentlemen, this is an interesting discussion, but I don't think we are getting anywhere. I suggest we bring in somebody with some infantry expertise and see if we can come up with a feasible air-ground operation. Does that make sense?"

Both men agreed.

Chapter 63 Recruiting a General

Florence was on the phone with President Melvin Graham of New Virginia, who she knew from her days in Washington. Graham had been on the same House subcommittee and like Florence had moved up since then.

"Hello, Florence. It is so good to hear from you. I hear you have your hands full right now with the drug war, but at least your secession was a little more straight forward. Would you believe that eight months after our secession, I am still involved in eliminating superfluous agencies and services?"

"Absolutely, Melvin. You and I both know government feeds on itself. I can well understand that those who have their own little kingdoms are not going to give them up without a fight."

"You got that right! And if that's not enough, being right next door to the crackpot and having to worry about what he may try next."

"Yes, Melvin. I totally understand, and I sure hope Campbell will not try anything foolish. But I too have a problem, which brings me to the purpose of my call. I am in need of a general, and I know you are a good friend of Lon Whitt. I understand that he is a tactical genius, and I know too that he has been heavily involved in your secessionist movement."

"Correct, Florence. Also his main job is director of the American Fossil Fuel Association. As you mentioned, he is well known for his military exploits, but he has been out of the military for a long time. On top of that, he is a wanted man, having been indicted for treason due to his efforts on secession."

"I understand, Melvin, but I would still like to talk to him."

"Yeah, persistent as ever. I will contact him and ask him to give you a call. On the number that you called from?"

"Perfect, thanks."

Within the hour, Florence picked up the call, which her caller ID showed Lon Whitt. "Good afternoon, Colonel Whitt. Thanks for getting back so quickly."

"You are welcome, Governor. I like to be prompt. And by the way, it is Mister, not Colonel, but Lon to you."

"Thanks, Lon, but your military reputation precedes you."

"That was a lifetime ago."

"Not quite, Lon. I assume President Graham filled you in on what I wanted to speak about."

"He did and I am flattered, but even if I were to consider it, I would have to check first with my boss."

"Lon, what would it take for you to consider it?

"Governor, you obviously don't mince words. I like that. If I were to consider your offer, I would want the freedom to run my operation as I see fit with no second guessing or delays subject to a committee's decision."

"Lon, you also don't mince words and I like that. As long as your operation conforms to the Arizona Constitution, you will have total freedom."

"Governor, I am afraid I am not familiar with the Arizona Constitution."

"Yes, you are, Lon. It conforms exactly to the original U.S. Constitution and the first ten amendments."

"O.K. Governor. Let me check with Robert Stephens."

"Excellent, Lon. But if there is a problem, I will want to talk to Mr. Stephens."

"Fine, Governor."

Chapter 64: General Whitt

A day later, Lon called Florence back with the news that Robert Stephens agreed to a temporary leave for him for up to ninety days. Florence did not like the time limit, but felt that she could persuade Stephens to grant an extension if necessary. "Lon, how quickly can you make it to Phoenix?"

"I've checked airline schedules and Columbia has a direct flight from Richmond to Phoenix, arriving at 12:00 noon tomorrow."

"Terrific Lon. I will meet you at the airport and brief you on the way back to my office. And by the way, I will need your suit, shoe, and hat sizes for your uniform, which I will ask to be expedited."

Lon gave her the information, told her he was looking forward to meeting her and they hung up.

The plane arrived on schedule and Lon was the first off at the gate. Florence had never met him, but knew it was Whitt from his imposing figure, posture, and stride. Florence spoke first, "So nice to finally meet you, Lon."

"The feeling is mutual, Governor."

After retrieving Lon's baggage, which consisted of one small suitcase, they headed to the parking garage to get her car, which was less than a ten minute walk to her assigned parking spot. She opened the trunk of her compact BMW , Lon threw his suitcase in and they got in with Florence on the driver's side. He told her he would have preferred to carry his suitcase, but regulations permitted only one carry on and he had a brief case. She told him she understood and that was why she was averse to flying other than in her own plane. "Lon, before we get started, I am curious as to what you do for Stephens. I know he owns what was the largest coal company and now I guess is the only coal company in the U.S."

"Correct, Governor. Stephens is also director of the North American Fossil Fuel Association, formerly known as the North American Coal Trade Organization, which works to counter the propaganda and pseudoscience of the anthropogenic global warming theory. I am the spokesperson for the association as well as the ex-officio coordinator of the secessionist movement."

"Lon, we do need to move on to your mission here, but lacking a science background, I am not sure I understand how what you said connects. Can you explain in a nutshell?"

Lon then briefly explained the tie in between the theory, fossil fuels, carbon dioxide emissions, and the EPA.

Florence replied, "It's clear now. Obviously, the EPA has no jurisdiction over states that are no longer in the Union."

"You got it, Guv."

Florence smiled and then filled him in on Ariel and developments since the kidnapping and torture of the border agent.

After taking it all in, Lon said, "I would like to have a meeting with Mr. Nelson, General O'Hara, and you this afternoon if possible."

"No problem at all, Lon. I anticipated that and have a meeting scheduled at 3:00 this afternoon in my office. It's about 1:20 right now and we're just about there. I have taken the liberty in booking you at this Marriott, which is only a couple of blocks away from the Capitol. I've also rented you a car that will be waiting for you at the hotel. I'll drop you off now and I think that should give you enough time."

"More than enough, Governor. Thanks."

It was 2:50 when Witt had announced himself to Sheila, who in turn called Florence,

"Mr.-I mean General Whitt is here, Governor."

"Excellent, Sheila. Please send him in."

"Hello, Lon. I trust your room is satisfactory."

"Absolutely, Governor. Very nice."

"You are slightly early, but I am sure Nelson and the General will be along shortly."

At that moment, Sheila was announcing the two others. When they entered her office, Florence did the introductions, "Gentlemen, I would like you to meet Major General Whitt, and General Whitt, please meet Brigadier General O'Hara, commander of Arizona's air force and Mr. Butch Fleming, formerly Assistant Director of the CIA and now Director of the Texas Information Agency on loan to us."

Since Whitt was not in uniform yet, Florence had intentionally stated the exact ranks of Whitt and O'Hara so that there would be no misunderstanding of who ranked whom. She knew that O'Hara wasn't happy with that arrangement, but O'Hara was going to have to swallow his pride and live with it. Florence invited Lon to lead the discussion.

"Thanks, Governor. Gentlemen and Governor, I am honored to have been asked to join with you in the eradication of this menace to society. The governor has been kind enough to brief me on the situation, but I would like to get a few more details. General "O'Hara, I understand that we have no idea as to the location of their airfield, but given the speed of those jets at something like twenty-five miles per minute, distance may be a secondary issue as compared to the time required to get the planes in the air and up to altitude from a dead sleep in the early hours. Is that correct?"

"No, General." O'Hara's face had suddenly changed from a frown to that of a smirk. "I, of course, don't know about Ariel's pilots, but in the U.S., pilots should be able to don their flight suits and have their planes in the air in ten minutes and up to altitude in one minute more. So distance could have a great bearing on how quickly they could be to target."

"Thanks for enlightening me, General. I had no idea reaction time could be that fast."

O'Hara's smirk had changed to a smile as he thought, "Maybe this guy won't be so bad after all."

Lon continued, "I think to be safe, we need to figure that their pilots are as good as ours and with the airfield probably less than two hundred miles away, we will need to work fast. I understand from the interrogation of one of their men that we know there is a back-up generator in the basement. Do we know the location of the door to the basement? And where is the fuel tank?"

No one knew the answer. "General, I had heard that before the previous attack, you were asking for more inteI, but were overruled by General Scott. Hindsight shows that you were correct. I think it might be a good idea to play a little more question and answer game with that fellow. Can you arrange that, General?"

An enthusiastic response, "Yes sir!"

Chapter 65: Second Interrogation

It had been just shy of six weeks since Ronaldo's first interrogation, but in that time he had been weaned off his drug habit, so the previous method of inducing his cooperation was not going to work. That presented no problem, however, to Butch Nelson, who was now doing the interrogation. "Ronaldo, I understand that you were very cooperative before and I trust you will be as helpful this time. I will tell you if you find that you cannot answer our questions, I will have to put you back on Cabbalo and after a few days we will go back to what worked so successfully the first time around. Do you understand?"

"Si, Senor."

"And you understand the consequences of untruthful answers?"

"Si Senor."

Questioning revolved around the back-up generator and the fuel tank. He knew the generator was in a secure room in the basement, but had only been there once and could not recall where the door to the basement was. Ronaldo did not know the location of the fuel tank, but had seen the gasoline tank truck unloading through a hose into a spigot in the ground towards the back of the palace just inside the wall. Nelson asked the two generals who were present for the questioning if they had anything else. They said they did not and Ronaldo was taken by a guard back to his cell. Nelson asked if he should bring another prisoner in to answer some of the questions that Ronaldo could not answer, and Lon told him that would not be necessary.

Chapter 66: New Strategy

The three left the interrogation room after Ronaldo was dismissed and headed to Florence's office. When they entered, Florence asked if they had learned anything new.

Lon answered, "Yes, Governor. I think we have enough. I will need twenty of your best Special Forces people for the plan."

Florence responded, "Lon, we have some Special Forces troopers left, but unfortunately, our best were lost in the failed attack."

Nelson spoke up, "Our Texas Rangers are the best, and I believe President Houston would be happy to contribute to the cause."

Lon spoke, "Governor, if you have no objection, I would like to have those men for this mission."

Florence replied, "None at all, let me run it by my friend, Jerry Collins, who is Houston's chief of staff." She dialed Collins, who picked up on the second ring.

"Hey Flo, I bet you're calling to thank me for getting you Butch Nelson."

"No, Jer, but I will tell you he's great and I appreciate it. I'm actually calling to see if I could borrow some more of your good people. We need twenty of your best Rangers for a daring mission against Ariel."

"Flo, I doubt that there is a problem, but let me check with Richard and get back to you ASAP."

"Thanks, Jer. Much appreciated.

While they waited for Collins' return call, Lon laid out his plan, "We will follow the path that your three troopers took when they went over to capture Ronaldo…"

Florence interrupted, "General, you don't mean 'we' as in you."

Lon replied, " Yes, Governor, 'we' as in we. I am going with my men."

"You can't be serious, Lon, I mean General."

"I am dead serious, Governor. You may recall the condition that I demanded to accept this job, and you consented."

"Yes, but…"

"Is there anything unconstitutional about my leading my men."

"No.

"Then it is settled, that is, unless you want to relieve me of command."

"You win, General.

"Thanks, Governor. Let me briefly go over the plan. We will wait for…"Lon was interrupted by the phone ringing. It was Jerry Collins calling back.

Florence answered, "Yes, Jer?… OK, Excellent! Thanks, Jer. With that, she hung up. "We're set. Houston gave the OK for the twenty rangers. All I need to do is tell Collins when we need them and where to report."

"Excellent, have them report to me at my hotel suite 7:30 AM Thursday two days from now. And General O'Hara, if you could join us as well since I would like to include some air power in the operation?"

"My pleasure, General."

"Great. We will cover the plan over breakfast and then take the Rangers out to Goldwater Training Ground for some mission training. We will be awaiting a moonless night, which will be coming up five days from now on Sunday."

"O.K. Lon, I will relay your request to Jerry Collins, but is there something more you can tell me about the mission to have me resting easier? I am concerned about those MIG's."

"Surely, Governor. We will come up from the rear of La Hacienda since the gate is in front and attacks are expected there. By the time the enemy jet fighters arrive they will find the villa totally blacked out with a heavy smoke screen to boot. Our people will be inside the villa and the MIG's will dare not take offensive action for fear of killing their own people. Our force will have gas masks and ultraviolet flash lights enabling us to see in the dark."

Florence responded, "It sounds too simple, Lon.

Lon replied, "It's really not too complicated, Governor."

Chapter 67 Operation Inferno

Thursday morning all were gathered for breakfast and a briefing on the upcoming operation, which was dubbed "Operation Inferno". It was to be a joint air ground operation, utilizing unmanned drones carrying inflammables. The whole idea was to knock out lighting and create enough smoke that when the enemy planes arrived they would not be able to see anything.

The operation began at 11:00 PM on a moonless Sunday night with the twenty Texas Rangers being led by General Lon Whitt. They took the same route through the tunnel that the three Arizona troopers had taken a couple of months earlier to capture Ronaldo. The element of surprise would be crucial to the success of the operation so the quiet and speedy Tesla bikes were again chosen as the means of transport.

When they were five miles away from La Hacienda, the task force took a detour to approach the villa from the rear as Lon had said in the meeting. What he had left out was some important information he had learned from Ronaldo's interrogation. Ronaldo had revealed that the transformer was on the back wall, enabling the Rangers to 'kill two birds with one stone' by planting explosives there.

At 12:51 AM, Lon radioed General O'Hara that he and his men were set behind the back wall and the explosives had been planted. O'Hara responded, "Roger." And with that sent the first of three drones, heavily laden with napalm, on its way. Forty –two minutes later, the first drone was crashed into the front gate of La Hacienda, setting off a huge fire and killing two guards at the gate. Following that, at two minute intervals, the other two drones crashed into the front wall, adding to the carnage, inferno and confusion. Figuring that the attack was coming from the front of the villa, the guards moved to the front with tanks as well. They had also alerted their air force to bring on the MIG's.

Concurrently, with the first crash at the gate, two rangers scaled the wall and planted explosives at the spigot to the fuel tank. Less than eight minutes later, when they were safely back outside the wall, the explosives were discharged taking out the transformer and generator concurrently and creating a mass of black smoke, which merged with the smoke from the front of the villa.

By the time that the MIG's arrived at 1:55 AM, twenty-two minutes after the alert, the darkened villa was covered in a dense black smoke screen, making it impossible for the enemy planes to determine a target. In addition, the Rangers had captured one of the anti-aircraft guns and had managed to knock out one of the MIG's. Unable to sense a target and coming under fire themselves, the jets retreated back to base to await daylight.

Meanwhile, on the ground, the Rangers had things well under control. Twelve guards were dead, including El Diablo's two body guards. There were four captives, including the grand prize, El Diablo, himself. It had been hoped that they would be able to rescue some of the prisoners from the first attack, but, unfortunately, they and General Scott were found asphyxiated in the dungeon from the smoke and lack of oxygen. Somehow, at least one of the guards had managed to elude capture, but nobody at the time considered that to be such a big deal.

By daylight, when the MIG's reappeared there was nothing left of the grand villa, but a burnt out hulk with nobody there.

Chapter 68: The Treaty

The guard who had escaped the inferno just happened to be a spy for President Montalban, so it was not long before word got back to the President about the attack. Not only that, but the guard had seen the insignia of one of the Rangers, identifying him as a Texas Ranger. This was all that Montalban needed. He had been looking for an excuse and now he had it.

Montalban placed a call to The White House and the receptionist answered, "Good afternoon, this is the White House. May I help you?"

"Si, Senorita. This is Juan de Carlo Montalban, President of Mexico. I wish to speak to President Campbell."

"Yes, Sir, I mean, Mr. President. Let me see if he is available."

"Gracias."

Campbell picked up, "Presidente Montalban, to what do I owe this honor?"

"Mr. President, there is a development that I think you should be made aware of."

"And what would that be, my friend?"

"Two of your states have invaded our country."

Laughing, Campbell replied, "You must mean Texas and Arizona."

"That is correct, but I fail to understand the joke."

"Surely, you have heard, that those states have declared their independence."

"Does that mean that you accept their independence?"

"Not on your life, but at the moment, there is nothing I can do."

"I may have a solution if you are interested."

"Indeed, I am. I am listening."

"I am sure you are aware that the state of Texas is the lynchpin in your secessionist movement."

"Yes, but please don't refer to it as 'my' movement!"

"Of course, but I think you know what I mean. If Texas were to back down, the other states would likely follow."

"That is an astute analysis, Mr. Presidente, and in agreement with our own analysis, but the question remains how to get Texas to back down."

"Ah, President Campbell, that was what I was getting to when you laughed. Texas and Arizona have committed an act of war on my country, and as a patriot, I feel I should respond in kind."

"So you are asking my reaction to your going to war with two of my states?"

"Exactly, Mr. President."

"I would tell you not to do it; not that I really give a 'rat's ass', but I cannot afford any more negative publicity like what I got when Russia took the Aleutians."

"What if I could propose a deal that would give you favorable publicity?"

"What do you have in mind, Mr. Presidente?"

"Give me a free hand in Texas and Arizona, and after we have defeated them, we will give Arizona back to you."

"And what about Texas?"

"Texas will revert back to its rightful and historic place, Mexico."

"You can't be serious!"

"President Campbell, I assure you I am very serious. Our loss of Texas in 1836 is a terrible blot on our glorious history. I intend to rectify that transgression."

"I am sorry, Mr. Presidente, that is unacceptable."

"If we declare war on Texas and Arizona, what will you do?"

"You will have put me in a very awkward situation. Even though I would not relish the idea, political pressure would be immense. We were very close to going to war with Russia over the Aleutians. Texas and Arizona would, I fear, be the last straw."

Montalban knew he was dealing with someone of low intelligence and sensed that he could make a deal even though he had no intention of giving back any territory after the war was won. "All right, President Campbell, you drive a hard bargain. Tell me what you think would be acceptable and fair."

"That is a very difficult question, Mr. Presidente. I dislike the idea of ceding any territory to Mexico, but…"

"What if I were to pretend ignorance of the fact that Texas had participated in the raid and just declare war on Arizona?"

"I think that Texas would probably come to Arizona's aid."

"And in the process, declare war on Mexico?"

"I suppose so."

"Would that not be more acceptable than Mexico declaring war on Texas first?"

"I suppose so."

"So do we have a deal? After the war is over, we will return Arizona to you."

"Mr. Presidente, let me have Texas back instead and we have a deal."

At this point, Montalban had the agreement he was seeking, i.e., that the U.S. would not interfere in a war between the two states and his country, but he was prepared to let Campbell feel even better about the deal that he had struck.

"Oh, President Campbell, will you not let me at least have San Antonio and the Alamo back?"

"Only if we get Arizona and the rest of Texas back."

The two shook hands and the deal was done. Montalban had gotten exactly what he had wanted, which was no interference from the U.S. when Mexico took Texas and Arizona back; and Campbell was delighted, thinking he had outwitted the President of Mexico in getting two states back in the Union and nipping the secessionist movement in the bud.

Chapter 69: Resignation

After Montalban had departed and Campbell called Allen Jefferson in to fill him in on the good news, Campbell was shocked, however, to learn that Jefferson did not share his exuberance. In fact, Jefferson expressed his disgust at the agreement. "Mr. President, I cannot believe that you have agreed to such a thing."

"Allen, am I hearing correctly, that you don't think an exchange of San Antonio for the states of Texas and Arizona is a good idea?"

"You have agreed to allow a foreign country to wage war on one of our states. No, I don't think it is a good idea; it is an atrocious idea and if you stand by the agreement, you can have my resignation right now!"

"Allen, I have to say that I am most disappointed in you; but because you have been a good and trusted advisor, I will allow you to think on this overnight."

"No consideration necessary, Mr. President." Jefferson replied as he left the Oval Office. Allen Jefferson had been unhappy in his job for a long time. Yes, it was a prestigious position with lots of perks, but enough was enough. His boss was grossly incompetent and at some point that incompetence would rub off on his advisor's reputation. He probably should have spoken up a lot sooner but held his tongue and basically betrayed his own values. At least for the moment he felt good about himself. He would start worrying about another job tomorrow. Surely with the contacts he had made, he could land a good position.

Campbell was flabbergasted and angry. Seething, he thought to himself, "I've treated that black boy with a lot more respect than he deserved." But he wasn't going to dwell on that. He was confident that he had made a decision that would ensure his place in history along with all the great Presidents.

Montalban's private plane landed in Mexico City at 10:00 that night. The next morning he had called in his chief advisor to inform him of the agreement. He asked him to find out from his joint military chiefs how much time it would take to be at full military capability for war.

To say he was unhappy to hear that it would be at least a month would be a gross understatement. He ordered them to re-think the situation and come back with an answer of one week at most. In the meantime, he sent the following message to Governor Florence Zimmerman:

November 18, 2043 9:05AM

Gobonara Zimmerman,

I am sure you are aware that members of your military have repeatedly violated Mexican sovereign territory without provocation over the last few months. We are reasonable people and do not desire any antagonism between our two countries, but under the circumstances we feel a war reparations fee of one billion dollars U.S. is in order. To avoid war, make your payment electronically to Banco de Mexico, Mexico City, within 24 hours.

Sincerely, Juan De Carlo Montalban, President of Mexico"

Florence was in her office attending to some inconsequential duties when the message came through. Unhesitatingly, she responded,

November 18, 2043 9:07AM

President Montalban,

We have never met, but I must compliment you on your sense of humor. Perhaps it is the language barrier that caused me to misinterpret. I am sure you are aware that we have rid your sovereign territory of the last drug cartel operating. One billion dollars U.S. does sound reasonable for our services. You may make your payment electronically to the Bank of Arizona Phoenix Arizona.

P.S. In the event that I have not misinterpreted, let me remind you that you were unable to defeat Ariel in over two years. Arizona was able to accomplish that in less than two months. If you are intent on waging war, it might be prudent to choose a weaker adversary.

Sincerely, Florence Zimmerman, Governor of Arizona

When Montalban received Florence's reply, he was furious. Not only had she refused his demand, which he had anticipated and hoped for to justify his declaration of war, she had tried to make him look like a fool. He knew she had a point, but many times pride overpowers logic. Mexico might well have gone to war except for the actions of Allen Jefferson.

When Jefferson left the Oval Office, he knew that he had to quickly dissociate himself from the President if he were to salvage his reputation and give himself a chance to stay among the governing elite. He placed a call to the Washington Post and asked if Kevin Chalmers was available. Chalmers was an old friend from Jefferson's undergraduate days at Tuskegee Institute. They had taken different paths since college, but Chalmers, like Jefferson, had done well for himself. He was regarded as one of the Post's best political reporters. They had been pretty close friends when they met up again in Washington three years ago, but had a falling out over a mutual girlfriend a few months later. The girl had long since left Washington for a wealthy New York real estate operator, who refused to leave his wife but kept the girl up in fine style. So the two college friends had reconciled, but were not nearly as close as they had been. So it was with some surprise that Chalmers received the call. "Hey A.J., what's going on?"

"Kev, I've got a hot story for you. Are you free this evening?"

"It just so happens that I am. Can you give me an advance clue?"

"It involves Campbell and me. I'll fill you in over dinner. Pizza and beer at my pad at 7:00?"

"Sounds good, but that wasn't much of a clue."

"I know. I didn't want to spoil the appetizer."

"You didn't. I'm looking forward to the meal."

"Me too."

Chalmers was at Jefferson's door at 7:00.

"Come in, old buddy. Good to see you."

"Good to see you too, A.J. So what's up?"

"I resigned today."

"You've got to be kidding!"

"Nope." Over the next two hours, Jefferson filled his friend in on all the frustrations he had endured working for the President and then the final straw. Jefferson was correct. This was a hot story for sure. In fact, it might be worth a Pulitzer Prize if handled correctly. Chalmers called his editor and asked him to stop the presses. He had a story that deserved top billing.

Chapter 70: Backlash

The next morning the Post came out with the following headline: "President cuts deal with Mexico." The story presented the details of the deal, but what was far worse from Campbell's perspective was the commentary that suggested that he had possibly committed an impeachable offense in bypassing Congress to create a treaty. The reaction to the article was immediate and fierce. The White House phone lines were tied in a knot with people all over the country expressing their indignation. Political cartoonists and comedians were having a ball making fun of the inept President.

Late that afternoon, Campbell put in a call to Montalban. When Montalban answered, Campbell quickly said, "I am sorry, but the deal is off."

Montalban replied, "President Campbell, you can't do that. I have already ordered our military to full readiness in preparation for the attack."

"Under the circumstances, Mr. Presidente, I think it would be wise to stand down. My citizens are very angry and I believe they are not likely to ignore a military action against Arizona and Texas. Again, I am sorry. I didn't anticipate this kind of reaction."

When the call ended, Montalban too was angry, but he could ill afford a war with the United States; and what Governor Zimmerman said had also begun to sink in.

After Campbell hung up from his call to Montalban, he asked his press agent to put out the following press release: *This is to correct a serious misunderstanding of a recent discussion President Campbell had had with President Montalban. While it is true that the Mexican president had visited the White House, the story has been grossly distorted to suggest that our President would sanction Mexico's declaration of war against Arizona and Texas in retaliation for intrusion into Mexican territory. President Campbell strongly protested and told him that he could give no assurance that we would ignore such an act. Montalban had said all he was interested in was to get San Antonio and the Alamo back as a matter of national pride. President Campbell continued to advise against it. Somehow, this discussion was taken out of context and suggested that our President had agreed. Our President denies that unequivocally.*

Despite the attempt to defuse the uproar, the population continued to believe that Campbell had agreed to the deal, particularly when his ex-advisor was on talk shows telling the public the truth. It was getting late in the year and the election less than a year away. Even before this episode, Campbell's poll numbers were not good, but since then his favorability rating had dropped to 38%. Campbell had to do something to reverse the tide or he would go down in history as the one-term President who had presided over the start of the break-up of the country. He now was about to make a disastrous decision that might have been avoided if he had had the level- headed Jefferson at his side.

Chapter 71: The Citizenship Act

Campbell called his Vice President in for a consultation, "Hector, what would your 'constituency' think if we revived the Immigration Bill?"

"Are you making fun of me, Mr. President?"

"Not at all, Hector. Not at all."

"In that case, I think you know the answer. Most of our citizens of Mexican descent have family among those who are undocumented, so they would be delighted and fully in favor."

"You know, Hector, that segment of our population has not been very supportive of our administration in the past."

"I think that stems from the feeling that you were not interested in the plight of the undocumented. "

"O.K, see what you can do to round up enough Senate and House members for a quorum so we can get this bill passed."

As the call went out, to say the members were unhappy would be a huge understatement. It was Monday November 23, three days since the start of the winter recess and they had to explain to their children and/or spouses why their vacation was to be cut short. In addition, many had hoped that the issue could be put off indefinitely. It was an issue that was so controversial that it could cost them re-election, and their tenure as always was the over-riding reason behind any legislation.

Finally by mid-December, enough Senators and House members were back to enact business. Both houses took up the bill immediately. On the Senate side, Majority Leader Randall Grayson asked for discussion. A Senator from Kentucky rose to express dissent. "Mr. Leader, my state is already unhappy with the restrictions on coal. If the Immigration Bill is passed, it might be enough to tip the balance to secession."

By mid-day and a break for lunch, twenty-one of the forty-six Senators present had spoken. Thirteen had expressed dissent, but only seven had raised the specter of secession, and of the seven, there were only four states represented. After lunch since there was no more discussion, a vote was taken, and the bill passed by more than a two to one ratio.

On the House side there was considerably more discussion, but by late afternoon, after sixty-one of the one hundred eighty nine members present had spoken, a vote was taken, and again, the tally was overwhelmingly in favor. Interestingly, the same four states' representatives mentioned the possibility of secession.

That evening, the bill was delivered to the White House by Ramirez and Holmes. Campbell congratulated the two and asked their feelings on the matter. As expected, Ramirez was totally positive, but Holmes had some reservations. "Mr. President, you know that I am in favor of the bill, but there are several members that expressed strong misgivings and suggested it just might push them over the edge to join the secession crowd."

"Gary, let's don't refer to the group as a 'crowd'. How many states are represented?"

"Four, sir."

"And how many in the Senate, Hector?"

"Also four, but Speaker Holmes and I have discussed the matter, and it is the same four."

"Not that it makes any difference, but which states are we talking about?"

Ramirez responded, "Alabama, Kentucky, Utah, and Wyoming."

"Ha, inconsequential states all. So we may lose four states to preserve the Union? I would say that's a pretty good deal. Hand me the bill so that I can sign and by the way let's change the name of the bill from 'Immigration' to 'Citizenship'. Now, we can have a drink on that." Campbell poured each of them a shot of his most expensive Brandy. "To the Union." They repeated in unison.

With the President's signature, the Citizenship Act SR 9073 became law, creating an estimated twenty million new citizens of voting age. And sure enough, four 'inconsequential' states had joined the ranks of secession by January 1.

Chapter 72: The Reform Candidate

Professor Jonas O'Leary had never supported secession, although he had continued his close relationship with his childhood friend, Lon Whitt, who was in the thick of the movement. Given his erudite standing in Constitutional law, his name had come up a couple of times as a possibility for the Supreme Court, but he was never seriously considered because of his strict conservative leanings.

As would be expected, Jonas had a long time interest in government and politics, but never an interest in entering politics. Circumstances have a habit of changing perspectives, however, and the precarious state of the union in late 2043 prompted Jonas to at least listen when several conservative friends invited him to a dinner meeting to discuss a possible candidacy for President.

It was the Monday after Thanksgiving at the Epicurean in Georgetown, one of Jonas' favorite restaurants. Reservations, this close to

Christmas, were at a premium even as brutally cold as it was, but Elton Crenshaw, who had instigated the meeting, had connections as a restaurateur. Crenshaw's educational background was finance, but he had found his niche in fancy restaurants. He had made his fortune in buying and turning around poorly managed restaurants in good locations by hiring top chefs, which he brought in as partners. Crenshaw had never held political office, but he was well known in political circles as a big donor for conservative candidates and causes. He, like Jonas, had a deep interest in education and had funded several charter schools in poor neighborhoods across the country. The one woman in the group of five, Melanie Hargrove, was a middle aged widow of a wealthy industrialist. While her husband was alive, there would have been no need for her to work, but she wasn't about to live on her husband's wealth. She started a successful executive placement agency exclusively for women in Georgetown and then franchised it around the country. By the time, her husband died, her income was several times that of her husband. She, too, was a philanthropist in education and conservative causes. The other two men were likewise philanthropists, Emil Gatterer, a real estate magnate; and Carl Axton, a retired airline pilot and stock broker. Axton had made his fortune through that uncanny ability to pick winners in their infancy. So the group was made up of people who had made it big, but were not at all reluctant to share their good fortune with good causes.

Jonas arrived right on time at 7:00 and the others were already seated at the round table. Jonas spoke first, "Wow, I am glad their heat is working.. Does anyone know what the temperature is?"

Melanie Hargrove responded, "Yes, I heard the weather report on the way over here about thirty minutes ago and it was eight degrees

Fahrenheit. They are expecting it to go down to six below by 2 or 3 in the morning, which will set another record for the day as well as the month."

Crenshaw commented, "At least, it's a clear night."

Another interjected, "But, a big snow storm is expected by weekend."

Another commented, "Wouldn't some 'global warming' be nice?"

They all laughed.

Jonas spoke, "Good to see you all and thanks to Elton for inviting me to my favorite restaurant. I have to say that I am impressed that you were able to make dinner reservations this close to Christmas."

Elton responded, "You are quite welcome, and as for the reservations, it always helps to have friends in high places. "Elton laughed and they all chuckled. "No, the truth of the matter is that this also has been one of my favorite restaurants, which I had been trying for years to purchase, certainly not that I thought it needed any improvements . A couple of months ago, one of the partners died and his widow was willing to sell me his piece of it." Elton continued, "Jonas, we all are appreciative of your taking time out of your busy schedule to hear us out."

Laughing, Jonas replied, "Elton, any time you would like to invite me for dinner at my favorite restaurant, I'll find time out of my busy schedule."

Elton responded, "O.K., now that we've all had our laughs, it's time for some serious business. Jonas, we are here tonight because our country is in deep trouble. The man in charge doesn't have a clue as to what's behind the problem or how to begin resolving it. We need someone with the reputation, the know-how, and the will to take charge. We are hoping that you will consider running for President as a third party candidate under the banner of Reform Party."

"I am honored and humbled even to be considered, but I sincerely question if I am the proper choice."

"O.K. Jonas, I am sure you agree that the country is in a mess and needs an alternative to that imbecile in the White House?"

"Absolutely."

"Alright then. Who would you say is the proper choice?"

"I am as clueless on the answer to that question as our fearless leader is to the situation facing our country."

"Do you respect the judgment of the people who are here tonight?"

"Of course."

"Well then. It is our considered judgment that you are the person we need. The question is if you will accept."

"Elton, I think you may have missed your calling as a trial lawyer." Laughs all around. "Yes, I accept."

Chapter 73: The Winter of Discontent

The mild summer temperatures of a few months before were now a distant memory, but for climate scientists an indicator of conditions to come. For the last several years, the sun had been going into one of its quiet spells and scientists knew that would portend cooler temperatures for at least three or four more years. January 22, 2044 was said to be the coldest day on record for the United States with all- time low temperature records being set in ninety- three different cities in thirty-two states. Miami and Death Valley tied for high temperature at thirty-three degrees Fahrenheit.

But the frigid temperatures were the least of the worries for President Oren Campbell. The National debt was at an all- time high of twenty trillion dollars, and interest on the debt was claiming 70% of the budget. Inflation was getting worse and unemployment as reported by the Federal Labor Board had hit 21% in December with the real number probably closer to 40% with so many of the unemployed who had given up looking for a job. The mass migration that had started almost a year ago had begun again as a result of the secession of the four additional states since the passage of the Citizenship Act. So now their neighbors were feeling the pressure of the migrants competing for the scarce jobs and it appeared that Indiana, Tennessee, Georgia, and Mississippi were likely to follow in secession in the next few days. Where is this business likely to end? The total disintegration of the country? Political cartoonists were having a ball, satirizing him. They all stung, but the worst came out in the Washington Post a few days earlier, characterizing Campbell as a Roman emperor playing a fiddle in front of the burning Capitol Building. The caption read, "Oren fiddles while the country burns."

Of utmost concern to Campbell was his place in history. Was he destined to be referred to in future history books as the one term President who had presided over the break-up of the United States? Despite the addition of all the new citizens of voting age, his approval ratings had barely budged. Didn't the newly enfranchised Hispanic voters appreciate what he had done for them? He had just concluded a meeting with several of the Party's bigwigs, concerned about his low approval ratings coupled with the surge of support for the new Reform Party candidate. They were now pressing him to drop out of the race to succeed himself.

Chapter 74: Panic

As predicted, the next wave of secession began a few days later. On February 1, Tennessee joined the ranks of secessionist states. creating a situation that might have had more importance psychologically than actually. The states of North Carolina, South Carolina, Georgia, and Florida had been cut off from their fellow states; and Mississippi was surrounded by states that had seceded. Over the next two weeks, Indiana, Kentucky, and Mississippi seceded, setting the stage for an even bigger psychological shock. Like many of the industrial states, Michigan had been hit hard by departing factories. Before secession, those factories had typically ended up in Mexico, but since secession, due to much more favorable tax rates and plentiful low cost energy, the factories were relocating to Texas, Arizona, New Virginia and other states that had more recently seceded.

The final blow for Michigan was the departure of the last of the

General Motors plants for Texas. The Chevrolet plant in Flint Michigan was regarded as the epitome of auto plants. GM had spent millions in renovating and automating so that it was clearly the most efficient in the world, using only slightly more than seven man-hours per car. The plant was turning out 330 cars per day with only 291 employees, so it was not the loss of a large number of jobs but the point that if the most efficient car plant in the world couldn't make it in Michigan, what hope was there for all the less efficient industry in the state? The plant was closed on May 15, 2044 and Michigan seceded on June 1. With that secession, the eastern states were cut off from the west, creating logistic problems and adding to the cost of goods which was already inflated.

Gangs were terrorizing residents of the larger cities with muggings and home invasions, and the suburbs were no longer the safe havens they used to be. Welfare recipients were organizing and demanding higher benefits to keep up with inflation, and too many of the productive middle class were out of jobs through no fault of their own.

By now the country was in a panic, and talk of secession had morphed into talk of revolution.

Chapter 75: Atlas Shrugged

After a while, those who produce get tired of supporting those who would rather continue to leach off those who do. This was the lesson of the classic by Ayn Rand. And so we are now at the stage of something more dreadful than secession. The states which had seceded had been producer states, contributing far more to the National treasury than they were getting back. So that with each state that seceded, less was coming in resulting in more financial responsibility for the remaining states. And within each state were the producers themselves having to shoulder ever more of the financial burden with less and less benefit.

Small business is the financial back bone of the country with individual entrepreneurs risking their own capital in hopes of a decent return and all the while supplying jobs. With the looting and shop lifting and little help from strained law enforcement, store owners finally decided that their efforts were just not worth it. Factory owners likewise were confronted with striking workers, worker slow-downs, strangling regulations from OSHA and EPA, and the onerous taxes that all of the producer class had to bear to support the non-producers. And farmers, who may well be the most independent and self- reliant people in the country also had given up, leaving farms that had been in their families for generations.

All the while, the one class that was oblivious to all the pain and frustration was the government class. Those in government continued to receive their pay checks and perks, so like the doctor or nurse administering a painful shot could truthfully say, "This won't hurt at all." What they meant was that the shot wouldn't hurt them.

Chapter 76: The Meeting

Campbell was paralyzed with fear at the rioting and looting going on. He briefly considered invoking martial law once again, but decided against it, recalling the result the last time. Governors were pleading with him to institute martial law, but he told them that they were free to do so in their own states. His approval rating continued to plummet and the pressure from his Party mounted for him to give up the notion of succeeding himself and support Marco Espinoza, a popular Hispanic congressman from San Francisco. Espinoza had been in the forefront of pushing immigration reform and was outspoken in his support of the Citizenship Act. Because of that he had tremendous following among Hispanics, and it was hoped that he could inspire the millions of new voters to register and vote in November.

On August 1, two weeks before the Party convention, the White House receptionist rang to let Campbell know he had a phone call from a

Mr. Jonas O'Leary. "What the hell does he want?"

"I don't know, Mr. President, other than he wants to speak to you." , The receptionist nervously replied.

"O.K., I'll take it. Professor O'Leary, to what do I owe this great honor?"

"Mr. President, it is I who am honored and I thank you for taking my call…."

Interrupting, Campbell said, "Enough of this bullshit, O'Leary You and I both know you are leading me by a two to one margin in the national polls and are ahead of the other candidate by three or four points. I doubt you had called to wish me a happy day."

"Absolutely correct, Mr. President. Far more serious than that. What I was hoping is that we could meet to discuss the situation and hopefully come up with a plan of action."

"I get the picture now. Something along the lines of my resigning the Presidency to set the stage for a special election so that you could take over now."

"No, Mr. President. Despite my candidacy, I have no aspirations for office. This was pushed on me. My entire interest at this point is in salvaging the country."

"And you are the man that can do it?"

"No, Mr. President, you are the man who can do it."

"O.K., Professor, you have my ear. When would you like to meet?"

"This afternoon if it suits your schedule?"

"Fine, Professor. Make it 1:30 in the Oval Office.

"Thanks, Mr. President. I will see you then."

Jonas arrived promptly and the two exchanged greetings. Campbell began, "O.K., Professor, you have piqued my curiosity. What do you have in mind?"

"Thanks again for agreeing to our meeting. The situation that the country finds itself in has been decades in the building and is the result of our straying from the Constitution that had been the instrument of our country's success. You just happened to be in office at the wrong time. Like Herbert Hoover, whose name is almost synonymous with the Great Depression, you may be destined to have your name attached to the Great Secession.."

Campbell interrupted, "Don't you think that has crossed my mind?"

"Absolutely, Mr. President, but many times we possess the power to alter history if we are pro-active rather than reactive. Despite the poll numbers, the office you occupy still has awesome power if you will but use it. My suggestion is for you to let the networks know that you will be making a major announcement tonight. Don't give them any hint as to the subject, and I guarantee you will have tremendous exposure across the continent. The subject of your speech will be the initiation of dialogue with the seceding states for reconciliation to determine if there is some course of action that will allow us all to work together for mutual benefit."

"And you think that will alter history?"

"I think that could set the stage, Mr. President."

Chapter 77: Change of Direction

Jonas O'Leary had hit a responsive chord with President Campbell, particularly when he mentioned that Campbell's place in history could be "the President who rescued the country from breaking apart." He asked Jonas if he would consider becoming Campbell's advisor, for a short time at least. Jonas said he would be honored, but first had to talk to his backers to convince them it would be best for him to exit the race.

That evening, having taken Jonas' advice after having contacted all the networks, Campbell went on the air with a major announcement. "Good evening, fellow citizens, As we approach the anniversary of our country's founding, I know the mood is far from celebratory. There are far too many out of work and far too many reliant on checks from the government. Many have given up hope and pessimism is pervasive. What I will tell you tonight is that I have been listening to the wrong advisors and I will be bringing in a new team of advisors, headed up by an individual, widely respected and whose name will be very familiar to most of you. I am not at liberty to divulge his identity tonight, but I expect to do so in the next day or two. There will be a radical change of direction that I feel will begin to heal the wounds that our nation has incurred. There had been the thought that the seceding states were in error and had broken the law. What is apparent now is that we should have been listening to them instead of our advisors. From this point forward, we will be making every attempt to address their concerns, which are the same as your concerns. We will not be looking at them as antagonists, but as friends who have been trying to tell us something. All sanctions will be lifted immediately and we will be reaching out as friends trying to come to an accommodation. Thank you for listening. God bless you and God bless America. Good night. "

When Lester Parsons heard the short speech, he could not believe his ears. He tried to call Campbell, but got the following recorded message, "The White House is taking no calls at this time, please call back later." After several tries, he decided to put it to rest till morning, but he could hardly sleep with all the cursing going on in his mind. The next morning after breakfast, he called again. When the White House secretary answered, he gruffly demanded to talk to the President, who then came on the line. "What's on your mind, Lester?"

"You damn well know what's on my mind, that idiotic speech of yours last night is what. I am just about ready to throw my support behind Espinoza."

"Lester, I rather thought my speech was a pretty good one, but you do what you want to do, and for a change, I intend to do what I want to do."

"You ungrateful bastard! If not for me, you would have been lucky to be elected county dog-catcher."

"If not for you, Parsons, the country wouldn't be in the mess it's in. I am done listening to you and don't bother calling again as you will not be connected to me." With that, Campbell hung up with a smile on his face. He actually felt Presidential for the first time.

Chapter 78: Comeuppance

Parsons was beside himself, but his day was to get worse. The Dow Jones average was up a record 1200 points on record volume; and what really hurt was Atlas stock, up 23% to a price per share of $1.92. Back, a few months earlier, Parsons and Simms had been able to close out a couple of thousand shares at $3.00 per share; but he was still short a little over three million shares, and another $0.20 per share dividend had been announced for holders of stock on record as of July 15. It was getting awfully expensive holding his short position, but what could he do? Stephens had told his minority stock holders to hang on to their stock, but that if they wished to divest themselves of any that he would take it off their hands at a premium. If Parsons only knew who they were, he could work a private deal, but he had no way of learning their identity. He dreaded the thought of a meeting with Stephens, but it appeared he was out of options. Sims was out on a limb as well, but at this point it was every man for himself.

He looked up the number, picked up the phone and dialed Atlas Energy. The receptionist answered, "Good morning, Atlas Energy. How may I direct your call?"

"Give me Robert Stephens III."

"Certainly, sir. And who may I say is calling?"

"Lester Parsons."

Stephens picked up. "Lester, good to hear from you."

"Yeah, I'll bet. Robert, this is not a social call. We need to do some business."

"Oh, and what might that be?"

"I need to close out a short position in your stock."

"That should be easy enough. Just contact your broker."

"Robert, you know full well that there are only a bit more than two hundred shares available and if I purchase them it will drive your stock price through the roof."

"So how many shares are you short, Lester?"

"Three million plus."

"Goodness, Lester. Hadn't someone ever warned you about the dangers of selling short?"

"Enough of that, Stephens. I didn't call to be ridiculed."

"All right, Lester. What are you prepared to offer?"

"Well, today's price is $1.92, so I figure a fair price would be $3.00 per share for the lot."

"Come on, Lester. You said yourself that the price would go through the roof if you bought the few shares being offered."

"So, what's your price?"

"I hadn't really thought about putting a price on the stock before your phone call, but I think maybe $30.00 per share would be fair."

"That's outrageous, and you damn well know it. I'll go $5.00 and that's my last offer."

"Lester, you are wasting your time as well as mine. If that's your final offer, I think our conversation has ended."

"You are trying to bankrupt me."

"Hardly, Lester. I am being far kinder to you than you were to my good friend, Oscar Welles."

"And who is Oscar Welles?"

"Welles was the CEO of Olympic Coal, who committed suicide after you pushed the company into bankruptcy."

"Don't blame me for that; it was a poorly managed company and deserved to go out of business."

"Watch it, Buster. Another statement like that and it will cost you an additional 10%."

"Forget it then. Let's do this thing for $7.00 per share. I can write you a check right now, which you can cash in a couple of days."

"No. You heard my price, but I will give you an alternative since you want to hold on to your cash. Turn over all your U.S. natural gas holdings, and we'll call it even."

"You are out of your fucking mind."

"Take it or leave it, Lester. I have business to attend to."

"O.K. Robert. Let's draw up a contract for $30.00 per share. I assume you will give me a few days to raise the cash."

"You have one week from today."

Chapter 79: Presidential Advisor

The next morning Jonas called the President to congratulate him on his speech and to give him the good news. His backers were disappointed but understood that as advisor to the President, he might be able to accomplish as much good as he might have as President, particularly since he would have a six month head start.

Campbell was elated. "So you're my man now?"

"Not quite yet, Mr. President. We have some terms to work out."

"I understand, Professor. I am sure we can meet your price. Let's plan on lunch at 12 noon in my private dining room and we can iron out the details."

"I will be happy to join you, but money is not the issue, Mr. President."

"Whatever it is, I am confident we can come to terms, Professor, or may I call you Jonas?"

"By all means, Mr. President. I am looking forward to our lunch."

"I too, Jonas. " Campbell smiled as he thought to himself about the way he had responded. "The Professor is rubbing off on me already. In the past, I might have replied with something like 'yeah, me too.'"

Campbell tried to think of what Jonas was wanting, if not money. "Was it the Vice-Presidency? Ramirez was certainly dispensable, but how could something like that be done constitutionally? Well, O'Leary was the Constitutional expert. He would let him figure that out."

Jonas arrived punctually, and the secretary announced his arrival. Campbell came out of his office to greet his guest. "Good to see you, Jonas."

"Nice to see you as well, Mr. President."

When they sat down to lunch, Campbell opened the discussion. "So Jonas, what do we need to do to bring you on board?"

"It's pretty simple actually. If I am to be your advisor, I want the final say on all decisions."

"Jonas, you have to remember that I am the President!"

"Absolutely, Mr. President. You still will have the power to fire me if you disagree with a decision, but if you cannot accept any of my decisions, you will not have to fire me; I will resign."

"I see; so what are your other conditions?"

"No other conditions."

"What about money, Jonas."

"No money, Mr. President. This is for love of country."

"Alright then, Jonas. As of right now you will head the advisory team so long as you remember I am the President."

"I won't forget, Sir, but there will be no 'team'. I do not need a committee, and think of the money that will be saved."

"But in my speech…"

Jonas interrupted, "Pardon me, Sir. I know you mentioned a team of advisors, but nobody needs to know."

"And what if the press wants to know who they are?"

"Just tell them that they wish to remain anonymous." And with that, Jonas had set the stage for his unquestioned authority.

Chapter 80: Reconciliation

After lunch, the President and his new advisor headed to the Oval Office to continue discussions. Again, Campbell opened the discussion, "So Jonas, what do you think our first order of business should be?"

"You mentioned it in your speech, Mr. President. You have already taken an important first step in removing sanctions. The next is in reaching out to the seceding states for some sort of accommodation."

"How do you propose we do that?"

"I think we can take a lesson from our history and invite them to a Constitutional convention."

"What makes you think that they would be interested?"

"Just a strong hunch, Mr. President. We talked about it in our meeting yesterday. Why, do you suppose that those states wanted to separate from the Union?"

"They obviously wanted to be independent."

"That is true, Mr. President, but why."

"They didn't like the way the country was going?"

"You nailed it, Sir. For a long time our country has been moving away from the Constitution and finally, they said, 'Enough'."

"O.K., Jonas. Let's see what they have to say."

"Thank you, Sir. I will get right on it."

After he left the Oval Office, Jonas' first call was to his old pal, Lon Whitt. It had been almost seven months since he had gotten back from his military assignment in Arizona, and the two had not spoken in that time. "Hello, old friend, or should I say General?"

"Old friend will do, Jonas. I think I am done with the military."

"Really, Lon. I heard you did pretty good with 'Operation Inferno'."

"Word does get around, but it was really those Texas Rangers that made it happen."

"With some good leadership, I might add."

"O.K., enough of that, Jonas. From what I hear in the latest poll numbers, I am probably speaking to the next President of the United States, so I doubt that your call is to request my support."

"Correct, Lon, but your information is outdated. I am no longer running for President, but as of today instead am working for President Oren Campbell as his chief advisor."

"So Campbell wasn't lying when he said he was headed in a new direction?"

"You are right, and I have some personal news for you, before we get into the meat of the discussion. You are no longer a wanted man. All charges have been dropped and the FBI has been ordered to immediately transmit that information to all law enforcement agencies."

"All kinds of surprises, Jonas, and I suspect the 'meat' of the discussion will contain an additional surprise or two."

"Just one, Lon. We are requesting your help in calling for a Constitutional convention of states."

"Jonas, assuming that you are including the states that have seceded in that call, it will never happen because that idiot boss of yours opened 'Pandora's box' with the "voting bloc for the same kind of big government that led to secession in the first place."

"Lon, I fully understand and must say that I disagreed with the act as well. I favored a pathway to legality, but not to citizenship."

"Too bad you were not advising the President back in November, but what's done is done, and there is no going back."

"But, Lon, what if the act could be reversed?"

"Jonas, there is no point in talking hypotheticals. I know you are a smart fellow, but I doubt that you can untie this 'Gordian knot'."

"I think I can, but the question remains that if the Citizenship Act is nullified, will you help with the call for a Constitutional convention of the states?

"Yes, I think I could support the call."

"Excellent, Lon. I will be back in touch."

When they hung up, Jonas redialed the President's private line.

"What do you have for me, Jonas?"

"I think some good news. Do you have some additional time for me today?"

"Certainly. It's 3:00 now. Do you want to do it now or this evening?"

"Now, Mr. President, if convenient. I can be there in twenty minutes."

"Fine, Jonas."

As Jonas was entering the Oval Office a short time later, Campbell asked excitedly,

"So what's the good news?"

"Lon Whitt will join us in the call for the Constitutional convention of the states under one condition."

"And what might that condition be, Jonas?"

"That the Citizenship Act be rescinded."

Campbell responded angrily, "Impossible! Whitt obviously has no intention of helping us. So that's what you call good news?"

"Yes, Sir. As you well know, Lon Whitt has been in the forefront of the secession movement and therefore carries a lot of credibility with that group. He is merely stating what he knows to be a fact, i.e., that there is no way that any of the states that have seceded would agree to a Constitutional convention without a revocation of the Citizenship Act."

"So Professor, tell me how you would go about stripping the citizenship of tens of millions?"

Jonas noted the change of address from 'Jonas' to 'Professor', but did not pause in his response. "Mr. President, 'stripping citizenship' may not be necessary, since they are probably not citizens right now anyway."

"That you are going to have to explain, Professor."

"Three points, Mr. President. The first is that Congress ignored immigration law, requiring candidates for naturalization to undergo tests for English literacy and knowledge of U.S. history. Furthermore, candidates for naturalization must have displayed good moral character during their time in the U.S. Respect for the nation's laws is one indicator of good moral character and insofar as their entering the nation illegally, it would disqualify them on that basis. The third point is that the House was one vote short of a quorum. Eight states had seceded over the past year, reducing the number of congressmen by seventy-five to 359.One hundred eighty were present, but forgotten was North Virginia's one congressional seat, requiring one hundred eighty-one for a majority. This is a case for the Supreme Court, but given my contacts and your bully pulpit, I think we can get this on the Court's agenda ASAP."

"Do you really think this is necessary, Jonas?"

"I do, Sir."

"There are going to be a lot of unhappy people out there, starting with my Vice President."

"Mr. President, I assure you there will be a lot more happy people out there."

Two weeks later after hearing the case, the Supreme Court nullified the Citizenship Act and the media had a heyday with the news. The liberal press and media catering to the Hispanic community was highly critical, but conservatives and even moderates felt that the ruling was correct. A day later, after the uproar had died down, Campbell gave the following speech over all the networks, written by Jonas. The speech was also simultaneously translated into Spanish:

"Good evening, fellow citizens.

By now you have heard the Supreme Court ruling on the Citizenship Act, and I am aware how controversial this law was. I am also hearing that the ruling was a political move. I assure you that there were no politics involved. We are a nation of immigrants, but we are a melting pot, not a salad bowl. What this means is that we welcome new citizens, but we expect them to return the favor by loving our country and demonstrate their love by learning our language, teaching their children our language, absorbing our culture, and last, but not least, observing our laws.

We are a nation of laws, and those known as "undocumented" are illegal immigrants. They have broken our law and must be willing to face the consequences. We are a nation of compassion as well. We fully understand why they want to improve their lives and that of their families. We are a nation of workers and we expect every able bodied adult to work and support himself and his family.

By executive order, here is our proposal to all undocumented immigrants:

1. If you have been here supporting yourself (and your family if applicable) and have committed no felonies since you have been here, you may apply for a special green card if you register by August 17, 2044, which is thirty days from now.

    a. When you register you will state where and when you crossed into the US, your place(s) of residence with dates of occupancy, your complete record of employment including amount earned. You will report all Federal and State financial assistance you have received, including any hospitalizations you did not pay for.

    b. You will be required to reimburse any entity from which you received financial assistance and will be given a reasonable time to do so. You will also be responsible for all taxes on earnings.

    c. You will also give the names and ages of any family members who accompanied you or came later with the dates of when they joined you and any hospitalizations that you or they did not pay for. Any family member, 21 or older must register himself.

    d. Any intentional misstatement on the registration will be grounds for revoking the green card privilege, immediate deportation and a permanent ban on future citizenship. This will also be the case for anyone failing to register by the deadline.

2. Current law allows for citizenship application after five years of green card status. This would not apply to special green cards issued under the above conditions. To apply for a regular green card with citizenship application rights, you must return to your home country and enter the U.S. legally. You must understand that it is not fair for you to jump in line ahead of people who have obeyed our immigration laws.

Thank you all for listening. Good night and God bless America.

Chapter 81: Reconciliation (part two)

Following the President's speech, Jonas called Lon Whitt. Lon answered on the first ring, "So you were able to untie 'Gordian's knot' after all. I shouldn't have underestimated you."

"You give me too much credit, Lon. What made it easy was that they were too hasty to get the job done; and in their haste, they made some big errors."

"Say what you will, Jonas. It took you to uncover the errors, but I know why you called. As I promised, I will work my contacts to see if we can get them to a Constitutional Convention, but I predict there will be some hesitation from a number of states."

"What do you anticipate the problem to be?"

"Basically, the uncertainty of the finished product."

"I understand, Lon, but make it clear that there will be no obligation for any state to sign on, if there is any disagreement on any part of the new Constitution.

"Will everything be on the table?"

"Yes."

"No exclusions?"

"No, although I think it reasonable to start with the Constitution as is, as a framework and work from there."

"Sounds reasonable. Let me get started."

"Great, Lon. Good luck."

When they hung up, Lon's first call was to Florence Zimmerman. She answered, "Hello, General, good to hear from you."

"Hello, Governor, how are things going?"

"Just peachy with Ariel gone, thanks to you."

"Thanks to those Texas Rangers, but let me not take too much of your time. I am sure you heard President Campbell's conciliatory speech of two weeks ago and yesterday's Supreme Court ruling on the Citizenship Act."

"I did. I have to say that I was surprised."

"Me too, but Campbell has a sharp new advisor. Professor Jonas O'Leary, a Constitutional expert, is responsible for the President's radical change in direction."

Florence asked, "Jonas O'Leary, where have I heard that name before?"

"He was considered for an appointment to the Supreme Court a couple of times, but he was considered too conservative."

Florence responded, "My kind of guy."

"Mine too, and just as an aside. "He's an old friend. He has asked me on behalf of the President to contact the states that have seceded in a call for a Constitutional Convention of states."

"Hmm, interesting. Who have you contacted before me?"

"You are number one."

"Any reason, other than thinking I might be a soft touch."

"On the contrary, Governor. If I can get you to agree, I think I may be able to bring some more along."

"I don't know about that, Lon, but you will have some tall convincing to get me to agree. As you know, secession would never have happened without people being very dissatisfied with the way things were. As things stand now, we are in pretty good shape; and when I look at conditions in the United States, we would be fools to go back. Now, if we were talking about a union of the seceded states; that is something that might be of interest."

"O.K., Governor. Let's take that as a starting point. If a union of the seceded states were to come about, would you be in favor of allowing other states to join the union?"

"You are a sly one, Lon. I see where you are going; but the only reason that I would be receptive to a union of the seceded states, is that we have much in common."

"And if I may, Governor, summarize the commonality as a desire to get back to the tenets of the Constitution?"

"In a nut shell, yes."

"So if other states agreed to commit to the Constitution..?"

"Yes, Lon, under certain conditions."

"All right then, Governor. Let's call for a Constitutional Convention of seceded states with an invitation to other states to join the proceedings with no strings attached. Campbell has agreed that everything will be on the table with no exclusions; and no state will be obligated to join without full acceptance."

"O.K., Lon. Let me bounce the idea off a couple of friends, and I will let you know."

Chapter 82: Constitutional Convention of States

When Florence hung up from the conversation with Lon, she first dialed Jerry Collins to explain the proposal. Collins admitted that the idea was interesting and that he would take it up with his boss. She then called her old friend from her days in Washington, Melvin Graham, President of New Virginia. "Hello, Melvin. Florence Zimmerman here.

"Hello, Florence. Good to hear from you again. I hear your pick of a general worked out pretty well."

"Indeed it did, and I thank you for helping me get in touch with Lon Whitt."

"No problem. Glad to be of assistance. How may I help today?"

"That's as good a lead in as any, I guess. I got off the phone with Lon about forty minutes ago discussing the possibility of a Constitutional Convention."

"Very interesting. A union of seceded states?"

"Not exactly, Melvin. It would be working toward a union, including states that have not seceded."

"Florence, if you are suggesting what I think you are, I have to say that I am not interested."

"Melvin, I totally understand, but please hear me out."

"Certainly, Florence, for old time's sake, but I have to tell you that you are probably wasting your time as well as mine."

"Fair enough, Melvin."

"From your earlier response, I gather that you may have some interest in a union of seceded states?"

"Possibly. We would have to be in agreement on a Constitution."

"I totally agree, Melvin. That was the position I expressed to Lon. Now what if other states that have not yet seceded wanted to join?"

"So long as they concurred on the Constitution as well."

"Again, we are in agreement, Melvin. All we are asking for is an open discussion. Everything on the table and no obligation for any state to join."

"OK, Florence. Let me speak to Jim Singer, my Vice President.

"Fair enough, Melvin, and you will get back to me?"

"Of course, Florence."

When she hung up, she saw that she had already received a call from Jerry and hoped that the news would be a bit more encouraging. And it definitely was. President Richard Houston was receptive and offered to host the convention in Austin. In addition, Houston had talked to President Bill Hubbard of Alaska and President Darren Prejean of Louisiana, both of whom were receptive. "Well, if nothing else", Florence mused, "we'll have a nice little get together in Austin."

Over the next few hours, however, the little get together had grown to all twelve of the seceded states and the five southeastern states that had not yet seceded. Also most of the governors and presidents were on their phones urging their counterparts to participate. By July 29, only nine states remained uncommitted, including California and New York, but interestingly, both of those states were threatening to split, as Virginia had done over a year earlier. The date of the convention was set for Monday, August 8, which was two weeks before the scheduled convention of President Oren Campbell's political party. His rival for the party's nomination, Espinoza, still had a substantial lead, but Campbell was focused on the Constitutional Convention of the states and his presidential legacy. He wanted to attend, but Jonas talked him out of it.

As the date approached, Jerry Collins and his secretary were busy with logistical preparations, such as hotel reservations for Sunday arrival and car rentals for the expected eighty or more attendees as there were to be two representatives for each state. President Richard Houston had sent out invitations for 7:00 PM dinner Sunday, at the Austin Country Club for those arriving early enough with a requested RSVP by 6:00 PM August 5 so that Collins could have an accurate count. By the deadline, there was a count of ninety- five people for dinner, including forty-three spouses, and all but six states had committed to the convention, with California and New York still questionable.

Proceedings were to begin at 9:00 AM in the Texas capitol building in the room where the Texas House of Representatives normally meets. President Richard Houston had agreed with Lon Whitt's recommendation that Jonas O'Leary be the chairman of the convention.

Chapter 83: Convention Convenes

Promptly at 9:00 AM August 8, President Richard Houston pounded the gavel. "May the Constitutional Convention of States come to order. We thank you all for coming. We are sorry that more of you could not make it to the dinner last night, but for those who did, I think I can speak for them in saying it was a memorable evening…"At that point a majority of the delegates rose and broke in with a round of applause. Houston continued, "Thank you, but the applause should be for each and every one of you, who have taken the time out of your busy schedules to meet for this historic occasion. Each of you has already heard the conditions for this convention; but I think it bears repeating, so no one will feel pressured to agree to anything that he or she is not totally comfortable with. With that, I will turn the gavel over to an individual many of you know, who was twice considered for the United States Supreme Court and is regarded as one of the foremost authorities on the U.S.

Constitution, Professor Jonas O'Leary."

Another round of applause. "Thank you, President Houston and delegates. I am honored to be here among such a distinguished group of statesmen. Two hundred fifty seven years ago our county's Founding Fathers met in Philadelphia to create the Constitution, which was a remarkable piece of work. They recognized that it was not perfect, and put in place the mechanism to amend it over time. That mechanism was intended to be difficult to preclude any frivolous tampering. But, over the years, men sometimes with the best intentions, and other times with nefarious designs; have altered this great document to the point where the founders might only barely recognize it as their creation.

We will start with the Constitution as is to save time, but only as a framework for discussion. As you have heard previously, everything is on the table with no exclusions. Motions for amendments will require a second from a different state; and after discussion a vote will be taken requiring three quarters of the states represented for passage. At this point, we have forty-three states present and remain hopeful that the other six states will join us before we have too many crucial votes. Until then, thirty-three states will constitute the required three quarters. We have to assume that most, if not all, proposed amendments will not be unanimous, but we ask that if you are unhappy with a particular amendment that you bear with us till the end of the convention to view the entire product before you make a decision. With that I will entertain motions from the floor. Use your buzzer to let me know you have a motion and when called on, please stand, identify yourself and your state."

The first to be recognized was a Tennessee delegate. "Thank you, Chairman O'Leary. Andrew Thornton, Vice President from the great and sovereign state of Tennessee. I move that the following amendment be adopted, 'Only immigrants who have entered the country legally, will be eligible for citizenship. Also, children born to illegal immigrants will not be citizens.'"

The motion was quickly seconded and discussion began. There was some dissent, but discussion ended an hour later. The amendment passed overwhelmingly with thirty-nine in favor. The next motion from the floor was to make a picture ID of every voter for federal elections mandatory. Several delegates from heavily Democratic states objected on the basis of discrimination against the poor; so that the motion was revised to allow any voter to obtain a state issued ID at no expense.. After that revision, a vote was taken and the amendment passed. The next amendment up for consideration was for the abolition of the Federal Income Tax and all other Federal taxes, to be replaced by a Federal sales tax with exemptions for food and prescriptions. After a second, a brisk discussion followed.

One delegate asked how Social Security would be affected. The answer was that Social Security would not be affected since it was considered to be too complex an issue to be resolved by amendment. The motion was therefore changed to specifically exclude Social Security from the amendment.

One delegate expressed concern that they would be voting on an amendment without knowing what the tax rate would be. At that point, President Richard Houston rose to comment. "We had anticipated a proposed amendment along those lines and therefore had invited our Secretary of the Treasury, Jimmy Phelps, to join us to help us with those kinds of questions. Mr. Chairman, with your permission, I will ask Secretary Phelps to address that question."

Jonas nodded his assent.

"Thank you, President Houston, Mr. Chairman, and delegates. I have developed a program to answer the tax rate question. The program is based on last year's figures, which of course included all forty-nine states until secession. If the Federal Income tax and all other Federal taxes, except for the Social Security payroll tax, were eliminated and replaced with a Federal Sales tax on all items, other than food and prescriptions, the tax rate would be 23%."

There was also concern that at some point in the future, an income tax could resurface by law. To preclude that possibility the proposed amendment's language was altered to include the wording that no income tax could be reinstated without a Constitutional amendment. That change still did not satisfy all the delegates, but a more contentious point had to do with the perceived regression of a sales tax, even with the exemptions. Some wanted the exemptions to be broadened to include over the counter medicines, clothing and gasoline. Others also wanted exemptions for automobiles, tires and parts. Conservatives pointed out that every exemption would result in a higher tax rate to compensate; and therefore were opposed to exemptions for candy, and some even for any snack foods. And that led to objections from some that exemptions for foods perceived as luxuries, such as caviar, lobster, and steak would benefit the wealthy. Finally, after four hours of intense debate with a short lunch break and no apparent consensus, Jonas broke in, "It appears that we are making no progress on this motion. I suggest that we table it for the time being and move on to a less controversial issue. All in favor of tabling the motion, say Aye, and those opposed say Nay. The Ayes have it. May I hear another motion for hopefully, a less contentious amendment?"

Collins was called on next. "Jerry Collins, Advisor to the President of the great and sovereign State of Texas. I move that the following amendment be adopted: 'Each and every state will have the legal right to secede from the union without any interference from any other state or states.'" President Graham of New Virginia seconded the motion and discussion followed. It was pointed out that without some limitations, the union would be too vulnerable to a break-up; so Collins altered his motion to make secession conditional on a change in the Constitution. A governor from one of the non-secessionist states pointed out that after the first change in the Constitution, no matter the amount of intervening time, any state would then be free to secede for the most whimsical reason. Collins' amendment was then revised again to say that any state desiring to secede could do so only in a timeframe no longer than 14 days after a change in the Constitution. After a short discussion, the amendment was easily passed. Since it was close to 5:00 PM, Jonas proposed that they adjourn for the evening and be ready to reconvene at 9:00 the next morning. He complimented the group on a very productive session, but reminded them that they still faced the controversial tax reform issue. He suggested having dinner with colleagues having different viewpoints to maybe facilitate coming to an agreement the next day.

The next morning they reconvened and a flurry of amendments, involving limitations on Federal power were passed with little discussion and dissent. They were as follows:

1. Term limits for Senators, Congressmen and Supreme Court Justices.

    a. Senate- two terms of six years.

    b. Congress- three terms of two years.

    c. Supreme Court –one term of twelve years.

    d. Combined service-maximum of twelve years.

2. All laws applied to citizenry to be applied equally to lawmakers.

    a. No government pension other than social security.

    b. No special health care.

3. Allow a 3/4 majority of the states to overturn a Federal law.

4. Allow a 3/4 majority of the states to overturn a Supreme Court decision.

By then it was time for a lunch break, and Jonas reminded the group that tax reform still remained to be resolved and to think about it over lunch. After lunch and no new motions, Jonas had the convention readdress the tabled motion of income tax abolition. Discussion for the first thirty minutes rehashed all the arguments of the day before and Jonas spoke, "It is clear that we are getting nowhere fast. I suggest that we take a vote right now to determine if it is the consensus of the convention that the Federal Income Tax and all other Federal taxes be replaced by a Federal Sales Tax with certain exemptions. If we do not have a consensus on that, we are wasting our time. Let me ask for one member of each delegation to stand if you are in favor…It appears that the vast majority are generally in favor. Just to make sure, all those against, please rise." Eleven individuals rose. Jonas continued, "OK, it is clearly the consensus of the convention that a Federal Sales Tax with certain exemptions should replace the Federal Income tax and all other Federal taxes. Let us take the proposed exemptions one by one. The first is food. May I hear a revision of the original motion addressing the exemption for food?"

There followed a motion that the exemption for food not include candy, steak, lobster, caviar, or restaurants, which passed after a brief discussion. Next came motions adding clothing to the list of exemptions, and modifying the prescription exemption to include medical equipment and over-the-counter medications. The medical exemption passed easily, but the clothing exemption had some dissent. Items that were clearly in the luxury category like furs were easily excluded from the exemption, but since pricing could vary widely on other items of clothing, it was difficult to reach a consensus. Phelps was called on again to inform the delegates the consequence of the above changes. The changes to the food and medical exemptions pretty much cancelled each other out, but the clothing exemption, even minus furs, would increase the tax rate to 26%.Ultimately, the clothing exemption narrowly passed with only furs excluded.

Then came automobiles, which appeared to be an irreconcilable matter. There was fairly wide agreement that an automobile was a necessity, but there were questions that complicated the issue. How many cars per family? How many workers outside the home? Price limits? How often can one trade in and still get the exemption? Phelps once more was asked to respond to the latest proposed exemption and shocked the delegates with his answer. "If all automobiles were exempted, the tax rate would have to be 38%."

After two more hours of discussion, it appeared that there was no consensus to be reached. On one side, including most of the secessionist states, was the position that there should be fewer exemptions. On the other side, more exemptions, but excepting certain items classified as "luxury". The side arguing for fewer exemptions, pointed out that every exemption raised the required tax rate to compensate. The other side argued the regression aspect of a sales tax.

A delegate from Georgia offered the following compromise, "The portion of the purchase price of a new automobile no greater than 10% above that of the least expensive sticker price would be exempt from the Federal Sales Tax and only one automobile exemption per individual of driving age per year would be allowed."

With this provision, the required tax rate would be 35%. Once again, the vote showed no consensus.

Finally, Jonas decided to step in to see if he could resolve the impasse. "Let me see if I can define the issue to determine if we can come to an agreement. If I get the sense of the deadlock; it is that the states that would be hit hardest by a sales tax with many exemptions do not have the bulk of the population, so that the few would be supporting the many. At present, a state's number of congressional districts is based on the population of a state. What if that were changed to be based on the amount of sales tax collected from that state? Let's have a re-vote on the Georgia compromise with the provision that the number of congressional districts of a state would be proportional to the Federal Sales Tax collected from that state."

This time the automobile exemption narrowly passed. After asking if there were any other modifications or additions to the original sales tax motion and determining that there were none, Jonas called for a vote on the motion incorporating all of the proposed changes. Surprisingly, after all the dissention, the amendment passed by a considerable margin. Perhaps, because like a jury that has deliberated for hours and hours; the individuals come to an agreement not so much because they really believe, but out of sheer exhaustion. Jonas then asked if there were any further motions, and when there were none, Jonas asked for a motion to adjourn, which came quickly with a second; and the Constitutional Convention thereby came to a close.

Chapter 84: Campaign for Ratification

At the conclusion of the convention of the states, Houston offered Jonas the use of his Presidential plane to fly to Dallas, where if he was lucky, he could catch a flight to Washington, arriving at a decent enough hour to get a good night's sleep for an early morning conference with his boss. The plane landed at 6:05 at Love Field and taxied right up to a plane destined for Ronald Reagan Washington Airport, scheduled to depart at 6:30 and arrive Washington at 9:00 PM EDT. And lo and behold, there was a first class seat reserved for Jonas. Talk about luck! Of course, the luck was for being associated with President Richard Houston.

The next morning at 8:30, Jonas was at the Oval office, briefing Campbell on the convention. Campbell interrupted, "OK, Jonas. Enough of the details. I want to know your feelings and if you think it has a chance in being ratified."

"Mr. President, on the whole I feel very good about it. There are always small details that I would have preferred, such as more exemptions to the Federal Sales Tax, but compromise is necessary if anything is to get done. As far as predicting the chance that it will be ratified, I cannot say. I am no clairvoyant, but I am hopeful."

"Well, what happens if it is not ratified? Where do we go from here?"

"Let's first see how close the vote is, and in the meantime, if you concur, I would like to start visiting some states that I think are on the fence. Also, I think you could help nudge this thing along with a speech tonight."

"OK, Jonas, you go ahead, but please keep me informed. And I will get working on my speech right now. But let me ask you something that I have been mulling over the past few days. Thanks to you, my approval ratings have improved, but still do not bode well for the general election, let alone my nomination. With the Party convention less than two weeks away, I have some real doubts that I would win the nomination. This would be a major embarrassment and probably set a historic precedent for a sitting President to not win his party's nomination for a second term. I am thinking that if I were to take myself out of the race, it might help the healing process."

"Mr. President, there are some historic precedents, but one has to go back to the nineteenth century to find them. However, I think your reasoning is sound. Your speech could go a long way to begin the healing."

That evening after letting all the networks know, Campbell went on the air. "Good evening, fellow citizens, I have had the honor of being President of this great nation for almost four years. I have worked tirelessly to do the best that I could do, but circumstances, timing, and perhaps, fate have intervened and frustrated my efforts. With this broadcast, I am hereby withdrawing my name as candidate to succeed myself in hopes that this action will serve to help make our country whole once again. You have no doubt heard the results of the Constitutional Convention of the States that just concluded yesterday. The congresses of each of the secessionist states are right now in the process of considering the new Constitution for adoption. I and my advisors have studied this document, and while there may be some who dislike certain elements, we consider it to be fair and in our country's best interests. I am therefore recommending to the states to accept this as our new Constitution. Our current Constitution requires three fourths of the states for ratification. At present, our country consists of thirty-three states so that twenty-five states will need to ratify. I am asking our states' governors to join with me in encouraging your legislatures to expeditiously meet and approve the new Constitution. Good night and God bless America."

Chapter 85: Campaign for Ratification (part two)

It had been a busy two days for Jonas after his meeting at the White House, and it had become apparent that getting the states to agree on ratification of the new constitution was not going to be an easy task. He had met with the governors of the six Mid-Atlantic States, and only Delaware was a fairly sure bet. Maryland appeared to be in play, but the populous states of New York, New Jersey, and Pennsylvania, as well as the new state of New Virginia were firmly against. That meant that unless one of those states could be won over, it would take only five more states to block ratification.

Jonas, however, was not the only one who had been busy since the convention concluded. Houston had asked the delegates of the independent states to remain behind for a short meeting to discuss forming their own union in the event that the new constitution failed to be ratified. Houston spoke, "Thanks for remaining. I will make this short so that ya'll can be on your way. I feel very good about this constitution. Sure, there are a few changes I would have liked, but all in all, I think it will be very good for Texas, and I think, for each of your states as well. We all departed from what had been a great country for much the same reason, i.e., that it had strayed way too far from what the Founding Fathers had envisioned. I feel that this constitution brings us back to that earlier vision of individual liberty and a government that is a servant of the people rather than the other way around. I am confident that our legislature will as well. We have much in common and will be stronger as a confederation. Thanks again and have a safe trip home."

By Friday afternoon, Texas and Arizona had ratified, and the legislatures of the other fourteen independent states were in session discussing ratification.

It was close to 5:00 PM on Friday and with it being rush hour on the weekend, Jonas was not sure he could get to the Albany airport and get checked in quick enough to make his 5:50 flight to Boston for his 7:30 dinner appointment with Governor McCarthy. Luck again was with him and he was on the plane with seven minutes to spare. The plane landed on time at 6:10. The governor had an assistant waiting for Jonas at the gate, who after picking up his luggage, transported him in the governor's limousine to the restaurant for the meeting.

The maître d' escorted Jonas to the governor's table in a private dining area. Governor McCarthy stood up and greeted Jonas. "Right on time, Professor, with a few minutes to spare."

"Thanks to you, Governor. I certainly would not have made it otherwise."

"Well, Sir, this is an important meeting."

"Indeed it is, Governor, and I appreciate your making time for me after hours and the invitation to such a fine restaurant."

"You are very welcome, Professor, but you should know that there is no such thing as 'after hours'."

"Of course".

With the pleasantries over, it was time to get down to business. Governor McCarthy opened the discussion. "Professor, I would really like to support the constitution…"

Jonas broke in, "That is very good to hear…"

The governor continued, "but I cannot accept the provision of changing the allocation of congressional districts based on Federal receipts. Strike that and I believe Massachusetts would approve."

"I understand, Governor, but I think that without that clause, the secessionist states would not ratify."

"Then, sad to say, I think we are at a stalemate, since I cannot foresee the big states relinquishing their power in the House."

Chapter 86: Stalemate

Over the next two weeks, Governor McCarthy's prediction appeared to becoming true. All but one state had completed their votes with the tally being twenty-four states for and eight states against. The bad news was that California had not yet come to a vote. There was strong support in Southern California, but that was outweighed by the more populous counties around Los Angeles and San Francisco. The debate was coming to an end and it did not look good for ratification.

In the meantime, the vote had been unanimous in the seceding states that were now in the process of forming a confederation. The Party convention had just ended with Espinoza being nominated to head the Party's ticket. Since Campbell had voluntarily forgone succeeding himself, this did not bother him nearly as much as a seemingly permanent break-up of the country and a legacy that would be an asterisk in the nation's history.

Jonas was with Campbell in the Oval Office when the word came through that California had just voted and ratification was defeated. "Damn, Jonas. If not for that Constitutional Convention, we might have had a chance to salvage the country."

"Mr. President, I wouldn't blame it on the convention, but in any event, the game is not over yet."

"Game? What game? This is as serious as it gets."

"I agree, Sir, and maybe that was a wrong choice of words. But all life is a game with choices and consequences."

"Consequences? So I'm to blame?"

"No, Mr. President. As we discussed before, the causes of secession had been building up for a lot of years before you ever came into office. The kindling was there. All it took was a match, and the match was the last mid-term election."

"OK, then why do you think the game is not over?"

"Because even in the states that voted against ratification, there was strong minority support in favor."

"Minority support? What good is that?"

"Fortunately, Mr. President, our system while constructed on the premise that majority rules, the minority is not powerless. As a good example, take secession itself."

"Jonas, are you suggesting that there will be more secessions?"

"Not necessarily, Sir. That was just an example. Let's give it some time and see how things shake out."

Chapter 87: A Republic Reborn

Meanwhile, in California, things were far from being settled. True enough, the legislature had just voted against ratification, but it was still in session. The Assembly minority leader, Jeffrey Palmer, had the floor. "Thank you, Mr. Speaker, for allowing me to speak. As you and the majority well know, we of the minority have strongly supported the new constitution for two reasons. The main reason, being that our country had strayed so far from what our Founding Fathers had envisioned, it was time and opportune to go back to their concept. The second reason, and not an insignificant one, is to put our country back together again. We are Americans and we want our country back. While we are also Californians, we have reached the point that if our fellow Californians do not agree, we will regrettably have to go our own way. As you no doubt know, we had been discussing the possibility of secession even before the Constitutional Convention. Our county councils have since voted for seceding from the state if the constitution is not ratified. A week from today, my county of San Diego will join Orange, Riverside, and San Bernardino counties and put the matter to a vote of our citizens to break away from the state of California to form our own state and join the Confederation of States. If polling data is even close to being accurate, we should win in a landslide."

Several assembly members argued that such an action would be illegal and unconstitutional.

Palmer took the floor again. "With all due respect to my colleagues, there is nothing in our state constitution that prohibits secession, and as a matter of fact, there is ample legal precedent. At the start of the civil war, western Virginia broke away from Virginia to form the new state of West Virginia; and earlier this year, the Virginia counties adjacent to the District of Columbia broke away from Virginia to form the new state of North Virginia. Furthermore, Article 4, section 3 of the U.S. Constitution recognizes the rights of individuals to break away from a state."

Discussion went on for some time, until one of the members made a motion to have a re-vote on ratification.

"We interrupt this broadcast for some late breaking news from the Oval Office."

"Good afternoon, and congratulations, Fellow Citizens. I am pleased to announce that the new Constitution has just been ratified. The legislature of the state of California has just completed a re- vote, and it being the twenty-fifth to approve, the new Constitution does now take effect. Since the states that had seceded had already individually ratified the Constitution, that means that our country has come back together There will be some details to be worked out on the transition, and I will leave that to Congress and the Supreme Court. I am proud to have been in this office for this historic moment. God bless the U.S.A. and before we sign off, I would like to hand the microphone to Secretary of the Interior, Nancy Larsen for an important announcement."

"Good afternoon, Ladies and Gentlemen. I have just received a letter of resignation from Alice Ridley, Director of the EPA. The resignation, which I have accepted is effective immediately. We thank her for her service and wish her well in whatever line of work she decides to pursue. Until we find her replacement, I will be filling in for her, but the activities of the EPA are to be scaled back significantly. There are currently 35,400 full time employees and even more on a contractual basis. Since its creation in 1970, it has grown unrestrained in both numbers and authority. Many have referred to it as our fourth branch of government. I will be asking for resignations from 10,000 within 30 days and an additional 20,000 in the following thirty days. By this time next year, I expect to have no more than 5000 working in the department.

"Regarding EPA's restrictions on coal and rumors of upcoming restrictions on other fossil fuels, I am announcing that as of today, all restrictions and fees on coal mining and the use of coal are hereby rescinded. Furthermore, I wish to put all rumors of future restrictions on fossil fuels to rest. Since the beginning of this century, the theory of anthropogenic global warming has been challenged by large numbers of notable and courageous scientists, but to no avail. Unfortunately, the UN and governments had bought into the concept despite overwhelming scientific evidence to the contrary. Sad to say, the tremendous amount of money available for research grants, led many otherwise respectable scientists to forget that the business of science is the pursuit of truth, not marketing their version of truth. Finally it is time to admit the grievous error made on the basis of faulty science."

Epilogue

With the revised allocation of congressional districts under the new constitution, the electoral power resided with the secessionist states, and their candidate won handily. They had offered the nomination to Governor Houston, but he declined, saying he appreciated the honor, but he preferred to remain governor of Texas, at least to the end of his term, and longer, if Texans wanted him for a second term. Florence Levin Zimmerman therefore was nominated and became the 51st President of the United States on January 20, 2045.

The House now was overwhelmingly Republican, but there was an unexpected and welcome surprise in the Senate. Prior to the election, the Democrats had enjoyed super majority status with sixty seats against the Republicans' thirty-eight. Thirty-three Senate seats had been up for election, with twenty-five of them held by Democrats. When the ballot count was complete, twenty-one of the Democratic Senators had been turned out of office, while all eight of the Republican Senators retained their seats.

What could possibly have changed to cause such a turn in events? Had the voters finally become so fed up with Democrat rule that they were ready for change? Or might the voter ID requirement have been at least partially responsible?

Whatever the cause, since the vacancy on the Supreme Court had never been filled, Jonas O'Leary was nominated by President Zimmerman the day she took office and confirmed by the Senate ten days later.

Lon Whitt was appointed Secretary of Defense with the mission of rebuilding the nation's military. Two years later, the U.S. military had been brought back to its strength of one hundred years earlier. President Zimmerman delivered an ultimatum to President Igor Segurin to withdraw Russia's forces from the Aleutians or suffer the consequences. The Russian troops were gone within a week.

Lester Parsons and Rex Morgan were in adjoining cells at Attica Federal Prison. Parsons had been convicted of stock market manipulation and money laundering. His partner, Bradley Simms, had plea bargained and turned state's evidence against him. Morgan was convicted of several counts of extortion and money laundering as well.

El Diablo never made it to trial. He was found murdered in his holding cell. He had been castrated and bled to death. The perpetrator was apparently one of the guards, but since all of them pled ignorance and there was no incriminating evidence, no one was ever charged.

Christina St. James had completed her movie about the Alamo and was involved in a new movie, based on the Ghost Storm incident. The watermelon farmer, who had recovered from his wounds, and his wife were included in the movie with a sizable retainer, enough so that they could forget about farming for the rest of their lives.

Nancy Larsen was last seen having dinner with President Segurin and was overheard to say, "Iggy, if I didn't know you better…"

And ex-President Oren Campbell and his wife returned to their palatial home in Blackwell Oklahoma and spent the last days of his life lecturing to high school students at the Oren Campbell Presidential Museum in his home town, content in the knowledge that he was destined to go down in history as the President who had saved the country.

Acknowledgements

This is to thank all the people who have contributed their time and effort to improve this work and bring it to its completion.

To my cousin and friend, Attorney Donald Dorfman. Don spent hours with me on the phone, editing a number of chapters and enlightening me on various aspects of the law.

To my good Facebook friend, Professor Andrea Silverman Share, who also spent long periods of time editing.

To my new friend, Professor Louise Leigh, for her assistance in editing.

To one of my good college friends, Major John Ridge in taking an early look and advising me on one of the chapters.

To Louise Harris, a Facebook friend, for her assistance in editing.

To Kathleen King, widow of my good friend and co-author, Don King, for her assistance in editing.

To Bobby Mathews for his persistence and excellence for cover and interior page design.

And last, but not least, to my darling wife, Sara, who has put up with me for the long hours I have ignored her while working on this book.